> **"Which side of the bed do you sleep on?" she asked**

The question startled him. "The right," Kieren said, humoring her.

"Do you squeeze the toothpaste from the middle or the bottom?"

"The middle." Then he added, "Until it starts to run out. Then I squeeze it from the bottom. Anything else you'd like to know?"

Samantha plunged ahead. "Do you wear pajamas or sleep in the nude?"

"That's getting a bit personal, don't you think?" he asked.

"This *is* serious," she said.

"What is?" Kieren honestly didn't believe that anything Samantha could say next would surprise him. Even though he'd only known her for a few hours, she could offer to spend the night with him and he wouldn't even bat an eye.

"Will you marry me?" she asked.

ABOUT THE AUTHOR

Unlike her heroine, Jacqueline Diamond has only walked down the aisle once, but the marriage has lasted sixteen years. During that time, she has produced two sons and twenty-nine novels. She's never had a close encounter with a mountain lion, but she does sometimes find stray cats in her garden in Brea, California.

Books by Jacqueline Diamond

HARLEQUIN AMERICAN ROMANCE

218—UNLIKELY PARTNERS
239—THE CINDERELLA DARE
270—CAPERS AND RAINBOWS
279—A GHOST OF A CHANCE
351—BY LEAPS AND BOUNDS
406—OLD DREAMS, NEW DREAMS
446—THE TROUBLE WITH TERRY
491—A DANGEROUS GUY

Don't miss any of our special offers. Write to us at the following address for information on our newest releases.

Harlequin Reader Service
U.S.: 3010 Walden Ave., P.O. Box 1325, Buffalo, NY 14269
Canadian: P.O. Box 609, Fort Erie, Ont. L2A 5X3

Jacqueline Diamond

THE RUNAWAY BRIDE

Harlequin Books

TORONTO • NEW YORK • LONDON
AMSTERDAM • PARIS • SYDNEY • HAMBURG
STOCKHOLM • ATHENS • TOKYO • MILAN
MADRID • WARSAW • BUDAPEST • AUCKLAND

For Kathryn Brockman

ISBN 0-373-16583-8

THE RUNAWAY BRIDE

Printed in U.S.A.

Chapter One

Samantha Avery couldn't believe her luck in finding the wedding dress.

She studied herself in the oxidized mirror of the church's changing room. Even in this dim light, the ivory tint flattered her cinnamon hair and amber eyes. She loved the high, lace-trimmed collar and sensual low back. The gown fit her slender frame as if tailor-made.

She'd found it after only two days of looking, which was a good thing, because that was all the time she'd had.

"It's unheard of," said Alice, the maid of honor, as she examined Samantha's corsage. "I mean, walking into the bridal shop and finding this dress unclaimed and put on sale that very day!"

"I guess so," Samantha agreed. "But then, I've never bought a wedding dress before."

"Well, I have. Two of them." Alice touched up Samantha's hair with a styling comb. "What you've done is nothing short of a miracle."

"Maybe it's a lucky sign," Samantha said.

"Of course it is." Alice's manner was reassuringly hearty.

They hadn't known each other long; they'd worked together as clerks at SpeedWest Airlines for three months. But then, Samantha rarely stayed in one place long enough to know anyone well, and she liked Alice's practical attitude.

Mary Anne, the bridesmaid and their co-worker, could be trusted to come up with a more romantic outlook. Now, bringing over Samantha's ivory hat, she said, "But it's kind of sad, too, don't you think? Someone must have called off her wedding at the last minute."

"Probably for the best." Alice, whose two marriages had ended in divorce, adjusted the hat atop Samantha's hair. "She probably took a good look at the guy and realized her mistake."

"Thanks." Samantha made a wry face. "You're so encouraging."

"You'll do fine," said Alice. "And if you don't, you can always get rid of him."

"I suppose." Staring into the mirror, Samantha was surprised to find she looked untroubled, even serene. In reality, she had mixed feelings about marriage in general and this one in particular.

She glanced around the room. It looked like what it was: a spare office in a small church, equipped with a few folding chairs, a desk, some hooks for clothing, a tarnished mirror and a vase of dusty artificial flowers.

What on earth was she doing here?

Since being consigned to a boarding school as a teenager, Samantha had never felt comfortable staying in one location long. Nothing invigorated her like getting on an airplane and heading for a country she hadn't seen before.

As a child, she'd believed in happily ever after; as an adult, she'd found that variety was the spice of life.

She loved sultry music, foreign languages, steamy climates, handsome men who kissed her hand, exotic restaurants and unusual wines. Throw in some historic sites and offbeat boutiques, and a job so she could afford it all, and Samantha was in heaven.

So what was she doing in San Diego, California, walking down the aisle with Hank Torrance, a man she'd met less than a week ago?

Getting married definitely hadn't been on Samantha's agenda when she landed in San Diego three months ago. The hotel where she'd been working in Costa Rica had closed unexpectedly, and her scant savings had carried her only this far north.

She'd been lucky to land the airline job, and had begun saving up for another venture to a land where dreams came true. The dreams usually involved a beach, a margarita and a darkly brooding man. And, of course, love at first sight.

Five days ago, she'd treated herself to a weekend at a resort in Acapulco. There, on a beach where attendants plied her with margaritas, she'd met darkly brooding Hank, a financial consultant who also lived in San Diego.

The night after they first met, he sent dozens of roses to fill Samantha's room. The second night, he hired a guitar player to serenade them while a waiter served a private meal on her balcony.

From the beginning, Hank had worn a dazed, smitten expression that she found touching. Samantha's previous suitors—and she'd been through her share—never treated her with such care. They waxed rhapsodic about her uptilted eyes, her full lips and her narrow waist, then acted as if she were a possession they hoped to buy. Hank, on the other hand, seemed to really care about her.

When he proposed, Samantha accepted on impulse. After all, he was wonderfully romantic. Besides, some of the best marriages she'd seen had resulted from brief courtships, while some of the worst came after years of living together.

A little of her confidence had ebbed since returning to San Diego, but it didn't pay to torture herself with doubts. She'd agreed to marry him, and that was that.

"Somebody turn on the radio," Samantha said. "Find some lively music. This feels too much like a funeral."

While Alice fiddled with the transistor, Mary Anne clucked disapprovingly. "This is the happiest day of your life! I wish I were in your place, Sam." A shy, heavyset woman in her early thirties, Mary Anne rarely dated.

Impulsively, Samantha hugged her. "If men had any brains, you'd have been snapped up long ago. You're a real prize!"

Mary Anne's delighted smile made her feel better. A whole lot better.

The song on the radio faded, and the announcer launched into the news. "Police claim to have found a key piece of evidence into yesterday's daring daylight robbery of a La Jolla jewelry store. So far, they won't say what it is.

"This was the third in a string of robberies by two masked bandits. Police say half-a-million dollars in jewels are missing. So far, no one has been hurt."

Mary Anne clicked the radio off. "Who needs to listen to that? How depressing."

"I hope they catch those jerks." Alice scowled. "They took my neighbor's ring; you should have heard her crying last night. It was a family heirloom she was having re-sized for her daughter. You've never seen anything so beautiful. A tiny circle of diamonds around the most gorgeous emerald. On the inside is the date, 1927, and her grandmother's name. Can you imagine handing that down for nearly seventy years and then some creep steals it?"

"I wonder what evidence they found at the robbery scene?" Samantha mused.

"Maybe the bozo dropped his wallet," suggested Mary Anne.

"Maybe he dropped his pants," said Alice, and they all laughed.

They could hear guests arriving in the foyer. It wasn't a big wedding by any stretch of the imagination. Not even medium-size. Samantha had invited her co-workers, but her father and stepmother couldn't come all the way from Germany, where her father worked for an American import company.

Hank hadn't said who he was inviting, except to mention that he and his parents didn't get along. At the time, Samantha hadn't thought much about it. Now, she wished she had met her future in-laws.

But she'd always trusted her instincts, and so far, they had led to an interesting life. She'd been a chambermaid in Florence, a translator in Düsseldorf, a companion to an elderly British lady in Bombay and a tour guide in Hong Kong. So what if she was jumping off the deep end with Hank? As Alice said, you could always get a divorce.

So far, Samantha noted with gratitude, she hadn't felt the panic that seized her whenever she felt trapped. She could trace the feeling back to her teenage years when her parents, afraid their globe-hopping would deprive her of an education, had committed Samantha to a boarding school in Switzerland.

Some girls thrived on the experience, but all Samantha had felt were the walls closing in. She'd spent endless hours sitting stick-straight while teachers droned on, then more endless hours in her room memorizing dry facts. Her few illicit forays into a nearby village had been punished with evenings of solitary confinement.

Since then, she hadn't been able to endure the thought of being chained to one place or one person. But this was different, she told herself. Marriage to Hank would be an adventure.

Mary Anne checked the foyer and tiptoed back. "They're all sitting down." Through the open door, Samantha heard the organist playing "We've Only Just Begun."

"The wedding march is next!" she said. "Come on, guys!"

Since there was no one to give her away, she and Hank had decided to march down the aisle together. But when she peered out, the entrance hall was empty.

Samantha wondered if she'd been left at the altar, and was surprised to feel a twinge of relief. Just nerves, she told herself. "Alice, peek out and see if you can spot him."

Alice sneaked over to the sanctuary door. "Oh, my gosh, he's standing by the minister! He must have forgotten your arrangement."

Samantha let out an exasperated sigh. How could Hank do this to her?

"There's something else," Alice muttered as she came back into the little room.

"What?" Samantha wasn't sure she wanted to hear this.

"He's bald."

"What?"

"Well, not entirely bald. He's got some hair around his ears. But the top part, well . . ."

Hank wore a toupee? Samantha was amazed he hadn't told her. What other secrets was he keeping?

She tried to shove aside her long-cherished image of a beach, a margarita and a man with a thick head of hair. The hair didn't really matter. She wasn't marrying his coiffure, for goodness' sake.

"We've Only Just Begun" ended and the organist segued into the wedding march.

"Oh, dear!" said Mary Anne. "Think of something!"

"We'll go down the aisle together," said Samantha. "Come on!" She linked arms with an amused Alice and an embarrassed Mary Anne, and dragged her friends forward.

The guests turned to stare as they sauntered down the aisle three abreast. It was a tight fit. Mary Anne turned sideways and scissored her way along, and Alice had to keep dodging the flower holders that jutted from the pews.

Samantha felt her cheeks redden. They must look like some consciousness-raising group gone mad.

Then Joey, the clerk-trainee from the office, let out an appreciative whistle, and Samantha felt her spirits rise. A wedding should be fun, shouldn't it?

Some of her lightheartedness dissipated as she noticed hardly anyone was sitting on the groom's side of the church. There were a couple of street people who had wandered in for a place to sit, and a woman in a peach-colored dress and a veil. Not much of a family she was joining, was it?

The panic hit her halfway down the aisle. A thick lump constricted Samantha's throat and she had to fight to breathe. She could hear the clang of a prison door slamming shut.

Stop it! she told herself, clinging to Alice and Mary Anne. You aren't signing your life away. If things don't work out, you can always leave.

Samantha sucked in a ragged gulp of air as her throat unclenched. The remnants of panic tingled through her fingertips and bled away.

Alice clucked to her encouragingly and quickened her step. Samantha tried to keep pace, but Mary Anne, who must have been woolgathering, had to break into a skip to avoid playing crack-the-whip.

When they reached the altar, the minister wore a slightly stunned expression, but Hank didn't seem to notice anything amiss. He beamed at Samantha like a rooster ready to crow with pride.

Where was the hint of uncertainty she'd cherished last weekend? It had mutated, ever so subtly, into an expression Samantha could only describe as possessive.

Catching her elbow, Hank whispered, "Lookin' good, baby."

"Where's your rug?" she whispered back.

He patted his smooth pate. "Little accident. Sorry."

Couldn't a financial adviser afford a spare toupee? she wondered, but the minister had begun speaking.

The words of the ceremony flew by. If Samantha hadn't heard them a hundred times in old movies, she could never have followed them.

Then came the climactic moment. "Do you, Samantha, take Hank..."

Her heartbeat speeded up and she felt dizzy. Every instinct cried out to turn tail and flee. But she couldn't and she wouldn't. This was irrational, and besides, surely every bride felt this way as she relinquished her freedom. "I do," Samantha said firmly.

"And do you, Hank..."

"Absolutely," he said. "You betcha."

Couldn't he just stick to the ceremony? Every hint of Hank's dark and brooding persona had vanished. He'd lost his toupee and forgotten to meet her in the foyer. She wondered if he had misplaced the ring, too.

But no, there it was, emerging from his pocket. With a showmanlike flourish, Hank slid it onto her finger.

Samantha was surprised to find the ring so heavy. It was a little too large, which wasn't surprising, since Hank hadn't asked her ring size. Or her preference in stones, either.

She glanced down, intrigued and then shocked to see a perfect circlet of diamonds around an old-fashioned, square-cut emerald.

How could this be? Had Hank bought a stolen ring? But the robbery had only been yesterday.

Samantha's fears ignited. *A financial consultant with no colleagues at the wedding? With no family to introduce her to? Without even enough money to replace a toupee?*

She slid off the ring and angled it so the light shone on the inscription inside. Everyone must be wondering what she was doing, but Samantha didn't care.

The inscription read: To Letitia, 1927.

She stepped back and glowered at Hank. His mouth tightened and his eyes narrowed as if in warning. She'd never seen this expression on his face before. He looked, well, threatening.

"Liar!" she shouted. "You aren't a financial consultant! You're a jewel thief!"

She flung the ring at him, picked up her skirt and raced down the aisle. As she ran into the street and flagged a startled motorist, it struck her that she knew what evidence the police had found at the jewelry store.

It was Hank's toupee.

Chapter Two

From the rise where Kieran French stood, the construction site resembled the ruins of an ancient city. Just as when he'd visited Pompeii one summer, years ago, he could see the outlines of streets and the shapes of buildings defined by their foundations.

But this was a town of the future, not the past—the realization of five years' hard work. He had never imagined that now, on the brink of bringing a new community to life, he might have to face losing it.

The edges of the fax paper cut into Kieran's callused palm. He wouldn't give up Hidden Hot Springs. Not even if he had to bankrupt himself fighting for it.

"Taking the day off?"

He swung around, startled, to see Pete Zuniga, the foreman, coming up the slope.

"Just daydreaming." Kieran felt himself lapse into a sheepish smile. The responsibility of developing Hidden Hot Springs weighed heavily on his shoulders, but he had a fond place for Pete, a college chum. "Something you needed to see me about?"

Pete's brown eyes twinkled in his tanned face. "Actually, I'm here as kind of a delegate."

Up the slope behind him trailed a couple of construction workers named Mack and Ernie. Hanging back, his thin face tinged with scarlet, was Lew Jolson, the project architect.

"What's this?" Kieran joked. "Palace revolt?"

"Hell, no." Pete took off his cap and wiped his forehead. It was only June, but the temperatures soared into the 90s. "I mean, not exactly."

"We're lonely," said Mack.

"Yeah?" Kieran shot him an amused glance. "You guys miss me that much? I've only been up here half an hour."

Lew chuckled. "He didn't mean for you."

Kieran had an idea what was coming. The men grumbled that their backbreaking schedule, six days a week, didn't leave time to meet women.

Besides, a lot of these guys were in their thirties, like Kieran. They didn't want to waste time hanging around bars. He'd heard them grumbling at night in the recreation hall: Where did you meet an old-fashioned girl, the kind who kept writing to Ann Landers saying she couldn't meet any decent men?

"I presume you have something to propose?" he said. Better to let them get this off their chests, although he didn't see how they could spare even a few days' vacation if they were to meet their construction schedule.

"Yeah, well . . . uh." Pete stuck his hands in his pockets like an embarrassed kid. "Some of the guys saw an article in the newspaper about a bunch of women who went up to Alaska looking for husbands. Kind of like mail-order brides in the old days."

"You planning to hijack their plane?" Kieran shook his head. "Our airstrip won't be ready for months. Besides, it's just for commuter craft."

"Hey!" Ernie objected. "We ain't going to hijack no airplane!"

"He's kidding," Lew said. "But Kieran, we're serious. Think about it. How much would it cost to put an ad in the

San Diego newspaper? Hold a dance at the rec hall, play some tapes, serve cookies and coffee?"

"Beer," said Mack. "Gotta have beer."

"What kind of girl you fixing to meet?" snapped Ernie. "What kind of girl's going to come out here and drink beer?"

"What kind of girl's going to come out here, period?" Kieran pointed out. "Come on, guys, I know how frustrated you are, but in four months we'll have this hotel built. Some of the shops will be opening, and there'll be jobs for women."

"The guys don't want to wait," Pete said. Below them, other workers huddled in the scant shade, eating their lunches. "And how many women will there be? We got over a hundred guys here, and considering they're all shareholders, they're pretty much stuck for the duration."

"The duration" could last years. The plans called for a movie theater, a minimall, private houses and condominiums to replace the trailers where most of the men lived, and eventually a school.

But unless something changed soon, there wouldn't be any children to attend it. A few married men had joined the project early on, but they'd all dropped out when their wives got tired of the isolation.

Kieran shrugged. "You guys want to hold a dance and advertise for dates, go right ahead. But you might want to wait until Halloween, because what shows up could be pretty scary."

"It's worth a try." Pete slapped his cap back into place. "Thanks, Kier."

"Think nothing of it," Kieran said.

As the men turned away, Lew added, "You should drop by. A little feminine companionship wouldn't do you any harm, either."

Kieran gave him a distant nod. Getting mixed up with a woman was the last thing he needed right now. It could be hard living alone; he had the normal masculine urges, but he tried to channel his energy into work.

By the time the men trooped out of earshot, Kieran's thoughts had returned to the letter.

Beatrice French Bartholomew. There was the kind of feminine companionship a man could do without. It was just like her to turn up now, trying to claim an inheritance to which she had no right.

Kieran's uncle, Albert French, had left him Hidden Hot Springs five years ago. It had been a low point in Kieran's life. His construction company was drowning in red ink, his fiancée had deserted him and he didn't know what he was going to do with a crumbling resort along the back roads of San Diego County.

Then, on a trip to clean up his uncle's possessions from the old shack where Albert lived, Kieran was struck by the possibilities of the hot springs and the surrounding canyon.

Secluded among weeping pepper trees, the site spoke of an older, gentler time. During the 1920s, it had been a popular getaway for the Hollywood set. The Great Depression had siphoned off its business, but the beauty remained.

The springwater ran hot and clear, a luxury for bathing and drinking. Furthermore, Hidden Hot Springs was only a few hours' drive from San Diego and Orange counties. With the right convention and resort facilities, it could turn into a money-maker.

But where was he going to get the capital?

Rejected by bankers and investors, Kieran hit on a scheme. Many of his friends were in construction and related fields. Like pioneers of old, they could pool their money and expertise to build the community themselves. He would offer shares in lieu of cash.

They'd spent years drawing up plans, securing permits and putting utilities in place. They'd broken ground last winter on a hotel and hoped to complete it by fall, when the tourist season began.

And now Albert's daughter, Beatrice French Bartholomew, had turned up again.

She'd been estranged from her father for more than a decade, since he caught her cheating some of his friends at cards. Since then, Albert had told Kieran, she'd stolen a friend's husband, spent all his money and then divorced him. A few years later, she'd been arrested in a fraudulent investment plan, but escaped prosecution by testifying against her partners. It wasn't surprising that Albert had excluded her from the will.

Then, this morning, Kieran had received news from his attorney that she'd filed suit, claiming he had taken advantage of his uncle when Albert was ill and feebleminded. Ill and feebleminded? That old coot had hiked three miles with Kieran a month before he died, and beaten him at Scrabble, too.

The problem was, the will had been handwritten and witnessed by a couple of transients who couldn't be found. The will was also imprecise, leaving the property to "Kieran French and his wife" in anticipation of a marriage that had never taken place.

Beatrice's suit included the contention that, since Kieran had no wife, the will was invalidated. Nonsense, but annoying nonsense. The woman would seize on any pretext to try to take his property.

Kieran would see Beatrice in hell before he gave her Hidden Hot Springs. Losing the land wouldn't just hurt him, it would cheat a lot of good men who'd trusted him.

Let them have their dance and their mail-order brides. Hey, he hoped that damn thing worked out. Maybe they'd get a few nice ladies, although that would surprise him. In any case, Kieran French didn't have time to get mixed up with women, nice or not.

Somehow, he had to prove that Uncle Albert really meant for him to have this property.

"MAIL-ORDER BRIDES? Somebody must be joking." Samantha's boss tossed the personal ads onto her desk. "Look at that!"

She glanced at the notice he'd circled in red.

"Mail-Order Brides! A hundred red-blooded men need WOMEN for serious relationships. Come to our mixer! Friday, 8 p.m., Recreation Hall, Hidden Hot Springs."

Directions followed. It looked like the place was at the back end of nowhere.

"Probably a mad mugger," Samantha said. "Luring naive women into the underbrush. I'll bet the place doesn't even exist."

Fred Low, owner of Low's Del Mar Travel, leaned on the edge of her desk. "I've heard of it. They're building a convention center out there."

"Well, I can't imagine who'd go for something like that." Samantha pictured a bunch of lonely, lusty men waiting to seize their hapless prey. "Certainly not me!"

Fred smiled. "Good. You're an excellent secretary. I'd like to keep you around a while longer."

"You will, if my ex-fiancé doesn't catch up with me." Samantha sighed.

In the weeks since her interrupted wedding, she'd changed jobs and moved a few miles north to the beach community of Del Mar. Although Hank was locked up, his accomplice had so far escaped detection, and Samantha remained the only witness.

She could have kicked herself for flinging that ring at him. It had disappeared, and the police hadn't been able to find any of the other loot. Only Samantha and the toupee could link Hank to the robbery. Without her testimony, he'd probably go free.

She missed her friends, but the deputy district attorney said it was too dangerous to contact them. The accomplice would probably be watching, and the trial was still a month away.

She'd even had her mail forwarded to a safe-deposit box rather than to her new apartment. It was a pain having to pick it up, but she'd do whatever it took to cover her tracks.

"You should be safe here." Fred gazed out the window, past shady residential streets to a glimmer of ocean barely visible beyond. "Del Mar's a quiet town."

"I'm counting on it." The phone rang and Samantha answered. "It's for you," she said. "That tour to the British Isles."

"Right." He retreated to his office.

Samantha glanced at the newspaper on her desk. It amused her that Fred always read the personals. He claimed he wanted to check on unauthorized resales of airline tickets that might cut into his business, but she suspected he enjoyed prying into other peoples' lives.

The only other person Samantha knew who read the personals was Mary Anne, who also enjoyed soap operas and gossipy talk shows. Still, since Fred left the classifieds lying open, Samantha sometimes flipped through them to the employment section, just out of curiosity.

That was how, last week, she'd come across an ad for her dream job. It involved working on the recreation staff of a cruise ship out of Miami.

Samantha had applied at once. What could be more fun than cruising from island to island on a boat full of delicious food? The job started in August, by which time

Hank's trial should be over. Every time she picked up her mail, she watched eagerly for a response.

Samantha glanced at the paper again, and the red-circled ad leapt out. *Mail-order brides!*

What kind of men would place an ad like that? Your brainless macho types, she supposed. *And what kind of woman would answer?*

The phone rang again. It was a customer checking on a cruise to Central America, and after that a man called wanting to book a trip to Nashville. Five o'clock came before Samantha knew it.

She tucked the newspaper under her arm. She hadn't had time to read the advice columns; she'd tackle those over a frozen dinner.

What a dull life, she reflected as she waved to Fred and let herself out onto the second-floor open-air walkway. Here it was Friday, and she didn't dare go out dancing or even to the movies.

Samantha could already hear the steel drums of the West Indies and taste the Jamaican rum. Her body yearned to sway with the swell of the ocean beneath the ship...

Her thoughts broke off as something moved below in the parking lot, near her red sports car. Samantha frowned. What was that blond man doing?

Sunlight gleamed off a crowbar as he swung it. He was going to smash the window!

"Stop!" Samantha yelled. "Robber! Robber!"

The man spun around, and she gasped. There was no mistaking the sharp planes of Hank's face beneath the shaggy wig.

What was he doing out of jail? How on earth had he found her?

The sensible thing would be to call the police, but a driving fury seized Samantha. *How* dare *he hunt her down? What was he planning to do, destroy her car for revenge?*

"You creep!" She clattered down the stairs, hearing her voice echo across the parking lot. "You get away from there! Thief! Liar!"

Several people paused while getting into their cars and turned to look.

Hank hefted the crowbar. "Stop right there! I'll use this on you if I have to."

Samantha stopped a few dozen feet away. *Why didn't he flee?* There were too many witnesses to attack her here, or at least she hoped so. *And why was he wearing that hideous wig?* A man with brown eyes and dark stubble on his chin had no business trying to look like one of the Beach Boys.

Hank darted forward, grabbing for her arm. "Unlock that car."

Samantha dodged back and braced herself. She'd taken a self-defense class a few months ago and she knew exactly what to do.

She screamed.

It wasn't some puny little "eek!" either. She'd practiced in her car on the freeway, like the instructor advised. What issued from Samantha's throat was a bloodcurdling, heart-pounding, rising-to-an-ear-rending howl guaranteed to raise blood pressure for miles around.

Upstairs, a door banged open. "What the hell is going on?" demanded Fred's nasal voice. "I'm calling the police!"

Hank balanced on the balls of his feet, weighing his options, and then turned and ran. His wiry body—*why had she ever thought he was well-built?*—vanished behind a parked truck.

"And don't come back!" yelled Samantha.

"Are you all right?"

She looked up toward the balcony. The setting sun blared into her field of vision and she couldn't see Fred's face. "Yes, thanks to you. Look, I'm sorry but—that was Hank. I have to find somewhere else to hide."

Her boss leaned over the railing and she could see disappointment in his eyes. "I don't suppose you'd consider coming back when this is over?"

"With any luck, I'll be headed for the Caribbean." Samantha waved. "Thanks for everything."

She imagined she could hear Fred's sigh resounding through the parking lot.

Not until she turned on the ignition and started to back out did Samantha realize her hands were shaking. She could have been killed! In her anger, she'd acted like an idiot.

There'd been too many witnesses this time. If Hank turned up again, she might not be that fortunate.

She had to find somewhere else to lie low. Someplace a whole lot more remote than Del Mar.

How had Hank tracked her? Nobody outside the district attorney's office knew her whereabouts. But then, Samantha supposed, there were always ways of tracing someone. It was almost impossible not to leave a trail in some computer.

She headed inland toward her apartment, traveling well in excess of the speed limit. If Hank knew where she worked, he might also know where she lived.

The underground parking garage had a locked gate, and Samantha let herself in with her card-key. She parked next to the stairs and ran up two flights.

Letting herself into the apartment, she checked for signs of an intruder. Then she called the district attorney's office.

As soon as the secretary, Mrs. Gray, answered, Samantha identified herself. "Where's Dick Enright?" He was the deputy D.A. assigned to Hank's case.

"I'm sorry, he's left for the weekend."

"Remember me?" Samantha pressed. "I'm the *only* witness to that string of jewel robberies, and Hank Torrance just tried to kill me!" A slight exaggeration, perhaps, but it made the desired impact.

"Oh, my God!" said Mrs. Gray. "A judge set bail this morning. He must have been released this afternoon. You should have been notified!"

"Well, I wasn't!" Samantha said.

"We'd better send a policeman out to keep an eye on you." The secretary had a dry voice with a Midwestern accent. The first time they spoke on the phone, Samantha had formed a mental image of a sedate lady with graying hair pulled into a bun. "Give me your location and I'll take care of it. I'll page Mr. Enright, too."

"Just give him a message," Samantha said. "I'm going into hiding again and this time there won't be *any* traces. Got that? I'll check in by phone."

"But Mr. Enright will want to know..."

"See you at the trial!" Samantha hung up, still burning with anger, but hoping she hadn't directed too much of it at poor Mrs. Gray.

Out of the closet came two suitcases covered with travel stickers. Racing around the apartment, Samantha threw her clothes and cosmetics into the bags with practiced speed. She'd escaped a revolution in a small African country once, and the only thing she'd left behind had been a collection of matchbook covers from local nightclubs.

There was no time to sort things. In went the blue garter, the white lace stockings, even the darn wedding dress she hadn't been able to return for fear Hank's accomplice would be watching. The hat wouldn't fit, so Samantha stuck it in a shopping bag and staggered out the door.

She piled everything into the car and zoomed onto the street, her heart thudding. All she could think of was to find a safe place where she could stop and formulate a plan.

She had to find a new home and a job where she'd be safe. How was she going to accomplish that when even the district attorney's office had let her down?

Maybe she was overreacting, Samantha told herself as she approached the freeway. Okay, so Hank had found her. It might have been dumb luck. She could head north a few miles toward Oceanside or beyond, to Orange County or Los Angeles. Among all those millions of people, she could easily disappear.

Then she spotted the gray sedan in her rearview mirror. She had never seen that particular vehicle before, but there was no mistaking Hank at the wheel. The wig had slipped to one side and he looked like a crazed refugee from a Marx Brothers movie.

The signal light ahead flicked to yellow. Samantha stomped on the gas and shot through.

Hank roared up on her tail. He must realize the sports car could outrun him on an open road, but he didn't intend to give her the chance.

Samantha remembered the evening before the wedding, the only time she'd let Hank drive her car. He'd spent a lot of time fussing with the seat to get it adjusted, then screeched away from the curb with breakneck acceleration. "Great wheels!" he'd shouted in exhilaration.

The jerk had probably been planning to use it for a getaway car.

Now Samantha's mind worked feverishly. The freeway was coming up. If she headed north, she'd be stuck on a straightaway with a lot of traffic and few exits. Too easy for Hank to force her over.

Instead, she went south. Maybe in the welter of freeways in and around San Diego, she could lose him.

Her hands felt slippery on the wheel. She couldn't keep this up for long. If Hank didn't kill her, an accident might.

Where could she go that was safe? A place where even if he showed up, people would protect her?

As she charged up a ramp and merged into traffic, a name popped into Samantha's mind. Hidden Hot Springs.

It sounded like the back end of nowhere, all right. Hidden was part of its name. A hundred burly construction workers awaited her. If they couldn't defend her, who could?

It was a bizarre idea, but she didn't have a better one. Besides, the directions were right there in the newspaper, on the seat beside her.

Samantha wove between two trucks, trying to stay out of bumping distance of Hank. He was probably mad enough to cause a crash, just for spite.

Why hadn't she sensed his true character during that wildly romantic interlude in Acapulco? Why on earth had she agreed to marry him?

Samantha gave a mental shrug as she shot past a bus into the fast lane. She'd followed lots of impulses in her twenty-eight years, and none had turned out as bad as this one. Chalk it up to the luck of the draw.

In another minute she could branch onto a freeway heading inland. From there, she'd be able to plot her way into the hinterlands where Hidden Hot Springs lay. But first she had to lose Hank.

A check of the mirrors showed him hanging a few feet behind her rear bumper. He flashed his headlights. She replied with a rude gesture.

The gray car edged forward. He was going to override her bumper!

Samantha stepped on the gas and the sports car leapt. She was about to give it another surge, when she realized Hank had suddenly dropped back.

It was easy to see why. A California Highway Patrol car—better known as a Chippie—was approaching on their right.

Samantha caught her breath, wondering if he would activate his flashers. Her speedometer read sixty-five, a good ten miles per hour over the limit but not yet in the realm where a ticket was inevitable.

Then it struck her that, for the first time in her life, she *wanted* to get stopped. The patrolman could protect her from Hank. On the other hand, he might also give her a ticket. Some cops were like that.

The freeway transition lay dead ahead. If she could reach it, she might escape Hank *and* avoid a ticket.

Samantha hit her turn signal, gave the Chippie a friendly wave and cut across four lanes of traffic. As she darted onto the connector ramp, she noticed a large truck blocking the patrol car from following.

The patrolman had missed the turnoff, and so had Hank.

Safe on the inland freeway, Samantha boosted her speed to seventy-five. She was running for her life.

When no gray sedan showed up during the next ten minutes, she let her speed slacken. Her heart rate slowly returned to normal.

So far so good. Now to carry out her plan.

Samantha peered at the newspaper, reading the numbers of the roads. She ought to be able to find them without too much trouble.

Settling back in her seat, she tried to imagine all those muscular guys crowding a recreation hall. She'd pick the biggest, beefiest one to be her protector. A huge hunk of muscle without a brain in his head.

That was what she needed. Brawn without brain.

Of course, there might be a few problems. Exactly what was she going to do with him? Marry the lug?

Oh, well, Samantha thought. As Alice had said, she could always get a divorce. And she already had the dress.

Chapter Three

Kieran let the men off at six on Friday, although they often worked later in summertime. Tonight there'd be showering and shaving like nobody's business around here.

He had to admit, placing the ad had given morale a boost. Even some of the toughest characters had sorted through their tapes and compact discs for dance music, and he'd surprised one big lug who'd been teaching another to dance behind some trees during lunch hour.

Even now, washing at the pump in front of his cabin, Kieran smiled at the memory of their red faces.

He'd been asked countless times if he were planning to show up tonight. His preference was to catch a "Star Trek" rerun via the satellite dish, but he supposed the owner of Hidden Hot Springs ought to make an appearance. And, in all honesty, he was curious to see what sort of women would arrive.

Although the ad hadn't included a phone number, several ladies had called construction headquarters to confirm it wasn't a joke. One mentioned she would be loading her girlfriends into a van for the trip.

Kieran hoped she meant it. He'd hate to see the men disappointed.

In the fading light, he scrubbed his bare chest with a towel. With no women around, he'd gotten used to wearing casual attire, and sometimes hardly any attire at all. Now, for instance, he'd thrown on ragged cutoffs and shoved his bare feet into a pair of huaraches.

Although water pipes led to the cabin, over the last few decades tree roots had reduced the flow to a trickle. For most uses, Kieran came outside to pump groundwater.

The cabin was located in a clearing, with a welcome sense of privacy. The nearness of other cabins was evinced, however, by the blare of a televised announcer from one direction and, from the other, off-key singing. That would be Lew Jolson, the architect, listening to the nightly news, while Pete Zuniga was wreaking havoc on "I Will Always Love You" with his whiskey tenor.

Kieran checked his waterproof, shatterproof watch. It was a few minutes past seven. Plenty of time to change clothes and shave before making his obligatory appearance.

A rustle of movement caught his attention, and he turned to see a mountain lion cub giving him an assessing gaze. The area abounded with squirrels, chipmunks, deer, foxes, possums and raccoons, but the larger animals rarely came this close.

What was a cub doing by itself? Its mother couldn't be far behind, and that spelled trouble.

The project's plans set aside a botanical and wildlife reserve where Kieran hoped man and animal might be able to coexist in peace. But he hadn't counted on big cats.

The cub pounced to one side, then stopped and stared at him again. The little fellow, a few sizes larger than a full-grown tomcat, didn't appear injured.

But if it wandered onto the main road a few hundred feet below, it might fall prey to traffic, especially with the cars expected tonight. Kieran began to circle downhill. If he approached from the opposite side, he might be able to shoo it to higher ground.

Before he reached position, however, Pete launched into another song. Wrinkling its nose in what looked for all the world like distaste, the cub padded down the hill.

"Wait!" Kieran called, knowing it was useless. His shout might even have annoyed the creature further, he reflected as he stomped after it.

A minute later, he pushed aside an overhead branch to see the cub sitting in the middle of the two-lane road, calmly licking its paws as it regarded the surroundings.

On the far side of the road lay the tumbledown shack where Uncle Albert had lived. He'd claimed it was the only remaining cabin where he could still get decent water pressure. In fact, Kieran suspected, the old man had enjoyed chatting with the occasional prospector or lost tourist whose vehicle chugged down the road.

To Kieran's left, a half mile east around a bend in the road, lay the small town of Hidden Hot Springs. A short ways across the highway, the spring-fed trees petered out into scrubby brush. Either way, the cub could get into trouble. It needed to run back past Kieran's cabin to the preserve.

He strolled toward the road, keeping his distance from the unfazed animal. He would try to circle around and come at the cub from the far side.

The thrum of a car engine whined into Kieran's nerves. *Blast it, why did some driver have to show up now?*

Too annoyed to care that his anger was irrational, Kieran planted himself in the middle of the road. *Let the damn fool run over him first!*

The cub quivered, ready to flee but unable to decide which way. From the west, a sports car raised a cloud of dust as it roared toward them well over the speed limit.

Squinting against the setting sun, Kieran shouted, "Stop, you numskull!" and waved his arms like windshield wipers.

At the last possible minute, brakes squealed and the car skidded to a halt. A door flew open and a woman jumped out.

With the sun in his eyes, Kieran could make out only her silhouette. She had a small, slender frame, with straight shoulders and gentle curves. It was the kind of body that made a man want to explore it—assuming, of course, that he liked the person inside.

He didn't suppose this young woman liked him very much at the moment. The way she stood with slim legs astride and hands on hips gave testimony to her fury. Kieran wouldn't have been surprised to see sparks fly from her eyes.

"Well?" the woman demanded. "If there's some kind of road construction ahead, I'll forgive you, but otherwise, get out of my way!"

Couldn't the maniac see that she'd nearly killed the cub? "If you weren't so busy trying to wear ruts in the pavement, you might have noticed..." He turned to indicate the lion, but it wasn't there.

Kieran surveyed the landscape. Not a trace. The little creature had made its getaway, and he could only hope it had chosen the right direction.

"Yes?" the woman snapped. "Noticed what?"

Beneath her withering gaze, Kieran became aware of his state of undress. He wouldn't even show up in front of his men wearing nothing but ripped cutoffs and sandals. *Come to think of it, he hadn't bothered to shave this morning, either.*

On the other hand, she'd ventured to Hidden Hot Springs seeking masculine companionship, hadn't she? Why should she look so offended when a specimen of the gender appeared half-naked in her path?

"Forgotten how to talk?" the woman challenged. "I guess living out here in the backwoods can do that to you. Well, let me remind you. This is a street. See, it's paved?

That means it's for wheels, not feet. So why don't you take your feet somewhere else and let me pass?''

The woman must think he was some kind of rube. Kieran fought back a smile. "Why, yes, ma'am." He made a bow. "We don't often see yer likes round these parts. Fact is, iffen we see us a good-lookin' cow, we figger it's party time.''

A low chuckle escaped her. "Okay, I guess I deserved that, but why the heck *are* you standing in the middle of nowhere waving your arms?''

"Just lonely, ma'am." Kieran favored her with what he hoped was a dirt-eating grin. "I put on my best duds and ever'thing. Been meanin' to get myself one o' them fancy tattoos, too, but we're a little behind the times in Hidden Hot Springs.''

"Hidden Hot Springs? You mean I'm there?'' She stared around in horror. "This is it? What did you do, place the ad yourself?''

He felt like teasing her all evening, or at least until the sun sank a little lower so he could get a better glimpse of her. "Sure thing, ma'am. I'm looking for a mate to drag into the bushes.''

"The thought already occurred to me, but I don't scare easily." The woman crouched in one of those pseudo-karate stances that self-defense instructors liked to teach women. "Don't try to get close.''

He could see her face now, small and heart-shaped, framed by soft wisps of brown hair. The eyes tilted slightly, giving them a hint of exoticism, and her lips were full and moist.

Her skin glowed with a healthy sheen, and he could follow the course of every breath she took, rippling along her silky print blouse. The way she lifted her chin and glared made him want to cup her face and taste her mouth.

Kieran chuckled. "Hey, I don't need to drag my women off. Usually I just whistle and they follow.''

"Let's get one thing straight," she snapped, straightening. "Just because I drove to the middle of nowhere to check out a mixer doesn't mean I'm for sale! So quit looking at me like some—like some cow you're planning to buy!"

Kieran shook his head. "Lady, no man in his right mind would pay good money for a temper like that!"

"Well, from all indications, your right mind is something you left back in civilization!" she countered. "Now is there really a town, or do I have to turn around and go back?"

"It's just around that bend," he said.

"You aren't…you aren't coming to the mixer, are you?" she ventured.

He really must look a fright, Kieran thought in amusement. Aloud, he drawled, "Naw, I guess I'll pitch me some hay and get a bit o' shut-eye. Now you be careful with that horseless carriage. We don't see too many of them in these parts. Yer likely to scare the chickens."

The woman shook her head, the sun making her hair glow with red highlights. "You're the most annoying man I've met in a long time!"

"Glad to be of service. No charge for the entertainment." He shot her a challenging look and strolled off the road.

Kieran paused to watch the visitor slide into the car and jerk it into gear. She hit the accelerator and shot down the road.

Whatever had possessed him to provoke her that way? He'd sensed she was enjoying it, but mostly he'd wanted to watch her reaction. In fact, he wouldn't have minded standing there for another half hour, enjoying the play of emotions that animated her face.

Maybe things wouldn't be so boring at the party tonight, after all. Kieran hadn't intended to dance, but he'd have to claim at least one turn around the floor with that young woman.

Just to annoy her, of course.

SAMANTHA GRITTED her teeth and forced herself to ease up on the accelerator.

Who did that big lout think he was? He'd stared at her as if she'd been put there for his express enjoyment. She almost hoped he'd show up tonight just so she could ignore him.

On the other hand, a woman couldn't help noticing the way the sunset gleamed on his tan skin and well-defined muscles. It wasn't the kind of self-consciously sculpted body a man got in a gym, either. This guy had come by his muscles the honest way—he'd worked for them.

She couldn't remember the last time she'd seen a physique like that, with a narrow waist and long, firm legs. This guy must think he was hot stuff. Well, maybe he was. His forehead had been covered with thick blond hair, and who could help noticing the chiseled planes of his cheeks? As for the blue-green eyes, if they hadn't been dancing with glee at her expense, Samantha supposed she might have found them riveting. And his mouth, well, you could only describe it as forceful.

What on earth was she doing, cataloging the guy's features as if he were the offering in a vacation brochure? If there was anywhere she planned to travel, it certainly wasn't into his bed!

On the other hand, if she *were* designing such a brochure, she knew precisely the words to describe him: Arrogant. Self-centered. Stubborn. Cute.

Cute? What was that doing in there?

Samantha hit the brakes and looked back. In her preoccupation, she'd scarcely noticed the handful of ramshackle buildings along the road, but the sign dead ahead said: "Leaving Hidden Hot Springs. Come Back Soon!"

Leaving Hidden Hot Springs? It wasn't much bigger than that spot where she'd run across the Wild Man of Borneo.

As she backed up, a couple of chickens squawked out of the way. The guy hadn't been kidding about the poultry.

Samantha found a space next to what looked like a hitching post and killed the motor. In the fading light, the place resembled something out of the Old West. Not a cleaned-up Hollywood version, either.

The building in front of her, hewn of rough timbers, bore a hand-painted sign: General Store. A porch rambled across the front, and there were two small, dusty windows. A skewed placard read Closed.

Across the street, an equally ramshackle adobe building was marked Public Restrooms. A whole building for public restrooms? This must be where clods like that guy in the road came to scrape off the dirt once a month.

Behind the showers, along a rise, sat several dozen trailers on crude foundations. So this was where the natives lived.

She had half a mind to leave right now. This was the last place on earth she would choose to stay.

Samantha sighed and got out of the car. The good part, she supposed, was that this might be the last place Hank would think to look for her.

Besides, she could endure anything for a month. Then would come the trial and then, with luck, she'd be off on the trip of her dreams. She'd have a steady source of income *and* a new island every few days. It was worth a month in Dullsville.

She checked her watch. Not even seven-thirty, yet. Half an hour till the mixer.

Across the street, two men leaned against the wall of the bathhouse, smoking cigarettes. One nodded politely, the other eyed Samantha with naked hunger. She clamped her lips shut and marched along the buildings.

This place didn't even have sidewalks. The uneven ground made her high heels wobble, and she could feel the men staring at her exposed legs. She wished she hadn't worn such a short skirt, but when she'd picked it out this morning, she'd figured her legs would spend most of the day hidden behind a desk.

Well, those guys ought to grow up. Women in the nineties dressed any way they pleased, and men were expected to control their baser instincts.

Was it really possible that they didn't have *any* women around here? she wondered, her thoughts drifting back to the half-naked man in the road. He hadn't looked like the type who'd find himself alone for long.

Surely there was a larger town within commuting distance, although Samantha had to admit she hadn't passed one. A guy with that kind of masculine self-confidence wouldn't allow himself to languish out here.

It was intriguing to reflect on what bottled passions might boil beneath the surface if he really had been celibate for months. She supposed she was lucky he hadn't propositioned her right there on the highway.

What would she have done if he had? Slapped his face? She could almost feel the stubble of his cheek beneath her hand. How would he have reacted? Would he have grabbed her wrist and pulled her close?

She didn't want to think such thoughts about that oaf. Especially when she had her doubts about his personal hygiene.

Past the general store, she noticed a large prefab structure marked Dining Hall. From inside came the clatter of dishes, but Samantha couldn't see anything without opening the door, and she had no intention of doing that.

She could imagine what lay inside: rows of scarred tables, a cafeteria serving line and overcooked food drenched with salt and fat. Exactly like the dining hall at her boarding school, except that the men were probably allowed to sit wherever they wanted.

By contrast, Samantha pictured her favorite sidewalk café in Paris. Patrons meandered from table to table, catching up on the news, while waiters darted between chairs with drinks and dinner plates. The flavors of wine, garlic and herbs blended in her memory, making her mouth water.

Now *that* was her idea of a place to eat.

She remembered she hadn't had dinner, except for a granola bar she'd found on the floor of the car. Well, she wouldn't find anything edible in this town, that was for sure.

The whole idea of coming here struck her as impossibly foolish. Mudville, U.S.A., that's what Hidden Hot Springs should have been named. It even came with its own resident Bigfoot planted on the highway.

As she gazed around dispiritedly, another thought occurred to Samantha. There wasn't a sign of any place to spend the night. The town might have once been a resort, but there didn't appear to be any public facilities at the moment.

She wasn't looking forward to driving back through the canyon in darkness. What were the other women planning to do?

Or would there be any other women?

At that moment, she felt her first quiver of fear. It hadn't occurred to her that she might find herself stranded in a remote town full of men. The idea might sound romantic, but it didn't feel that way.

She was edging toward her car when the rumble of a motor made her turn. Beyond the dining hall lay another building, an adobe structure that, judging from the bell tower, might once have been a church. The sign in front read: Recreation Hall/Library.

A familiar blue Saturn stopped in front and a chubby figure in pink slacks and a flowered blouse slid out. Even with the setting sun in her eyes, Samantha knew who it was.

"Mary Anne!" Despite the tremors in her high heels, she bounded down the dirt walkway. "It's me!"

"Samantha!" Her friend grabbed her in a hug. "Oh, we've been so worried! You just disappeared. I know you had to hide from Hank, but couldn't you let us know you were all right?"

Stepping back, Samantha gazed at her friend in apology. "The district attorney's office told me not to contact anyone. But you know what? Hank found me, anyway."

"He did?" Mary Anne's gray eyes widened. "Are you all right?"

She nodded. "That's why I'm here. It's as good a place to hide as any. Or, at least, that was the idea."

Lights flicked on inside the adobe building, and Samantha heard intermittent blares of music as someone checked out the sound system. "What about you? What brings you here?"

Mary Anne bit her lip. "You always told me that if I wanted something, I had to make it happen myself. When I saw the ad in the personals, I almost felt as if you'd reached out and tapped my shoulder. I knew I had to come."

"I'm proud of you!" Samantha said. "But why drive all the way out here? There are singles events in San Diego."

Mary Anne smiled ruefully. "I tried one last week. Everybody seemed so busy trying to impress each other. I'm not good at that."

Samantha hoped with all her heart that Mary Anne wouldn't be disappointed tonight, but so far, this town didn't seem very promising. "What about Alice?"

Mary Anne sighed. "I didn't tell her. I couldn't. You know how cynical she is about marriage."

"I can see how a person could get that way. Cynical about marriage, I mean." Samantha still shuddered whenever she thought of her close call with Hank.

From the cafeteria and the trailers, men began drifting toward the church building. Samantha linked her arm with Mary Anne's. "Maybe we should go inside," she began when, with a clatter and a thump, an aging minivan roared toward them down the road.

Pink crepe paper floated out the window, Barbra Streisand's voice soared from the radio, and Samantha could have sworn she caught a whiff of perfume.

The van screeched to a halt next to Mary Anne's car, and a tall brunette leaned out the driver's window. "The Love Bug is here!" she cried. "At 'em, girls!"

Doors flew open and women poured out. Samantha thought she counted eight, but she couldn't be sure.

"You can say one thing for them, they're not shy," she observed.

Mary Anne smiled. "I like having a lot of people around. This way no one will notice me."

"I thought that was the idea," said Samantha.

Her friend ducked her head. "I mean—well—I wouldn't want a *lot* of attention."

More cars, and more women, followed. Samantha had to admit, they looked downright presentable. What could have attracted them to this out-of-the-way place? They couldn't all be running from vengeful ex-fiancé's.

"Let's go in," urged Mary Anne, and Samantha nodded.

Inside, they found a large, open room with an arched ceiling. The adobe walls bore faded frescoes of Spanish missionaries and Native Americans.

Along one wall stood a bookcase filled with tattered volumes, and Samantha remembered the sign out front had referred to a library. On the other side, a long table had been rigged, covered with a vinyl cloth and set with cans of soda and beer.

How typical, she thought. The men hadn't fixed anything to eat, and she was starving.

She felt a surge of gratitude as the tall woman from the van plopped a tray of cupcakes on the table. "You sure are enterprising," Samantha said, taking one. "Hope you don't mind. I missed dinner."

"They're carrot cakes," said the woman. "Full of vitamins. Sugar, too. Don't forget to brush your teeth." To Samantha's raised eyebrow, she explained, "I'm a teacher. Second grade."

Samantha stuck out her hand, the one without a cupcake in it. "Samantha Avery. Unemployed you-name-it-I've-done-it. This is my friend Mary Anne Montgomery."

The dark-haired woman shook their hands. "I'm Beth Bonning. You guys from San Diego?"

They nodded.

"We're from Chula Vista. Right on the border." Beth gazed around. "I hope these guys' idea of a serious relationship isn't wham, bam, thank you ma'am. I've met enough creeps in the last five years to last me a lifetime."

"I've met enough creeps in the last five weeks," said Samantha. "One in particular."

"I haven't even met any creeps," said Mary Anne.

Samantha put an arm around her. "You will," she said with mock reassurance.

The place was getting full, and someone turned up the sound system until Samantha's eardrums threatened to pop. The music featured a pulsating rhythm, shrieking guitars and incomprehensible vocals.

Despite all the arrivals, the women were outnumbered three to one. Finally, even shy Mary Anne was dodging around the jammed dance floor in the arms of a man.

Samantha took refuge behind the refreshment table, pouring drinks into paper cups. She wanted time to get her bearings before she fended off masculine attention.

Assessing the men in these cramped circumstances was difficult. For one thing, they blurred together in a sweaty mass. She approved of the heavy tans, but wasn't impressed by their idea of dress-up clothes: blue jeans and T-shirts.

For another thing, none of them matched her image of a burly bodyguard. The only guy who fit the bill had been the human roadblock she'd met earlier, and she had no intention of signing on the dotted line with a mutton-headed specimen like that.

She didn't want to think about the mischievous glint in his aquamarine eyes, or the grin that teased the edges of his mouth. What she needed was a protector, not some good-looking dunce.

Gazing around the hall, she observed a tall, gangly fellow dancing with Beth, while Mary Anne was being squired by a short man with a lively face.

The short man wore a tweed sports jacket, while the tall fellow was dressed in a loose-fitting navy blazer and slacks. Samantha decided they must be some kind of supervisors.

A guy in management ought to be in a position to keep her safe, she reflected. At least his trailer might have a private bathroom. On the other hand, both Mr. Short and Mr. Gangly looked like earnest types. Once they hauled a woman down the aisle, they'd expect her to stay married.

A few minutes later, the screaming music blew out a fuse, and there was a lot of milling around while the men vied for the right to fix it.

Beth and Mary Anne retreated to the refreshment table, accompanied by the two management types. Mary Anne introduced her companion as Pete Zuniga, the project foreman.

"Guess you're the boss, huh?" said Samantha as they shook hands.

"No, he's not here, yet." Pete shrugged. "Kieran's kind of a loner."

"But he'll probably show up. He knows it would be good for morale," added the tall man in the blazer. He thrust out his hand. "I'm Lew Jolson."

"He's the architect," said Beth.

"What exactly is this Mr. Kieran's function?" Samantha had only the vaguest idea of what people did on a building project. "Is he the owner?"

"We're all the owners," Lew said, starting to drape an arm around Beth and then thinking the better of it. "But he's the main owner. He inherited the land around here, and he put the project together. If it weren't for him, we wouldn't be here."

"By the way, Kieran's his first name," added Pete. He gave Mary Anne a fond look. "Would you like to walk down to the dining hall and grab a cup of coffee? We can come back when the music starts."

"Sure." Mary Anne smiled in astonished delight. They walked out together.

"So when is this Kieran character going to show up?" Samantha figured he must be older, maybe in his fifties. "Is he married?"

Lew shook his head. "The way he works eighteen hours a day, I doubt a marriage could survive."

Perfect, Samantha thought. *Never home. He'd hardly notice he had a wife.*

"Is he—easy to get along with?" she asked.

"He's a hell of a guy," the architect said. "When I first heard about this project, I didn't think he could get it off the ground, but he did, against tremendous odds. He's one tough customer, let me tell you."

Better and better, Samantha mused.

The music started up, and Beth tapped Lew's arm. "Are we or aren't we?" she asked.

"Definitely, we are," he said, and led her back to the dance floor.

Samantha drummed her fingers on the table. Kieran French. It was an unusual name and she liked it. She didn't like the image it conjured, though, of someone slender and sophisticated, more at home at the theater than in the boxing ring. But surrounded by loyal construction workers, he might qualify as a protector.

The air was getting thick, and men who didn't appeal to her were giving Samantha the eye. She dodged her way to the front door.

As she stepped outside, she heard someone say, "There's Mr. French."

Finally! Samantha followed the man's gaze to a tall, broad-shouldered figure with his back to her, standing beside a pickup truck.

Might as well walk over and introduce herself. Around here, boldness appeared to be the order of the day.

As she approached, she realized the man was talking on a cellular phone. His baritone drifted back, the words blurred but the forceful tone unmistakable. She caught the phrases "...due this morning...behind schedule... expect you to deliver on time..."

A take-charge guy, the kind who got things done. Not only that, but even in the fading light his jacket was unmistakably tailored to a powerful frame. Well-cut slacks draped over tight, muscular buttocks, dropping to sturdy leather shoes equipped with rubber tread.

This guy had found the sophisticated man's approach to dressing up in Mudville. Samantha could picture him equally at home at a Broadway play or at Carnival in Rio. She'd never expected to find anyone like him in the back end of nowhere.

"Get that damn shipment out here if you have to hire the bloody Marines!" snapped Kieran French, and clicked off the phone.

He leaned against the truck, fury radiating through his taut body. Samantha waited for a moment, then cleared her throat.

"Mr. French?" she said. "I've been wanting to meet you."

"Yes?" He swung around, shaggy blond hair framing a face still clouded with anger. "And you are—?"

They both stopped in shock.

"Bigfoot," gasped Samantha, and then wished she could disappear into the dirt track that passed for a sidewalk.

Chapter Four

Kieran had been hoping to encounter the lady in the short skirt again, but he hadn't expected her to corral him at his pickup.

He had felt his blood pressure nearing a boil as he'd talked to the "what me worry?" contractor who had failed to deliver the building supplies on time. That kind of ineptitude threatened the future of Hidden Hot Springs as much as his greedy cousin Beatrice did.

Turning around and finding this pretty lady was exactly what Kieran needed to take his mind off his problems. Damn, but he liked the way she skewered him with those amber eyes. She'd be a pleasant diversion for the evening, and by the time he got home, he'd have pushed that damn contractor right out of his thoughts.

"Bigfoot?" he repeated.

It was hard to tell in the dim light, but he could have sworn she was blushing. "Just a joke," she said. "I'm Samantha Avery."

She thrust out her hand. It felt small but firm in Kieran's grasp. In fact, every movement she made reflected a fierce sense of self-awareness. She might be a foot shorter than his six-one, but this lady was a tough cookie. He decided then and there that the trick with Samantha Avery was never to let her get the upper hand.

"You've been wanting to meet me?" he challenged.

Samantha's mouth twisted in a rueful smile. "Actually, I guess we already met, didn't we?"

"In a manner of speaking."

Now that she didn't have the setting sun behind her, he caught the full impact of her shape. The sleeveless print blouse clung to full breasts, then tapered to a slim waistline. The blues and scarlets of the print were repeated in a brief skirt that failed to cover her slender legs.

"You like my outfit?" Samantha teased.

"Very sensible," Kieran said. "Hot day."

She regarded him assessingly. What was on the woman's mind, anyway? Kieran could almost have sworn she was doing what she'd accused him of earlier: viewing him as some kind of product for purchase.

Nope, that must be his imagination running wild. He'd spent too much time alone. He'd almost forgotten how to act around a lady. She'd come here to dance, maybe meet a man she'd like to see again. Nothing wrong with that.

Music started inside the rec hall, as if to prompt him. "Care to dance?"

"Sure." She swung around on one of her impossibly high heels and led the way inside.

Kieran couldn't help noticing the glances she attracted from the men wandering in and out of the rec hall. He wondered why on earth she had sought him out.

He would just have to let Samantha tell him in her own sweet time.

MAYBE KIERAN FRENCH wasn't such a hopeless prospect after all, Samantha mused as she walked. Where else was she going to find a man with both the mental and physical strength to protect her if Hank showed up?

Freshly brushed, the shaggy hair looked stylish instead of sloppy. Clean-shaven, the strong planes of Kieran's face made him resemble a take-charge manager instead of a mountain man. As for that mouth, it might be grinning with amusement at her expense, but it could also bark orders and make men obey.

She wasn't sure how an executive developed shoulders and upper arms like that. Maybe he strode around the construction site snapping commands into his cellular phone, pausing only to hoist a large beam with a single hand before moving on to the next heroic task.

In short, maybe he was exactly the guardian she'd been looking for. Certainly Hidden Hot Springs was remote enough to meet her requirements, and full of rough-looking men, as well.

Kieran French wouldn't be an easy man to twist around her little finger, but Samantha had had her share of experience with the opposite sex. This man could be brought around to her point of view with a little persuasion, she had no doubt.

KIERAN TRIED NOT to pay too much attention to Samantha's soft form, swaying with feminine grace ahead of him as she led the way. He forced himself to nod and acknowledge the greetings of his men, calling each one by name. It was a matter of pride to him that Hidden Hot Springs would be built by a real community and not just hired hands.

In the flat lighting of the former church, he caught sight of Lew Jolson waltzing with a tall, dark-haired woman. A moment later, Pete Zuniga strolled in the door with a chunky young woman and whirled her onto the dance floor.

As Kieran and Samantha found a small clear space, the music changed from vibrant rock 'n' roll to a sultry tango. Other couples retreated, unfamiliar with the steps.

"Who the hell picked that one?" muttered Lew as he led his companion toward the food table.

Samantha's eyes dared Kieran. "Know how to tango?" she asked.

"Try me," he said.

He doubted she'd be able to keep up. The tango was one of the most difficult ballroom dances. It had taken him and Michele, his former fiancée, months to master as part of their weekly ballroom dance outings.

When performed correctly, it was both theatrical and sensuous. In Kieran's mind, the tango put all other dances in the shade.

What did this fresh-faced, smart-mouthed young woman know of the intricacies of Latin American rhythms? She'd probably spent her whole social life in San Diego nightclubs and, until not long ago, from the looks of her, at high school proms.

To Kieran's surprise, Samantha moved smoothly into position, close against him. He slid his right arm tightly around her waist and claimed her free hand in his.

Kieran could feel each taut muscle of her body as every tantalizing curve pressed against him. He struggled to control his response. The last thing he needed was to get turned on with all his men watching. They'd be making jokes at his expense for weeks.

To test her reflexes, he whirled Samantha around without warning. She almost lost her balance but caught on quickly, then nearly threw *him* off-balance by draping herself over his arm, head thrown back in a pose.

The onlookers applauded. Kieran realized a crowd had gathered to watch them.

He twirled Samantha upright and she straightened against him. The rules of the dance called for allowing no light between them, and she certainly didn't.

Then the music took over, awakening long-dormant responses. Feeling Samantha undulate in perfect harmony with him, Kieran moved into the drama of the tango.

Knees flexed, bodies rigid, they covered the floor with a series of languorous long steps and staccato short ones. Cheek to cheek, they melted into the provocative cadences born in the depths of Buenos Aires.

Samantha felt feather-light in his arms. How did she know which way he was going to turn as soon as he thought of it? She keyed into every twitch of his muscles, right down to the electrical impulses jolting his nerves.

Kieran tried not to think about what might happen if he held her in his arms without the intrusion of all these onlookers. How she would tantalize his mouth and arouse his passion, sensitive to every breath of desire and every thrust of passion.

Samantha's knowing gaze, the slight curve of her lips told him she was a far more experienced woman than he'd imagined. What other surprises did she hold in store?

The tempo quickened and he felt her body answer his own with faster steps and sharper turns. There was a question in her eyes, one that probed at him as he spun her and flung her away, then drew her back.

She wanted something from him. He could see it in the way she tilted her head and pressed her lips together. She hadn't come to Hidden Hot Springs from idle curiosity but, in some way Kieran didn't understand, to find him.

He had underestimated Samantha Avery. Now he must bide his time through the tantalizing intimacy of the tango until she faced him with her question.

He almost laughed aloud, thinking of the response his body was preparing.

WHERE HAD KIERAN FRENCH learned to dance like this?

Samantha had always loved to dance. In every city she visited, the ballrooms became her source of release, and her hope of finding her own Fred Astaire.

Never in any man's arms had Samantha felt the elegance and confidence that Ginger Rogers must have known. Until tonight.

She'd never dreamed her body possessed such grace. She'd never felt a man balance her this way, allowing her to instinctively share his power.

For a backwoods Romeo, Kieran had a lot going on upstairs, and probably downstairs, too. Samantha could feel the eyes of a dozen hungry women burning holes in her back. The sensation reminded her of the fact that Kieran French was a guy in search of a mail-order wife.

Why should he settle for letting her hide out in his cabin—and on a platonic basis at that—when he could have his pick of brides? If she didn't snap him up, somebody else surely would.

Besides, becoming Mrs. French instead of Ms. Avery would be a definite advantage in covering her tracks. True, she'd have to deal with that business of their sleeping arrangements, but Samantha figured she could squirm out of anything if she really put her mind to it.

In that moment she made up her mind to marry Kieran French until Hank's trial did them part.

KIERAN FELT AS IF HE might explode from the energy pounding through his arteries when the dance ended much too soon, but instead he had to stand there accepting the praise and good-natured teasing of his friends. Aware of Samantha growing restless at his side, he finally managed to escape with her toward the door.

Just when he thought they would get away, they stumbled into Pete. "Hey, Kier," said his friend. "Aren't you glad we went ahead with the mixer?"

Kieran nodded, realizing it was useless to fight the inevitable. He had about as much chance of fleeing anonymously into the night as he did of performing the mazurka upside down on the ceiling.

The redhead on Pete's arm beamed at Kieran. After a moment, he realized her affection was targeted at Samantha, not him.

"You two know each other?" he said.

"I was a bridesmaid at—" The woman stopped. "I mean, I'm Mary Anne Montgomery." She gazed at Samantha as if in appeal.

"I almost got married recently," Samantha said. "Fortunately I discovered my fiancé's true nature before it was too late."

"That makes two of us," said Kieran.

"You know Hank?" Mary Anne asked in astonishment.

"I was referring to my own fiancée." Something still didn't click for Kieran. "You two didn't drive down together, though?"

"I didn't know she was coming," Samantha said. "But I'm glad she did."

"You're both staying over for the picnic tomorrow, aren't you?" Pete put in.

To a flurry of questions, he explained that Lew and the tall brunette, Beth, had decided to organize a picnic for the following day. The men were rounding up tents and sleeping bags in the hope that the women would stay.

"Wait a minute." Kieran shook his head. "Since when do the men take Saturdays off?"

"Since we don't have the supplies we need," answered Pete. "Come on, give everybody a break."

Kieran had spent the better part of the afternoon trying in vain to figure out how to work around the missing supplies. Pete had a point.

"All right," he said. "But we'll have to work extra next week to make up for it."

"Slave driver," commented Lew, approaching from one side.

"Damn right." Kieran noticed that the dark-haired woman seemed perfectly at home with her arm linked through the architect's. Both his pals had lucked out tonight.

Oddly, the thought made Kieran uncomfortable. He realized with a start what was really bothering him—tonight marked a new stage in the life of Hidden Hot Springs.

Five years ago, after he'd hit on the scheme of providing shares in exchange for services, the project had belonged only to Kieran, Lew, Pete and an attorney friend, Joel Phillips. Together they'd drawn up the plans and estimated the financing, the number of workers and a tentative timetable.

In the second stage, after securing the necessary permits and pooling their credit, the three of them had been joined by construction workers, plumbers and other specialists who had a taste for adventure and were willing to work for minimum wage in exchange for shares.

Although the hoped for completion of the hotel this fall loomed large in Kieran's plans, he hadn't given much thought to the other alterations in store. The masculine camaraderie and frontier-camp mentality of the town were bound to change.

Now the transition had begun sooner than expected. For this weekend, at least, he'd have to think about what he was wearing, what language he used and who might be occupying the public bathing facilities.

His friends wouldn't always be available at the drop of a hat for poker or softball. Hell, somebody might even object to keeping the TV in the rec hall permanently tuned to a sports channel.

And, now that Kieran considered it, hadn't the objective been for the men to get married? Things might never return to what he'd come to consider normal.

He took a deep breath. He was letting himself get carried away. The only thing at stake was his peace of mind for one weekend, and he could survive that.

"Are you staying over?" he asked Samantha.

After the briefest of pauses, she said, "Of course."

"Without even a toothbrush?" he joked.

Samantha bit her lip as if fighting a smile. "I have more than a toothbrush. Actually, I have a whole suitcase . . . or two."

"Oh, who cares, anyway?" Beth tossed back an errant strand of dark hair. "The whole bunch of us are staying and we haven't got so much as a change of underwear. We'll just wash everything in the rest room."

Kieran could picture it already. One dance, and he'd wake up to see the entire town strewn with lingerie. However, he doubted any of the men would object.

Samantha tapped his arm. "Could we take a walk?"

"Sure." The heat generated by the tango had dissipated, but he wouldn't mind a stroll in the evening breeze. He particularly wouldn't mind walking beside Samantha. Even though he was giving the men the next day off, Kieran never relaxed his own work schedule, so he doubted he'd see much of her tomorrow.

Unless, of course, she cared to share his bed tonight. That was a possibility he was more than willing to entertain.

Still, he wasn't looking for anyone who needed a lot of time and attention; those were in short supply these days. On Tuesday, Kieran had a meeting scheduled with his lawyer and Beatrice. The last thing he needed was to get distracted.

"Tell me about Hidden Hot Springs," Samantha said as they stepped outside. "How old is the church?"

"It dates from the last century," Kieran replied. "It was the first structure in Hidden Hot Springs."

As they walked, he told her about the Indian legends that the hot springs had restorative powers, and how the region had been occupied by missionaries and ranchers for several centuries.

Then, in the nineteenth century, gold had been discovered in some of the canyons of San Diego County. Prospectors rushed in. A few made their fortune, most lost everything, and some disappeared, giving rise to ghost stories and tales of hidden treasure.

Despite Samantha's occasional questions, Kieran could tell she wasn't concentrating on his words. From the tightness of her mouth, he gathered she was holding something back.

For someone with as much sheer nerve as she'd displayed when she confronted him on the highway, she was proving mighty elusive tonight. What the hell was on her mind, anyway?

They reached the edge of town and sat on a boulder beside the road. Beyond them, tufts of brush escorted the two-lane road into the canyon.

A few miles farther, Kieran knew, the road turned into a dirt path, ending in a small, rugged campground. The only people who traveled this way were naturalists and, rarely, a prospector.

They sat in silence for a while, and then Samantha said, "Mind if I ask a few things?"

"Shoot." Kieran had a store of knowledge about these parts, all learned from his uncle, but he couldn't imagine what else she would want to know.

"Which side of the bed do you sleep on?"

That startled him. He couldn't believe the woman was propositioning him so baldly, although with her temperament, he wouldn't put anything past her. But this was a heck of a cold-blooded way to go about it.

"The right," he said, humoring her.

"Do you squeeze the toothpaste from the middle or the bottom?" she asked.

It had to be some kind of game. "The middle." Then he added, "Until it starts to run out. Then I squeeze from the bottom."

From far off came the plaintive wail of a coyote, quickly joined by a chorus of barks and howls. The cacophony echoed off the canyon walls.

Samantha shivered and pressed against Kieran. Slipping his arm around her, he discovered she was trembling.

Until this moment he'd never thought of her as vulnerable. Despite her small size, Samantha possessed grit and tenacity that made her seem a fair match for Kieran. And, in spirit, she certainly was. But here on the edge of the wilderness, he realized how much men and women needed each other, just as in frontier days.

"Are you the jealous type?" she asked.

It took Kieran a moment to recover his aplomb. "I don't think so," he said. "If I can't trust someone, I don't want to be involved with her."

Samantha nodded, the faint breeze ruffling her curly hair. The moon rising over the canyon walls gave her an ethereal air, like a woman from another time.

"Anything else you'd like to know?" He tried to keep his tone serious, but it wasn't easy. He hoped this wasn't a joke at his expense.

"Yes!" Samantha plunged ahead. "Do you wear pajamas or sleep in the nude?"

"That's getting a bit personal, don't you think?" he said.

"Just answer the question."

"Look, what's going on?" Kieran demanded. "Are you writing a book about men's sleep habits, or what?"

"You don't smoke, do you?" she said.

"No."

"I noticed you don't smell of tobacco, so I figured you didn't, but I had to make sure."

He tried to reclaim his train of thought, which was proving more difficult than expected. Talking to Samantha was like trying to negotiate a maze. "Why should you care?"

The breeze carried the faint scent of some night-blooming flower. Behind them in the brush Kieran heard a swish, and wondered if it might be the cub from this afternoon. It was more likely a raccoon. It certainly wasn't a possum—they made almost no noise when they moved.

He bent over, picked up a small rock and chucked it toward the bushes. There was another swish, moving away through the bushes.

"You could have hurt it! Whatever it is!" Samantha protested.

Kieran looked at her in surprise. "If it was an animal, I doubt it. I aimed too high. If someone was spying on us, I devoutly hope so."

"You think I'm setting you up?" she asked.

He met her level gaze for a moment. "No," he said. "But that doesn't mean someone couldn't be spying on us. However, apparently they aren't."

"Good." Samantha let out a long breath. "That would be awful."

"It would?"

"This is serious," she said.

"What is?"

Kieran honestly didn't believe that anything Samantha could say next would surprise him. She could offer to spend the night with him, ask for a job or demand to interview him for a newspaper, and he wouldn't bat an eye.

"Will you marry me?" she asked.

Chapter Five

It took several seconds for Kieran to clear his throat. "Beg pardon?" he said.

"You guys did advertise for brides, right?" Samantha glared at him. "Well, am I right?"

"Yes, in a manner of speaking." He had to concede that he'd been prepared for anything but this. "I didn't expect to have one drop in my lap the first night."

"Have I offered to drop in your lap?" she snapped.

"Indulge me in a little idle curiosity," he said. "Why the hell do you want to marry me?"

"I like the way you tango," Samantha said.

"A good reason," he remarked sarcastically. "Well, can you cook?"

"Cook?" She wrinkled her nose in distaste. "Honestly, in this day of frozen dinners and takeout, I'm surprised you'd care."

"If I'm going to get married, I prefer service with a smile," Kieran said.

"Of all the chauvinist..." She stopped herself. "We'll work it out."

"Which?" he said. "The service or the smiling?"

"I'm grouchy in the morning." Samantha grimaced, as if to demonstrate. "Sometimes I smile by noon. That's the best I can promise."

"And the service?"

"You'll get what you deserve," she said.

"Then I'll get the best."

Kieran was about to end the conversation by dismissing the entire subject, when something occurred to him.

Beatrice's suit claimed the will should be invalidated because it referred to Kieran *and* his wife, who didn't exist. It was merely a diversion from her main point, that her uncle had been incompetent, but Kieran wouldn't mind depriving his cousin of at least one piece of ammunition.

The will didn't specify which wife, nor when they had to get married. If he were married, even briefly, the term would be fulfilled.

Of course, that would give Samantha a half-interest in Hidden Hot Springs, but she could deed it right back to him. That would be one of his terms—if he decided to marry her.

Apparently, the woman had come here with matrimony in mind and happened to fix on him. Was she desperate to have children? Trying to please her family? He supposed either motive was as good as the reasons a lot of people got married.

Kieran also had to acknowledge a certain appealing irony. One fiancée had abandoned him after a relationship lasting over a year, while a new one had arrived ready to marry him on a moment's notice.

"Maybe we should sleep on this." He caught Samantha's look of dismay. "I wasn't propositioning you, but a test drive might not be a bad idea."

"Test drive?" she sputtered. "By the time I got done with you, you'd have two flat tires and a dead battery."

Kieran threw back his head and laughed. "Nobody's ever accused me of having a dead battery."

He heard her quick intake of breath. When their eyes met, her lips were parted slightly, as if she'd just contemplated what it would mean to take him up on his offer.

"Care to check me out?" he challenged.

"I already drove for two hours today. I wouldn't want my sports car to think I'm fickle."

Samantha stood up and stretched. The movement pressed her breasts against her blouse, and this time Kieran realized it was his breath that came too fast.

She swung around and began walking toward the cabins. He allowed himself a moment to enjoy the sight of her wonderfully curved silhouette, then caught up with her in long, easy strides.

"The ground gets awfully hard at night in those tents," Kieran teased.

"And something's going to be awfully hard tonight in your cabin, too," she tossed at him.

"I wish you'd tell me why you want to marry me when you're obviously not swooning with passion," he said as they neared the buildings.

"I will tell you," she said, "after you say yes."

Kieran was about to point out the unfairness of this position, when he remembered his own ulterior motive. "I'd have to impose a few conditions of my own."

"I can just imagine what—" Samantha stopped as they came within earshot of half a dozen men hanging around outside the rec hall. From the ragged edge of their voices as they argued about the merits of their favorite baseball teams, Kieran sensed he might have to break up some fights later.

No wonder. The guys who'd found lady friends were busy across the road, raising tents and rolling out sleeping bags. These men were angry because they'd lost out.

Kieran greeted the workers, feeling their gazes travel longingly to Samantha. He didn't blame them. Much as he liked to think that he functioned just fine by himself, he wouldn't be too happy tonight to see her on some other guy's arm.

"What do you fellows say?" he asked. "Should we try this again? Maybe advertise up north in Orange County? Lot more women up there."

"Waste of time," grumbled Mack, one of the men who'd championed the mixer in the first place.

"It's kind of discouraging," Kieran agreed. "We really had them outnumbered tonight. But I'll bet this was just the tip of the iceberg."

The men's expressions began to clear. "Yeah, why not?" said another guy. "It wasn't that much work to set up."

"I'm a gambling man myself," added a fellow beside him. "If you get the odds enough in your favor, you're sure to win sooner or later."

"Maybe you could run a phone number in the ad and help the ladies organize carpools," suggested Samantha. "Some women might not drive all this way by themselves."

Soon the men were discussing how to go about organizing the next get-together. Kieran drew Samantha away.

"Good suggestion," he said.

"I have to admit, you did a good job of handling them yourself." Her earlier breeziness had given way to a more serious mood. "You sure redirected their thoughts in a hurry."

Not everyone would have noticed, Kieran reflected. "You ever worked in management?"

She shook her head. "I never stay at one job long enough. I like to keep moving."

If she liked to keep moving, why did she want to marry a man who obviously wasn't going anywhere? Kieran was beginning to wonder if this lady might be running from the law. What could her crime be—lying about her age on her driver's license?

They had reached the impromptu campsite. "I haven't slept in a tent since I was a kid," Samantha grumbled as

Kieran helped her over the uneven terrain. "I'm going to need a chiropractor after sleeping on this."

"You turned down a perfectly good alternative," he reminded her. "Did I mention that I give an excellent back rub?"

She groaned and stretched her shoulders. "I'll bet you say that to all the ladies."

"It usually works, too."

Mary Anne beamed as they approached. "This is going to be fun!" she chortled. "Samantha, look—we can share this one. It's like a dollhouse inside!"

Samantha peered into the tiny tent. "Too bad we're not the size of dolls."

"Don't worry." Pete plumped a pillow and tossed it into the tent. "In this fresh air, you'll sleep like babies. You won't notice a thing."

Kieran felt a protective instinct, and chalked it up to being responsible for whatever happened at Hidden Hot Springs. Nevertheless, he said, "It might be wise for some of the guys to sleep out here, as well. Just in case anybody needs anything in the night."

Pete nodded. "We thought of that. We'll take good care of them, boss."

Kieran briefly wondered if he ought to volunteer to stick around, but even if the men were taking tomorrow off, he couldn't afford to. And he certainly wasn't going to lose sleep over a stubborn woman. If she didn't like tents, she could perfectly well stay at his cabin.

He debated whether to leave Samantha to her own devices, and decided she'd probably break her citified neck stumbling around in the semidarkness. "Can I bring anything from your car?"

The answer turned out to be two large suitcases. The woman must have packed every stitch of clothing and pair of shoes she owned.

She'd certainly come prepared. The question was, prepared for what?

Finally Kieran told Samantha good-night and began the hike to his cabin. The last thing he saw, looking back, was a slim figure with curly hair standing on a rise of ground. She gazed across the canyon as if wondering what the hell she'd gotten herself into.

SAMANTHA AWAKENED SLOWLY. The first thing she noticed was Mary Anne's regular breathing, then the murmur of voices a ways off.

Her shoulders and back felt stiff, and her feet ached. Why did people sing about the joys of camping? What were they, masochists? She hadn't felt this uncomfortable since she was twelve years old and spending the week at Girl Scout camp.

She sighed at the memory. It had been one of those experiences that distinguish real life from the cheery optimism of children's books and movies.

If Disney Studios had produced the story, Samantha would have discovered the joy of living in harmony with nature. Instead, she'd antagonized the camp counselors by falling out of her canoe, weaving the words "Camp Sucks" into her beadwork and ordering pizza delivered from town. The last straw came when she dyed her hair, and that of her two best friends, bright purple. It was the most shocking color she could find at the local drugstore.

Samantha was sent home in disgrace. The last thing she remembered seeing were the smirking faces of her worst enemies, two girls who wore only designer sportswear and made snide remarks about the less attractive campers. Samantha's only regret was that she hadn't stayed long enough to give them boot-camp haircuts in their sleep.

She rolled over and realized she wasn't in a bunk bed and that her red-haired companion was long past age twelve. Oh, yes, Mary Anne. Hidden Hot Springs. Kieran.

The memory of last night made Samantha sit upright with a start. Good heavens, had she really proposed to a total stranger?

Her body could still feel Kieran's hard chest pressed against her as they tangoed. She would never forget the way he moved, masterful yet gentle, knowing just when to release her and when to seize her again. She pictured his face in the moonlight, provocative and amused.

And arrogant. She'd never met a man so cocksure of himself. It made her want to take him down a peg, or two or three.

How could she possibly marry a man like that? Of course, from her experience with men, Samantha didn't doubt that she could make the amorous Mr. French tow the line. But a month-long prizefight wasn't going to leave her in good shape for her courtroom confrontation with Hank.

What she'd been looking for was someone easy to manipulate, a brainless hunk who would adore her, protect her and then let her go. She'd gotten the strong impression that Kieran was not that man.

Her proposal had been a mistake. Thank goodness there was still time to rectify it.

Samantha glanced around, wondering how she was going to handle her usual morning ritual of washing up. At this moment, even figuring out how to get dressed without waking Mary Anne struck her as a tricky task.

There hadn't been room in the tent for her suitcases, so she'd left them outside. Pulling on her robe, Samantha poked her head out of the tent.

For a stunned moment, she didn't see the cases anywhere. Then she spotted them several dozen feet down the slope. Who had moved them?

Shoving her feet into sandals, she padded down the hill. When she reached the luggage, Samantha discovered to her horror that one latch had popped open on the larger suitcase, and a T-shirt was sticking into view. Had someone rummaged through her belongings last night? Who would do such a thing?

The first face that came to mind was Hank's, but he would have invaded her tent, not just her baggage. Samantha knelt and opened the case, surprised to find nothing had been disturbed. This was definitely puzzling.

"Something wrong?" The masculine voice drifted down from overhead. Samantha knew without looking, from the suppressed mirth underlying the deep tone, that it had to be Kieran.

When she twisted around to see him, a dozen stiff muscles protested. "Ouch. Darn it."

In the daylight, his eyes glimmered a serene shade of blue. "Is this the morning grumpiness I've heard so much about?"

Samantha gestured at the suitcase. "Somebody messed with my things."

His expression darkened. "I find that hard to believe. Not around here."

"The latch was open. Maybe some of the disappointed guys decided to play hockey with my stuff." Samantha couldn't think of any other explanation.

Kieran knelt and examined the ground. At this angle, a shaft of sun raised golden highlights in his dark blond hair. The shaggy ends reached the collar of his polo shirt, which was stretched taut across broad shoulders.

How would it feel to touch that powerful body? Samantha's fingers flexed instinctively, and she shoved her hand into her robe's pocket.

Kieran hadn't stirred. Studying the ground that way, he looked like a tracker on the trail of a bad guy. She half expected him to make a Sherlock Holmes pronouncement. *Joe Blow from Trailer Nine hails from Savannah, and there's a trace of red Georgia clay in the tread of these shoes....*

"Here's your culprit."

Samantha followed his gaze to the bare dirt. She didn't see any footprints. "What? The wind? An earthquake? Continental drift?"

"Right here." Squatting on his heels, Kieran indicated a faint depression. "I know it's hard for a city girl like you, but it should be obvious."

Samantha squinted at it. She felt as if she ought to grasp his meaning to prove she wasn't an airhead, but the small dent didn't mean anything no matter how hard she stared. "I give up."

"Mountain lion," Kieran said, standing and brushing off his slacks. "From the size of it, a cub. I saw one yesterday. I was hoping it had gone back to the hills."

"I should have figured it out right away. Small dent equals mountain lion. Everybody knows that." Then it struck Samantha that this was no joking matter. "You mean they come into your camps?"

"Not usually," Kieran said. "We make it a point not to leave food scraps around." He indicated an open bag of potato chips and a candy wrapper on the ground. "Apparently people weren't so careful last night."

Samantha's initial fears eased. "Oh, well, how much harm could a cub do?"

"Not much," Kieran agreed. "The only problem is, the mother won't be far behind."

"This is a real fun place, I can see that." Samantha felt as if a giant cosmic boot should swing from the sky and plant itself in her rear end, for her foolishness in thinking she could ever live in Hidden Hot Springs. "I'm just not the Jane Goodall type."

"Gee, from your reaction on the highway yesterday, I could have sworn you find apes a real turn on," Kieran murmured. "Wasn't that what you mistook me for?"

Samantha was trying to frame a reply when the murmur of voices from below brought her back to reality.

What was she doing, standing in her bathrobe chatting with Kieran in full view of the whole town? "Is it safe to use the bathhouse?" she asked.

"Squeamish, are we?" He carried her suitcases down the slope for her. "I'll see what I can do."

Kieran strode into the structure first and shooed out a few lingering workmen. They grinned with embarrassment as they emerged, nodding to Samantha and a couple of other women who were waiting.

"All clear." Kieran waved them in.

Beth was among the early risers. "Reminds me of a trailer trip my family took one summer," she said, gazing around the large, concrete-floored bathroom with its rows of sinks, toilets and showers.

"Yeah, but I'll bet *they* had shower curtains," rejoined one of the women.

"And doors on the toilet stalls," muttered another.

They noticed with relief that the men had left them a stack of towels, along with soap and shampoo.

"Thoughtful bunch," Samantha said.

"I suggested it to Lew last night," Beth replied. "We teachers plan ahead."

Mary Anne trundled in, yawning. She wore her clothes from yesterday, like most of the women. "I guess a lot of the guys have private bathrooms in their trailers and cabins," she said. "I sure hope so. It's going to take a long hot shower to get me going. I'd hate to think some guy was standing out there waiting."

"They won't mind," Samantha returned cheerfully. In her experience, men seemed able to last indefinite periods without a bathroom.

"You came prepared," one of the women said, eyeing Samantha's bathrobe.

"I'm always prepared," she said. "I'm a defrocked Girl Scout."

The women carried on a general conversation while showering, which made them less self-conscious about the lack of privacy. Samantha was surprised how little most of them seemed to mind the primitive surroundings.

One woman rhapsodized about the small-town atmosphere. Another admitted to feeling like a kid in a candy shop, in the presence of so many available males. Beth had already figured out the logistics of organizing weekly shopping trips to another town.

As she tried to restore some shape to her mashed hair, Samantha realized that if she stayed in Hidden Hot Springs, she wouldn't be alone. Some of the other women would be visiting here, maybe even marrying their new-found Romeos.

What about her?

Impressions of Kieran floated through her mind. That deep masculine voice, the strong shoulders, the protective way he'd made sure she was settled yesterday evening.

With a start she realized that, in one of her dreams last night, she'd imagined someone leaning over her. In her imagination, it had been first her father, then Indiana Jones.

Had Kieran checked on her while she was sleeping? Maybe he'd been curious to see if she snored. Or afraid of the liability if anything happened to one of the campers.

Or maybe that hadn't been him at all.

Samantha finished cleaning up and changed into a pair of form-fitting green shorts. A print camp shirt completed the outfit. Her first intention had been to put on jeans and an old T-shirt, but that no longer seemed appropriate. If today were going to be her last with Kieran, she wanted him to remember her with at least a trace of regret.

For some reason, the prospect of leaving troubled Samantha. She told herself it was because of the risk of encountering Hank. Well, with the trial almost a month away, she could put some distance between herself and San Diego. Surely she'd be safe in Los Angeles, or better yet, Las Vegas, across the state line.

But if Hank had found her once, he could do it again. Among strangers, how could she count on anyone to help her?

When she emerged from the bathhouse, Kieran helped store her suitcases in her trunk. "About last night," she said. "You know, what I asked you. Well, everybody makes mistakes." She shrugged. "Let's forget it, okay?"

Kieran leaned against her car, which looked smaller than usual beside his large frame. Most of the others had gone into the dining hall, and they were alone for the moment. "Well, *my* offer still stands. You can take me up on it tonight."

"You have a lot of nerve, bringing that up again." She tried not to let her gaze linger on his square jaw and tanned face. Yes, they tangoed together like Fred and Ginger. Yes, he made her quiver when he rubbed his thumb across her cheek, as he was doing now. But he was also obstinate, obtuse and infuriating. "You are the most self-centered—"

Without warning, Kieran lowered his mouth to hers. Surprise melted into pleasure as his lips parted hers and his tongue explored the sensitive inner rim of her teeth.

His hand found the small of her back and moved her against him. Samantha became intimately aware of the ripple of his muscles and the power in his arms.

Caught off guard by an urge to yield, she felt her nipples harden against his chest. *Damn, the man was dangerous.*

After a moment, Kieran lifted his head. "So what do you say?"

"Was that supposed to be a free sample?"

He caught her face in his hands and kissed her again, with deliberate thoroughness. A hot liquid sensation rioted through Samantha's veins, draining away her strength to resist.

Kieran drew back. "Hungry?"

Reluctantly, Samantha nodded.

"Good. It smells like breakfast's ready." He caught her hand and tugged her toward the dining hall.

Darn him, he knew perfectly well that wasn't the kind of hunger she'd meant! Samantha thought grumpily. Chalk one up for Kieran, but it was the last point she'd let him score.

Inside the dining hall, the large space had been painted a warm mint green, and an all-weather carpet helped absorb the chatter from dozens of diners. It didn't feel at all like the austere, silent room where the boarding school students had taken their meals.

Samantha downed a muffin and some fresh fruit in a haze of sensory overload. She wasn't used to a man who could stimulate her with the barest of touches. She could hardly look at Kieran now, because if she did, he would almost certainly notice her confusion. He might also see from her flushed skin and overbright eyes that she wanted more of him.

Looking back at that crazy weekend in Acapulco with Hank, Samantha understood that she'd been lost in a happy buzz born of margaritas, sunshine and ocean breezes. She'd mistaken Hank's calculated attentiveness for sex appeal and his compliments for caring.

Hank hadn't fallen in love with Samantha Avery as a person, he'd wanted to collect her as a trophy. And she hadn't fallen in love, either; she'd made the mistake of believing in a shallow fantasy.

Hank had never come close to arousing the passion she'd felt a few minutes ago for Kieran—which was a good reason to head out of here today and find somewhere else to hide. The last thing Samantha needed was another man tangling up her life.

She snapped out of her reverie to see Kieran regarding her with a mischievous grin. "Something on your mind? I've asked you twice to pass the salt."

"For someone who was nearly mauled by mountain lions, I think I'm doing all right," she snapped, and plopped the saltshaker in front of him so hard it shook crystals onto the table. "Want the pepper, too?"

"I'm not that desperate." He brushed off the front of his shirt, and she realized some of the flying salt had hit him.

"Sorry." She blurted out the word as if it were a dare.

"Done eating?" he asked.

She studied her half-empty plate. "Well . . ."

"Good." He pulled her to her feet. "I think we're overdue for a chat."

Samantha felt as if she were being marched off to be shot, but she let Kieran draw her out of the dining hall. He escorted her across the street, up the rise and onto a path.

"Where are we going?" she asked.

"My place."

"I have no intention of—"

"Don't flatter yourself." He caught her wrist as she stumbled over a protruding tree root. "We need a private place to talk."

"I thought I made it clear I changed my mind. There's nothing to discuss."

"Yes, there is," he said. "Our wedding plans."

Chapter Six

"There isn't going to be any wedding," Samantha protested as Kieran guided her around a bend in the path. "I've decided getting married wasn't a good idea."

The path narrowed as they headed toward his cabin, until they could barely walk side by side. The ground was covered with such lush undergrowth, she was forced to stumble against him several times.

"You refused to tell me why you wanted to marry me until I said yes." Kieran enjoyed the rapidly changing expressions on Samantha's face—confusion, irritation, uncertainty. "So I'm saying yes."

"But it was only a strategy to find out why I made such a fool of myself."

"I wouldn't think of prying into why you made a fool of yourself. However, I do have a few requirements, which I'll explain later."

"You can't be serious," she said.

"Let's just say I've had time to mull the benefits as well as the drawbacks."

Alone in the silence of the cabin last night, Kieran had, indeed, given Samantha's proposal some thought. The more he considered it, the more it made sense to take a wife. He was tired of eating every meal at the dining hall, tired of his musty unkempt cabin and tired of sleeping alone.

And when he faced Beatrice on Tuesday, he'd love to have a wife to flaunt.

"Did you check on me last night?" Samantha asked unexpectedly.

Kieran ignored the question and gestured north. "That's where the hotel will be, over there." Only a construction crane was visible above the manzanita trees.

"Well, did you?"

"We'll pass the hot springs in a minute," Kieran went on. "The hotel will have springwater piped to a pool in the courtyard. We'll bottle the water, too, but only for sale locally."

"Why not ship it to supermarkets?" Samantha asked, momentarily distracted. "That stuff's popular."

"We'd have to butt heads with the giant soft-drink companies just to get shelf space," Kieran explained. "Plus we'd have to go industrial in a big way, and I don't want to ruin the canyon."

"Did you check on me?" she repeated.

"Yes." Kieran ground out the word reluctantly. "I woke up around midnight and heard some coyotes howling. Just thought I'd check to be sure everyone was safe."

"You looked in on everyone?" Samantha demanded.

"A few tents selected at random," Kieran said.

He couldn't even explain to himself why he'd gone slipping into her tent to make sure she was safe. The truth was that coyotes howled almost every night.

Gazing down at her as she lay quiet in slumber, he'd noticed that her face had softened into a childlike sweetness. It had charmed Kieran, and yet he'd missed the liveliness that animated her expressions when she was awake. He especially liked the way her mouth sometimes twisted into a half smile, as if she held her amusement barely in check and it might burst out at any moment.

It bothered him that he hadn't been around when the cub showed up. Had its mother made an appearance, Samantha might have been in real danger.

But, he reflected as they crossed a gravel road and continued on their path, the lion hadn't come. And there couldn't be much else that a sharp-tongued woman like Samantha needed protection from.

"What's that?" She indicated a thick grove where steam rose into the cool morning air.

"The springs," Kieran said. "Want to take a dip? The sulphur smell takes a little getting used to, but the hot water feels great. I'll bet you've got a swimsuit in one of those bags of yours. Perhaps you prefer to do it the natural way, of course. . . ."

He caught her steely look. "I agreed to talk in private. If you want to go skinny-dipping afterward, you're on your own."

Kieran grinned. "I can do that any time. I'd rather make the most of your company."

Samantha folded her arms, then immediately unfolded them as she stumbled and had to grab a branch for support. "Couldn't you pave this alley? It's a health hazard."

"It isn't an alley, it's a path, and it's supposed to be rustic," Kieran informed her. "It dates back to when they built the tourist cabins, in the twenties. There's only four still standing, three in use and one down by the road where my uncle lived."

Kieran's unit needed some work, he mused as they neared it. Usually the ramshackle appearance didn't bother him, but he couldn't help seeing it through Samantha's eyes as they turned up the last walkway.

They emerged into the clearing. The cabin had a gray, beaten look, and the pump sat in front amid dry grasses scattered with yellow wildflowers.

Kieran pointed Samantha to a glider on the porch. She strode ahead and whacked the cushions, sending dust flying.

The corners of her mouth twitched. "I guess modern detergents haven't reached this corner of the backwoods, yet."

"What we need are cleaning ladies," Kieran grumped. "Or wives."

Before she could respond, he marched into the house. A few rags and a bottle of cleanser later, the glider was fit to sit on.

He tossed the cleaning supplies aside, as Samantha settled onto the glider. She curled one leg under her and, with the other foot, rocked herself.

As she leaned back and closed her eyes, Kieran was reminded of a cat making itself at home. He'd never pictured a woman living here, but come to think of it, Samantha might fit in comfortably.

Kieran had to smile, imagining her stomping through his life, rearranging it to suit herself. Of course, the only rearranging he planned to allow involved furniture, dust and dishes.

Two birds twittered overhead, then darted off in a mating dance. "Dinosaurs," said Samantha.

"I beg your pardon?" Once again, she'd managed to say the last thing on earth he expected.

"Scientists believe birds are descended from dinosaurs," she explained.

"You mean I've got a brontosaurus nesting in my peppertree?" Kieran clucked his tongue in pretended dismay. "I wondered what was making such a mess."

"You said you wanted to talk," she prompted.

"I'm just waiting for you to fulfill your promise."

"You mean to tell you why I want to marry you? Well, I've changed my mind, so there's nothing to talk about. If that's all you wanted, I'll be heading back to town now."

Kieran had no intention of letting her off the hook so easily. "Do I intimidate you? Is that the problem?"

"Heck no."

"Then what's holding you back?" he challenged.

Samantha gave a shrug of surrender. "Nothing, I suppose. Well, it's simple. Someone's trying to kill me and I need a place to hide."

Kieran braced one hand against a post. "You call that simple?"

"Sure. I need to hide out for a month until the trial."

"Whose trial?" He couldn't quite take her seriously. "What did you do, get involved with the Mafia?"

"It's Hank Torrance," she snapped, clearly embarrassed. "The man I almost married. He turned out to be a jewel thief. I found out when he tried to give me a stolen emerald ring. You know, at the wedding."

Kieran was having a hard time picturing this. "You were at the altar and he tried to slip a hot rock on your finger? That takes quite a nerve, wouldn't you say? I'd give the guy some credit."

"This isn't a joke." She glared at him. "I'm the only witness and he wants to get rid of me. He's got an uncanny ability to track me down. I can't figure out how he does it."

Pieces of the puzzle began to slip into place. "So you came to the most remote spot you could find, and decided to hook up with Flatfoot for protection?"

"Bigfoot," she said.

Despite his pleasure in toying with her, Kieran could see this was no light matter. "If he's such a threat, why isn't he locked up?"

"He made bail," Samantha said. "I've complained to the D.A.'s office—they didn't even tell me he'd been released."

"You're probably leaving a trail a mile wide," Kieran told her. "Use a little caution—like staying away from your old friends—and you'll be fine."

Her rocking sped up, the glider springs creaking as if to give voice to her irritation. "I *have* been cautious. Mary Anne didn't know where I was; she showed up here by coincidence. The problem is that Hank's got a partner, someone the police haven't found. I think the guy must be a computer whiz. I didn't tell anyone about my new job or apartment, but Hank found me."

"So here you are." Kieran sat beside her on the glider. In the tight space, he could feel his hip wedge against hers. She squirmed but had nowhere to move. "You planned to sign me up as your marital bodyguard, then dump me?"

"No!" she protested. "I mean, I was going to tell you the truth before we got married."

"What changed your mind?" he said.

"Marriage is too complicated," Samantha answered. "I've got another plan. I'll go to Vegas and hide out."

"Get a waitressing job?" Kieran suggested. "At one of the casinos?"

She nodded.

"They screen their help so thoroughly they'll record every groove of your fingerprints and whether your navel is an innie or an outie," he said. "Hank's computer-whiz pal, if that's what he is, will have you pegged within hours."

"Got a better idea?" grumbled Samantha.

"Sure. Marry me."

"Right."

"I'll make it simple." He stretched his legs, letting one overlap hers with a touch of possessiveness. "You can leave whenever you like. No strings attached. Well, maybe one."

"I can just guess." She tried to wiggle into the corner, but the space was too tight.

"All you have to do is sign two documents," he said. "A marriage license and a quitclaim. And come with me to San Diego next Tuesday."

Samantha bit her lip as she tried to puzzle out his meaning. Finally she shook her head. "I don't get it. What are you up to?"

"I could lose Hidden Hot Springs." Kieran caught his breath, realizing it was the first time he had spoken those words out loud. "My cousin Beatrice claims she should have inherited the property. She's questioning my uncle's soundness of mind and whether he really intended to disinherit her."

"So where do I fit in?" she asked.

"The will specified that the property was to go to me and my wife." Kieran grimaced. "I was engaged at the time Uncle Albert made out the will. My lawyer says that the provision is null and void, but Beatrice claims it invalidates the whole will."

"So you want to show up with a wife," Samantha murmured.

"Couldn't hurt."

She started to laugh. "I don't believe it. You're willing to marry me just to score points with your cousin? That still leaves her other contention, which has to be much more serious."

"True." Kieran felt his jaw tensing the way it always did when he thought about Beatrice. "But I'm going to fight her every step of the way."

"There must be a way to prove your uncle was sane," Samantha said. "Have you looked for character witnesses?"

"My uncle was a modern-day hermit," Kieran explained. "My best bet lies right here in Hidden Hot Springs. I remember seeing him writing in a diary, and I've never been able to find it. It's possible he destroyed it, I suppose."

"Not likely," she said. "People almost never destroy their diaries. It's their bid for immortality."

"You could help me look," he suggested. "In any case, I want to kick out that portion of the suit. It would be one less thing I have to deal with."

She bit her lip. "Let me see if I get this straight. You're willing to marry me for a month?"

"That's right." He wondered if he'd overlooked some complication. "Husband and wife. That way, my men will leap to your defense if Hank shows up. I'll even help you myself if it doesn't interfere with my work."

"Gee, thanks."

"It's what they call a win-win situation."

"What about that other paper you mentioned?" Samantha prodded. "The one I have to sign?"

"A quitclaim," he explained. "I'm not planning to let you keep a half-interest in Hidden Hot Springs. It isn't actually mine any longer, anyway. What hasn't been signed over to my men has been put up as security to the banks."

Samantha leaned her head back on the glider. "A half-interest in Hidden Hot Springs."

"Don't get greedy."

She shot him a mischievous grin. "I was just contemplating the possibilities. Now as for *my* terms..."

"Terms?" Kieran arched an eyebrow. "Your terms are that you get protected, and go free in the end."

"That isn't all."

"And you can plan whatever kind of wedding you like. Hanging upside down in the trees or bathing at the spa, but I draw the line at skydiving. And if there's any way we can pull the thing off before Tuesday—"

Her mouth quirked mischievously. "How about today?"

"Today?" Kieran admired efficiency, but this was pushing matters a bit. "Aren't there a few, well, accessories we'll need?"

Samantha peered at him impishly. "Hey, I've already got the wedding dress. And a hat, too."

Kieran remembered the tuxedo he'd saved from his ballroom-dancing forays years ago. He recalled storing it with some other rarely used possessions in a spare closet at the office. "Well, then, what are we waiting for?"

THE TANTALIZING AROMA of grilling charcoal wafted into the bathhouse. "I hope we have enough potato chips to go with the hamburgers," Samantha said.

Beth glanced up from pinning the hem on the wedding dress. In the past few weeks, Samantha had lost five pounds, which made the dress hang differently. "They've got truckloads of potato chips."

"And coleslaw. You never saw so much coleslaw!" said Mary Anne as she arranged a bouquet of wildflowers over one of the sinks. "I can't believe I didn't bring my bridesmaid's dress."

"Why on earth would you?" demanded Samantha. "You didn't even know I was going to be here, let alone that I'd get married."

"Alice will be so sorry she missed—" Mary Anne caught herself. "I'm sorry. Of course I can't tell anyone."

"You'll be hearing wedding bells yourself pretty soon." Beth winked at her.

"Oh, I don't know. But you will, Beth, for sure."

An appealing thought occurred to Samantha. "We'll be neighbors! The three cabins are right together!"

The other women exchanged glances. "How close together?" asked Beth.

Samantha threw back her head and laughed, then had to readjust her hat. "We'll have our privacy, I assure you."

Her friends looked relieved.

THE MEN AND WOMEN had pitched in to decorate the old church. It hadn't been used as a church in years, Kieran had informed Samantha, but its lovely stained-glass window made it perfect for today.

White crepe paper draped the walls, and flowers mixed with greenery had been set about in pots. Walking in with Beth and Mary Anne, Samantha felt emotion squeeze her stomach.

Why had these people gone to so much trouble for a stranger? It was amazing how quickly this place had begun to feel like a community.

It must seem odd to have a wedding the very day after the mixer. She supposed a newspaper would have a great time writing up the story if they found out about it, which they wouldn't, she profoundly hoped.

Even more ironic, Kieran hadn't liked the idea of advertising for brides in the first place, she'd learned this morning from Beth. How strange that he was the first to be married!

She took a deep breath to settle her nerves as she gazed between the rows of seats to where Kieran stood by the altar. He wore a tuxedo, which had to mean he owned it. Samantha couldn't remember ever knowing a man who actually owned a tuxedo.

Due to the haste, there was no music and no rehearsal. At Samantha's nod, Mary Anne went first down the aisle, then Beth, taking their places across from Pete, as best man.

At the altar, Lew stood ready to officiate, dressed in a dark suit. He had studied for the ministry and served as assistant pastor at a church before realizing that his real vocation lay in architecture. Apparently he performed ministerial duties in the town on the rare occasions that they were required.

Kieran's expression remained cool as Samantha reached him. Was he regretting his offer to serve as a temporary husband?

She brushed her doubts aside. Okay, so people might joke that she should have bought a rubber dress, the way she bounced from man to man. Well, she'd never lived her life to please the gossips, and she wouldn't now.

Besides, nobody in Hidden Hot Springs struck her as a gossip.

The ceremony flew by. Before she knew it, Kieran was slipping a ring on her finger. Samantha's heartbeat sped as she glanced down. The ring was heavy and bore an emblem. After a split second, she realized it was Kieran's class ring from UCLA.

Without warning, a sheer wall of panic slammed into her stomach. What had she let herself in for? What if she really found herself trapped in Mudville, doomed to spend the rest of her life eating mess-hall food and shopping out of catalogs?

No, Samantha told herself sternly. A deal is a deal. Once the trial is over, I'll be drinking rum and Cokes, and dancing my nights away to the beat of steel drums.

Lew was saying, "I now declare you husband and wife. You may kiss the bride."

Applause washed over them as Kieran tipped up Samantha's chin. She barely had time to prepare herself before his lips grazed hers, and then it was over.

She wished the kiss had lasted longer. Not much longer, with so many people watching. But long enough to imprint his mouth on hers. He'd left her wanting more, and it wasn't a sensation Samantha appreciated.

They strode down the aisle together and she relaxed at seeing the happy faces of her new friends. Oh, heck, this was fun. How many women got to have two weddings without having to endure even a single marriage?

Samantha changed into a sundress for the picnic. She wanted to keep the wedding dress in good shape for any of the future brides who wore the same size.

The picnic lasted all afternoon. The food wasn't spectacular but satisfying, and everyone enjoyed such activities as a tug-of-war, an egg toss and a three-legged race. Before long, most of the people were covered with dirt, laughing and much better acquainted.

Samantha kept sneaking glances at Kieran, enjoying his reaction to his men's high spirits. His strong face with its high cheekbones warmed with pleasure as he observed the couples pairing off. The man could be attractive when he wasn't acting arrogant and high-handed.

He'd make some woman a good husband, she decided. But not her.

Lew and Beth were lost in a world of their own as they sat to one side, talking. Pete kept one arm around Mary Anne's waist as he scurried about organizing activities and wisecracking with the participants.

Even the odd men out pitched in. They took turns operating the grill and, later, a man named Mack produced a banjo and provided a passable rendition of the latest country hits. Then Beth led the women in singing "Amazing Grace" and "'Tis the Gift to Be Simple."

Samantha sighed. "I feel like I should be wearing a gingham dress and a bonnet," she confided. "Then I could go home and tend to the spinning wheel. Not!"

A laugh welled from Kieran's throat. "Don't you think you'd have made a good pioneer?" he teased. "In some ways, my Uncle Albert was one." He glanced at Pete and Mary Anne, who were organizing a sack race. "It's kind of a cliché, but women do civilize a town. And Pete's been shriveling up inside, alone out here."

"How about you?" Samantha teased.

A startled expression crossed his face. "Shriveling? Hardly. And hey, now that I'm a married man . . ." He let the words trail off, leaving the implication loud and clear.

Wait a minute, Samantha thought frantically. Hadn't she made it a condition of the marriage that they keep things platonic?

She tried to recall exactly what they'd said earlier on the porch. Kieran had specified that she sign the quitclaim—which they would take care of at his lawyer's office Tuesday—and she'd said . . . she'd said . . . what *had* she said?

Samantha got the uncomfortable feeling that Kieran had managed to sidetrack her. Well, it didn't matter. She was his wife in name only, and that's the way they were going to keep it.

"Looks like people are leaving," Kieran said, and she saw couples wandering down the hill toward town. The two of them followed.

Samantha felt a pang of regret at saying goodbye to her friends. Mary Anne had to leave because she'd promised to sing in her church choir on Sunday, and Beth needed to drive her vanful of pals home.

The town wouldn't be the same. Samantha realized she hadn't given much thought to how it would feel, being the only woman in Hidden Hot Springs.

What would she do all day without a job or even a place to window-shop? She wasn't the sort of person to sit around for nearly a month.

She'd think of something. She certainly wasn't going to let Kieran think of it for her.

Studying him from beneath lowered lashes, she wondered what was going through his mind. Everyone said he worked eighteen hours a day, but that was when he'd been single. He didn't plan to slack off just because he'd put a ring on her finger, did he?

He certainly didn't expect to disappear with her into the bedroom and not show his face again for days. If that's what was on his mind, Samantha would set him right in short order.

She could feel the gentle weight of his arm around her waist, slipped there as if by instinct. Otherwise, he scarcely seemed to notice her as they strolled across the grounds making sure all fires were extinguished and that no food was left to attract animals.

Samantha began to relax. They'd pulled it off. She'd become the protected Mrs. French and he'd become an heir with a wife.

"That cub bothers me a little," Kieran admitted. "I don't know where it's gone."

Samantha stepped over a rock protruding from the ground. "I'm glad I won't be sleeping outside tonight."

"So am I."

"That's what you think."

He laughed.

From a high point, they waved at the last of the cars disappearing down the dusty road. As they turned away, Kieran began warning the men to stay indoors after dark and keep their screen doors shut.

"I was worried about Hank. I never thought about mountain lions," Samantha said.

"Normally they give humans a wide berth." Kieran's thumb stroked her shoulder blade. Samantha stiffened against the pressure, but it felt good on her tight muscles. "I hope last night's excursion was a one-time thing. Mountain lions can be relocated, but this is their native habitat and in a way they belong here more than we do."

"Just not in my tent," said Samantha.

He chuckled. "Well, are you hungry? Ready for a bridal feast?"

"Sure." Before she could wonder what he had in mind, Kieran guided her to the dining hall.

"We have an excellent staff," he said. "Our cook is Australian. He was having a bit of trouble getting his visa renewed, so I sponsored him. He likes this area. Says it beats the Outback."

The dinner was better than Samantha expected: chicken with wine sauce, scalloped potatoes and green salad, with an alternate meal of a sandwich plate.

At the long table, the men treated her like a sister, with good-natured teasing about being the only female in town. She was told to expect endless buttons to sew and love letters to write. Recognizing the good will behind the kidding, Samantha jokingly promised to serve as den mother.

"I even give haircuts," she told a couple of burly guys who'd joined Kieran for an after-dinner beer. "If you like nicks in your ears and sideburns that don't match."

The dining hall began emptying by seven o'clock. "Mostly the men go to the rec hall and watch TV," Kieran said. "But I expect they'll be tired tonight."

And you? Samantha wanted to ask as they stepped into the rapidly cooling air. The image she'd been suppressing all day popped into her mind, of her and Kieran walking into his cabin and locking the door behind them. A shiver of dread ran through her.

"Cold?" he asked.

"Nothing I can't fix all by myself," she said.

His eyebrows lifted, but he made no other response as they walked home a few dozen feet ahead of Lew and Pete.

Hidden Hot Springs felt different this evening as it settled back into its routine. Samantha could hear the buzzes and chirps of wildlife and catch the tangy scent of wildflowers drifting on a breeze.

A sense of isolation fell over her. In all her travels, she'd rarely ventured beyond cities. Here in the canyon, they were a good hundred miles from what she considered civilization.

Then she glanced at Kieran, who matched his stride to hers as they headed up the path. She was safer here, with him, than in any city. Safe from everything *but* him, anyway.

Lew turned off first, waving good-night, and a short distance later they themselves veered onto the trail that led to Kieran's cabin.

"Enjoy your wedding night!" called Pete. "I'm sure you'll get lots of nice, healthy sleep!"

Then he was gone. Samantha was alone with Kieran, and she wasn't at all eager to see what would happen next.

Chapter Seven

Kieran pushed open the door and reached in to snap on a light. Then he turned to Samantha.

Roguish glee flashed into his eyes. Before she could grasp the reason, he swung her up and carried her across the threshold.

Caught off guard, Samantha clung to Kieran, aware of the strength in his arms. Pressed to his chest, she could feel the beat of his heart.

It was hard to think straight suspended in midair, but she tried to muster a protest. "If you don't mind..."

"I don't mind at all." He plopped her onto her feet. "Just providing the bride's traditional welcome."

"Being hauled through the air like a sack of potatoes isn't my idea of a welcome," Samantha snapped.

"You mean that didn't make you feel at home?" Kieran murmured.

Samantha's response died as she took her first look around. This was where she was going to live?

The dominant feature in the modest-size front room was a fireplace of chipped red brick. Before it lay a matted rug of indeterminate color, barely noticeable in the mud-colored expanse of wooden floor.

Remembering that this had been a tourist cabin, Samantha doubted anyone had ever polished that floor till it gleamed. She'd usually moved before a place needed a thorough cleaning, and she didn't intend to break the habit.

In the dim light of an overhead fixture, the walls, too, looked gray. The only decoration was a photograph of people in 1930s bathing suits wading through a pool.

The furnishings consisted of a scarred table, four mismatched chairs, a lumpy brown couch and a coffee table made from the cut end of a log. Atop a rickety stand in one corner sat a small television set and a VCR.

The front window sported a threadbare set of beige curtains. The glass looked cloudy from a mixture of dust and spiderwebs.

"It's, uh, rustic," Kieran noted.

"Rusty is more like it." Samantha grimaced. "I'm almost afraid to look in the kitchen."

"You should be."

Deciding to leave that treat for morning, Samantha turned to her left, where a doorway led into what must be the bedroom. A small bathroom lay en route, and she forced herself to check inside.

It turned out to be better than expected. The old clawfooted tub gleamed as if refinished, and someone had laid white tile patterned with flowers on the floor. Even the sink and commode appeared new.

"Not bad," she said.

"It was hopeless when I moved in," Kieran conceded from the doorway. "I didn't so much redecorate as rehabilitate."

"Too bad you didn't get to the rest of the house," Samantha said. "I don't suppose they have health inspectors in Hidden Hot Springs, though, so you're probably safe."

She started to edge out of the bathroom, but Kieran's bulky frame was blocking the way and she had to brush against him. As she did, Samantha could feel his body go rigid in a very interesting place. She tried to convince herself she'd bumped into his wallet.

Wiggling past, she veered right and flicked on a switch. Light gleamed from a bedside lamp, revealing every yellowed crevice of its aging shade and every unappetizing detail of the bedroom.

Against one wall stood a pressed-wood chest of drawers that sagged in the middle. Next to it stood Samantha's two suitcases, which Kieran had brought up earlier. Worn from years of travel, they fit right in with the decor.

A narrow door led to the closet, which didn't look big enough to hold more than a couple of hangers. The double-hung window had been fitted with dusty miniblinds.

The bed itself resembled an oversize cot, covered with a worn quilt. Samantha couldn't imagine two people sleeping there unless they were on *very* intimate terms.

"The place could use some fixing up," Kieran admitted. "A little paint, maybe, and some new curtains. I don't suppose you sew?"

"Anything more complicated than a button, I send to the tailor," Samantha said. "And any painting more extensive than my nails, I hire out."

He clucked disapprovingly. "If you're going to be a housewife for a month, you ought to act like one."

"Housewife?" said Samantha. "I married a house?"

"You do intend to earn your keep, don't you?" Kieran took a step forward, pressing Samantha against the bed.

"I'll tell you what," she said. "I'll pay you room and board. Let's see—would a half-interest in Hidden Hot Springs do the trick? I suppose I could sell it to someone else and give you the money, if you'd prefer."

"I simply thought you might prefer to stay in a house that's clean and spruced up," Kieran answered, not moving.

Samantha surveyed the room over his shoulder. "I've slept in worse places."

That was an understatement. She had lain awake one night in a tropical hotel listening to mosquitoes munch holes in the netting over the bed. Then there'd been the French boarding house where she'd discovered her room abutted the communal bathroom and that the pipes roared like a 747 taking off whenever anyone flushed the toilet.

"Great. I'm glad you like it." Kieran reached down and pulled his polo shirt off straight over his head, baring a broad chest that, at close range, completely filled Samantha's range of vision.

"Excuse me." She tried to pretend she didn't notice the pectoral muscles monopolizing her personal landscape. "Where exactly were you planning to sleep?"

"With my wife." Kieran flung the shirt onto the floor and slipped his hands around her waist.

An alarming welter of sensations assaulted Samantha. The most powerful was the scent of spicy masculinity blended with the sun-ripened richness of her own skin. Then she became aware of his fingers probing her waist.

She lifted her hands to push him back. "We had a deal."

The stroking stopped. Kieran's face came down until his breath whispered across her cheek. "Deals have to be consummated, don't they?"

"Not tonight."

"Especially tonight."

"That was one of my conditions," she protested.

"It was?" He cleared his throat in mock bewilderment. "I don't recall any such condition."

"You interrupted me," Samantha reminded him. "On the porch. I was about to tell you, and you asked me something else. But it's still valid."

Kieran released a long breath of annoyance. "You can't be serious. You mean I'm expected to read minds?"

"Just read my lips," she said, and mouthed the words: "Go away."

After a moment's internal debate, Kieran retreated across the room and pulled something from the closet. He marched back and thrust a stack of sheets and a blanket into Samantha's arms.

"There you go," he said. "I'm sure you'll find the couch reasonably comfortable."

"You mean that lumpy thing in the living room?"

"Surely you weren't expecting to find a couch in the kitchen?"

Samantha thrust the sheets back into his arms. "I don't expect to find a couch at all. I am not the idiot who chose that sagging piece of garbage. If this were my cabin, it would be properly furnished with a *large* bed and a convertible sofa. You own that monstrosity so *you* get to sleep on it."

"I'd love to humor you, but the couch is much too short for me." Kieran turned as if to set the sheets on a chair.

Samantha placed both hands on the small of his back and pushed. "I'm sure you'll manage. Besides, you made a point of telling me how early you get up." She panted, feeling like a mouse trying to move a mountain. "Surely you wouldn't want to wake me."

Maybe the pile of sheets was handicapping him, but with only a moderate amount of strain she managed to propel Kieran toward the door as he said, "And my clothes are in the bedroom closet."

"I'll be happy to toss them out," she offered. "Now do sleep well." With a last burst of energy, she shoved him through the door and slammed it.

Samantha thought she detected a low chuckle as Kieran's footsteps retreated across the wooden floor. A moment later, she heard the rustling of old springs and the plumping of cushions.

She hoped sleeping on the sofa gave him a crick in his back as big as the one she'd just incurred in her shoulders.

THEY ATE SUNDAY BRUNCH in the dining hall. The cook had set out food with a Mexican flair: scrambled eggs and salsa, spicy sausage, flour tortillas and sugary tubes of fried dough that tasted like doughnuts.

"I thought the cook was Australian," Samantha observed as she filled her plate.

"Some people eat Mexican food in Australia." Kieran heaped his plate twice as high.

Pete joined them at the table, but Lew, she learned, was out jogging. "It gets too hot later in the day," Pete explained. "I hope Beth likes to exercise. He's a real fanatic."

"She looks in good shape." Samantha missed her new-found friend. She wondered what the other women were doing this morning.

If she were back in Del Mar, Samantha reflected, she'd be taking a leisurely walk down to a café for breakfast. Then she'd read the newspaper—something she wouldn't find out here unless it came two days late—and drink coffee. Afterward, she'd go home, change and head for the beach.

"What do you guys usually do on Sunday?" she asked.

Kieran looked baffled. "I try to catch up on paperwork. I don't know what everyone else does."

"I play softball," offered Pete. "Some guys drive to one of the towns for church. On special occasions, they go to San Diego, but usually we're too lazy."

"I'd like to see the rest of Hidden Hot Springs," Samantha said, despairing of finding anything more interesting to do. "Kieran?"

He stopped, a forkful of sausage halfway to his mouth, and stared into space as if he hadn't heard.

"Is he always like this?" Samantha asked.

Pete just beamed, as if delighting in the pair of lovebirds. Samantha sighed and finished her breakfast.

KIERAN DIDN'T KNOW what was wrong with him. He couldn't concentrate on the conversation, his plans for the day or even the food.

He kept thinking about how Samantha had looked last night when he left the bedroom: defiant with an edge of triumph. There sure was a lot of energy packed into that tiny frame—energy that he'd like to put to a much more rewarding use.

Hell, she wasn't a kid. She must have had experience with men before, and he could tell she was attracted to him. He didn't understand. Why couldn't she simply enjoy having an affair for a month?

He'd felt like a lusty teenager last night, returning his date safely home when he yearned with every pounding inch of his adolescent body to take her to a motel instead.

He'd lain awake on the sofa for hours, not even able to toss and turn on its narrow width. He'd dreamt of her mouth opening to receive his tongue; a moment later, they tangoed down an endless corridor, her nipples coming erect against his chest, his hand feeling every twist of her waist through the thin silk of her gown.

He'd pictured them naked in a secluded glade. She laughed and arched her back among the flowers, inviting him, and his mouth had touched every inch of those luscious breasts. His knee had slipped between her thighs and—

"Well?" Samantha demanded.

Kieran nearly choked on his eggs. "I beg your pardon?"

"Aren't you going to show me around?" she said. "Or are you going to sit there all day chewing on your fork?"

Kieran took a deep draft of coffee, which went down the wrong way. He sputtered and choked, and Pete whacked him on the back until his fillings nearly flew from his teeth.

"Not my day," Kieran gasped as he regained his breath. "Just—distracted." He stood up and carried his tray to the conveyer belt, Samantha hurrying behind him.

He couldn't look at her. He didn't want that fantasy to return, the one about the private glen and his knee gently parting her legs. Not until he had the chance to take Samantha in his arms and persuade her to make it all real.

He strode outside, nearly colliding with a couple of men arriving for a late meal. "Sorry, guys."

"No big deal," they said.

Samantha caught up with him. "Having a problem?"

"What? No." Damn, he didn't sound coherent even to himself. "Let's take a walk. I'll show you the construction site."

They crossed the highway and set off along the path. He steered Samantha onto a gravel road that ran through a grove of jacaranda trees. Their elegant branches raised a cloud of lavender blossoms against the sky.

"My Uncle Albert planted those," Kieran said, pointing them out. "He loved this place."

Samantha stepped through a drift of colorful blossoms that mirrored the shape of the jacarandas overhead. "There's got to be someone who could vouch for your uncle's sanity. How about a doctor?"

"He was healthy as a horse," Kieran said. "My uncle didn't go to a hospital until the very end, and by then he was in no shape to convince anyone of his sound mind. He suffered a series of strokes. By the time I got him to a doctor, he could hardly remember his own name."

"Didn't your uncle correspond with anyone?" Samantha said. "That would indicate he was of sound mind, at least."

"If he did, I can't find out who. And his diary, well, it's vanished into thin air."

They emerged from the trees into the sweep of what would become a grand driveway. Before them rose the framework of the hotel, a series of interconnected buildings designed to provide maximum exposure to the open air. In a central courtyard lay a large hole that would be transformed into an inviting pool of mineral water.

Wondering at her unaccustomed silence, Kieran guided Samantha around the structures, showing her the future lobby, the ballrooms, the massage and exercise rooms, the wings of guest rooms and the restaurants. It took an active imagination to picture what it would all look like; the structures were at different phases of development, from holes in the ground to skeletal frames.

"It fits into the land," Samantha mused. "When it's landscaped, I'll bet it will blend right in."

"That's our goal," Kieran agreed, surprised that she could visualize the ultimate results. "I have to give most of the credit to Lew. He's always had a reverence for the natural landscape."

As Kieran pointed out the future wildlife reserve on the slopes leading to the canyon walls, he saw a flash of brown between the trees. It might have been a deer, but the movement had been sinuous and collected, more like that of a big cat. Just what he needed, that mountain lion cub again. Or worse, yet, its mother.

With luck, it would stay in the brush. On a weekday, the noise around here was enough to scare them both back to a more remote area.

Samantha recalled him to the conversation by asking, "Where would the papers be? I mean, if they do exist."

"In his cabin, I would assume." Kieran tucked the mountain lion sighting among the thousand and one details in his mental filing system. "It's that tumbledown shack by the highway. But I've searched it top to bottom.

There were almost no records or legal papers at all. It created a real paperwork mess when I started out.''

"Maybe I could take a look," Samantha said.

"Why so interested?" asked Kieran.

"Oh—as you pointed out, there's not a lot to do around here," she murmured.

This uncharacteristic altruism raised hackles of suspicion along Kieran's back. "You aren't starting to feel possessive about this place, are you?"

"Possessive?" Samantha repeated the word as if she'd never heard it before.

Kieran caught her by the shoulders and forced her to face him. "You're signing that quitclaim on Tuesday."

"Don't squeeze me too hard, or I could say I was forced to sign under duress," Samantha retorted. "Then my signature wouldn't be valid."

Kieran released her abruptly. He didn't really think Samantha would try to blackmail him for her half of the property, but how well did he know her?

It struck him that he'd placed himself in a delicate position. In his drive to get the best of Beatrice, and under the mind-clouding fog of desire inspired by too many years of living alone, he'd married a woman he hardly knew.

As Beatrice had demonstrated, even the most unreasonable of claims could cause major legal headaches. And Samantha's claim, he realized with a start, was far from unreasonable.

"Kieran French and his wife." That was how the will read.

There was only one way he could make sure Samantha never went back on her word. And she'd brought it on herself.

His thoughts broke off as a group of men trotted into the cleared area, Pete in the lead. They carried bats, softballs and catcher's mitts.

"Sorry to disturb you, but you're standing in the middle of our playing field," Pete said. "Care to join us?"

"I'd love to." Samantha peered at Kieran. "How about you?"

He shook his head. "I've got a lot of work to catch up on. Why don't you play?"

She gave him a flick of a smile. "See you later."

Kieran retreated to his office trailer. As he strode away, he forced himself not to look back at her slender figure in the sunlight.

Thank goodness he hadn't made love to Samantha last night. And now he didn't intend to.

So long as the marriage hadn't been consummated, it didn't really exist. Legally, they'd entered into a union that wasn't a marriage because neither of them intended it to be. He wanted to one-up Beatrice, and Samantha wanted protection from that creep Hank.

As long as they didn't make love, Kieran could annul the marriage any time he wanted to. And Samantha could never successfully press a claim to half-ownership of Hidden Hot Springs.

As he stretched his legs beneath his desk, a none-too-subtle masculine urging reminded him that his body hadn't promised to go along with his decision. Damn it, he could tough this out. There was no other choice.

The morning flew by, and in the afternoon Lew had arranged for a movie to be shown in the recreation hall. It was *Ben-Hur*, which everyone had seen but seemed eager to see again. Once more, Kieran spent the hours buried in his office. The more time he spent away from Samantha, the better.

When he joined her for dinner, he found her surrounded by men. Trays crowded the long table as Samantha and the guys swapped jokes.

"Did you see the sign that says 'Illiterate? Write For Free Help,'" Samantha tossed out as Kieran set his tray next to hers.

"I spotted a bumper sticker on an old Mercedes that said, 'The Pieces Falling Off This Vehicle Are Of The Finest British Manufacture,'" returned Mack.

"Oh, that's nothing..." called somebody else, and the diners continued trying to top each other while Kieran wolfed down his *spaghetti alla bolognese*.

Even when the meal was finished, the men seemed in no hurry to depart. Despite his earlier resolve, Kieran began to find their presence annoying. Just because he'd sworn off sex didn't mean he couldn't enjoy a little female companionship.

At last he drew Samantha away with the promise of showing her yet another aspect of Hidden Hot Springs.

"What is it?" she asked, bouncing out the door beside him.

"You did bring a swimsuit, didn't you?" he asked.

"In Southern California?" she replied. "Of course I brought one. In fact, I brought two." Then she hesitated. "You mean the hot springs, right? You're not getting me out there half-naked in the moonlight."

Kieran flexed his shoulders, knotted from eight hours at a desk. "Give me a break. I'm stiff all over."

"I can just bet," she said.

He laughed. "Actually, you have nothing to fear."

"Oh?" Samantha stood on the path, hands on hips. "What's the next line? 'Nothing is going to happen that you don't want to happen?' I wasn't born yesterday."

"I meant it. I've changed my mind." Kieran nudged her up the path. "No sex. I promise."

She eyed him uncertainly. "What brought this on?"

He debated whether to invent some excuse, but decided she'd see through it. "I want us to be able to annul our marriage with no strings attached."

"Oh, really?" Mistrust dripped from her words. "This just occurred to you? Come on, Kieran, it's a trick, isn't it?"

"Absolutely not." He was going to have to come clean all the way. "What you said this afternoon made me realize that I don't want us to consummate our marriage. Not that I really think you'd try to hang onto your half-interest in Hidden Hot Springs, but I'm not taking any chances."

She started to laugh. "I don't believe it. You mean no matter what I do, even if I walk around in a see-through negligee, you'll keep your hands to yourself?"

Kieran groaned inwardly. He was beginning to fear he'd created a monster. "That's right," he grumbled.

"Well, well," said Samantha, and skipped ahead of him toward the cabin.

Twenty minutes later, Kieran realized he'd made his first mistake.

Maybe it was overfamiliarity with that photograph of people bathing in 1930s costumes, but he hadn't given any thought to what *kind* of swimsuit Samantha had brought. He'd assumed it would be one of those maillot things you saw in the Olympics.

He was returning from the utility room with towels when she exited the bedroom in the poorest excuse for a cover-up since Watergate.

The black-mesh top dropped straight from her shoulders to the upper thighs. Plainly visible beneath it shimmered two tiny strips of space-age fabric and a lot of gloriously curved flesh.

She had the nerve to stare straight at *him,* as if there were anything unusual about the sight of a man in short black trunks. Kieran never bothered with a T-shirt in Hidden Hot Springs, but her gaze made him suddenly aware of his state of undress. Well, it was nowhere near as spectacular as hers.

"Don't you have anything a little more conservative?" he asked.

"What's wrong with this?" She gazed at him with feigned innocence.

"It's not designed for swimming," Kieran said. "One dive and the thing would fall off."

"I wasn't planning to dive." Samantha bit back a grin.

She was right, of course. He took another stab at it. "The other guys might get the wrong idea."

"The other guys are having a poker tournament," she said. "First prize is a weekend at Universal Studios. I heard Pete talking about it."

"Pete has a big mouth."

In truth, the tournament had been Kieran's idea, intended to make it up to the guys if their mixer proved a bust. They would each be issued free poker chips to compete for tickets and gift certificates.

He wouldn't have to worry about anyone interrupting them at the hot springs, although he wasn't so sure going there was a good idea. But he couldn't back out now.

Samantha lifted one leg to show him the cork-soled sandals she wore. "Are these sturdy enough?"

"They're fine." Kieran tried not to look overly interested in the slim leg and delicate ankle. "Let's head out."

In the doorway, she said, "You aren't worried about that mountain lion showing up, are you?"

"There's a watering hole in the preserve area," Kieran said. "Animals usually stay up there."

Just in case, however, he took an oversize flashlight and a megaphone that he sometimes used on the construction site. Loud noises and lights were reputed to discourage even a big cat.

They didn't see or hear anyone on their short trip to the springs. Samantha bounced ahead of Kieran, the glow from her flashlight silhouetting her slender body.

Kieran wished he dared reach out and stroke the curve of her waist and the flare of her hips, but he didn't want to push his luck. He might consider himself a man of iron will, but even iron could melt if it were held too long in the fire.

The springs lay off the trail, amid a thick clump of manzanita shrubs. As soon as they stepped through the bushes, the rest of the world vanished.

The burble of water blocked out all noise, and the warm sulphur smell washed away the scents of aromatic plants. Kieran set the towels and his gear on a large flat rock.

"This is great." Samantha inhaled the steam. "The world's biggest Jacuzzi."

The springs weren't all that large, more of a pond where the underground stream broke to the surface. Kieran knew from experience that it was no more than four feet deep even at the point where the water boiled up. But he supposed it looked large to a city girl.

"Be careful." He pointed to the heart of the springs. "Right there it gets very hot."

"I'll watch out." Samantha shrugged off her cover-up and Kieran swung around, checking the area. Once he'd arrived at the hot springs at the same time as a family of skunks, and he was taking no chances tonight.

There was no wildlife in evidence, however. He turned back to the springs just as the moon broke through the clouds and washed the scene with silver.

Samantha's minuscule bikini glittered in the enchanted light, and droplets of water danced across her skin as she advanced into the pool. She stretched and then swiveled to look at Kieran.

He paused at the edge of the water, struck by her sensuality. Moonlight danced in her eyes and played across her breasts and hips. Her skin glowed like velvet, and in that instant his fantasy from last night felt real.

Chapter Eight

Samantha's breath caught in her throat at the sight of Kieran's powerful body poised on the rocks, moonlight shimmering around him. Each muscle of his chest and shoulders stood out in clear definition.

She'd seen the tensing of his jaw muscles and heard his quickened breathing when she appeared in her swimsuit, yet he'd kept his distance. He obviously had meant what he said.

Then why, she wondered as she sank back into the water, did she feel an irresistible urge to tempt him? What on earth would she do if he took her up on it?

She'd never met a man so maddening. The guy had an ego the size of Mount Palomar.

But Samantha couldn't help wondering how it would feel if he let loose that iron resolve and yielded to his healthy male instincts. It was ironic, but she'd been much better able to keep her own feelings in check when Kieran was the one trying to corral her into bed.

Now that he'd changed his mind, Samantha realized ruefully, she was discovering that she wanted him in a very fundamental feminine way. Or maybe, she admitted silently, she just loved a challenge.

In Acapulco, Hank had done all he could to seduce her, and Samantha had felt only a mild sense of stimulation.

And even that had been due more to their romantic surroundings than to her suitor, she could see now.

They'd almost made love, but Hank had been overcome by too many drinks. The result had been embarrassment on his part and, on Samantha's, a wave of sympathy that she'd mistaken for affection.

There was no need to wonder what she was feeling about Kieran. As he turned to survey the rest of their surroundings, she could hardly keep her eyes off the hard cords of muscle banding across his chest and upper arms.

He was her husband, after all. Not in a permanent sense, perhaps, but pioneers had always made the best of things, taking life as it came. Why shouldn't she?

Samantha lay back in the water, letting the heat penetrate. It soothed away the aches left from a day spent playing softball, followed by hours on a hard folding chair watching *Ben-Hur*. Visions of the chariot race flashed through her mind, all that sweat and Charlton Heston's amazing physical condition. She'd never met a man who could match him, until Kieran.

If only he knew that he had nothing to fear. Samantha wasn't going to try to claim half of Hidden Hot Springs. First of all, she wasn't the greedy type. And second, she didn't want to stay any longer than necessary in this remote town, no matter how gorgeous its master. Not when the Caribbean sang to her with calypso rhythms, and the perfect job lay almost within her reach.

Kieran meant to leave her alone, and that was for the best, Samantha told herself. At least they'd finally agreed on something.

Through languorous eyelids, she gazed into a sky so starry it might have been surreal. Alive with constellations, it reminded her that ancient peoples had revered the celestial bodies. She could see why: in the untamed night, their brilliance and depth made them seem incredibly powerful, almost alive.

She closed her eyes and let the water support her. The sulfuric smell reminded her of the spring's source deep within the earth, and the heat of buried fires washed away the day's strain.

Slowly, as her tension dissipated, Samantha became more aware of her own body. Every inch of skin reveled in the heated water and the contrasting sharpness of night air. Steam wafting upward enclosed and isolated her meandering thoughts.

She detected a ripple as Kieran entered the water. Secure in the knowledge that he wouldn't approach, she didn't bother to look up.

Floating freely, she realized she might be drifting in Kieran's direction. It was probably an illusion, and, if not, he would soon move away.

This all seemed like a dream, anyway, the heat and the steam and the fierce power of Kieran's body so tantalizingly near. Samantha didn't want to spoil it by opening her eyes.

Yet the pool's eddies conspired to waft her even farther toward the point where Kieran had entered the water. As she drew closer, she imagined she could detect the thrum of his pulse.

Unexpectedly, her foot brushed the hardness of his leg. The energy she sensed in Kieran jolted her as if her nervous system had just been fused with his. For one dazed moment, Samantha lost track of time and space. She started to sink, and thrashed around, unsure which way was up.

Strong arms caught her. One supported her back, while a large hand gripped her thigh, holding her steady.

The vertigo passed, but the current kept swinging her toward Kieran, pressing her bare side against the sturdy expanse of his stomach. Her lids were still closed, as she felt his fingers tighten around her thigh.

She told herself she must not gaze into his eyes. She knew she would see a naked hunger that mirrored her own. She had to leave Kieran free to withdraw, to pretend that nothing had happened between them. That was what both of them wanted, wasn't it?

Instead, he lifted Samantha until his mouth closed over hers. With a moan, she wound her arms around his neck and answered Kieran's passion with her own.

As his tongue invited her into a tantalizing game, he lowered them both onto a rocky shelf. Heated water embraced them as Samantha's body curved against Kieran's, half on his lap and half afloat.

The spring played its tricks, pressing her closer to Kieran and then drawing her away, as if to tease him. Even he couldn't resist the lure of the eddies; she felt his hands brush the bare skin of her waist and his fingers explore the lower edge of her bikini bra.

As she floated, the current conspired to arch her back and open her to Kieran. And he was there, right there, no longer a captive of desire but its lord.

Through her bikini bottom, Samantha felt his hardness against her tender core. At the same time, he stroked the silky bra upwards, baring the taut tips of her breasts. He bent over her with barely restrained ferocity, his mouth claiming her nipples as his hands seized her waist, holding her against him.

She gasped at the sensations rocketing through her body. The heat of the water magnified them, until the only thing she wanted was for him to ravage her with his masculine strength, and then to do it again.

With a shock, she felt suddenly only emptiness where Kieran had been. No strong hands gripped her as an eddy carried her away.

"Hey!" She blinked away the steam.

Kieran had retreated a few feet. "I meant what I said, Samantha."

"Oh, for heaven's sake!" She found her footing on the rocks and stood. Cool night air snapped over her shoulders as she pulled her bra into place. "What do you think I am, a black widow spider who's going to turn you into dinner when we're finished?"

"I don't know what you are," Kieran said. "I don't know how you really got into trouble with this Hank. I have only your word that you were an innocent bystander. I don't even know if Hank exists."

"You think I'm some kind of con artist?" Torn between laughter and outrage, Samantha glared at him. "Who knows, maybe I'm working for Beatrice!"

"Let's just say I was foolish to put my entire project in unnecessary jeopardy. What's done is done, but I'm not going to make things worse."

Kieran tossed her a towel and draped one over his own shoulders. Silver moon rays turned his physique to pewter, highlighting the sculpted manliness of his torso.

Those trunks might as well have been painted on his slim hips, Samantha noticed. She could see that, despite his words, he hadn't lost his desire for her.

She reached up and toweled her hair with deliberate slowness, knowing the motion elongated her body and outlined each curve. Darn it, if she had to suffer, so did he.

Something flew through the air. Startled, Samantha dropped her towel and grabbed it.

She found herself clutching a flashlight. "Good reflexes," said Kieran, starting up the path. "Coming?"

She didn't believe he would leave her here, at the mercy of wild animals, ankle-twisting loose stones and wrong turns, but she was in no mood to find out. She snatched up her towel and snapped him with it, or tried to, but Kieran ducked away. Powered by sheer irritation, Samantha chased him all the way to the cabin.

He flung open the door and strode inside, not pausing to hold it for her. Samantha had to admit that, had he stopped in the doorway, she couldn't have resisted the temptation to brush against him just to remind him of what he was missing. And he knew it.

The man was developing a maddening ability to read her mind. It was a dangerous trait and one she wanted to discourage.

Kieran switched on the lamp, filling the room with glare and shadows. The cabin needed better lighting, Samantha reflected as she entered. Not to mention a good cleaning and a few homey touches.

She wondered what it would take to turn this place into a real home. It would only be her home for a few weeks, but then, all the homes in Samantha's life had been temporary. She supposed Kieran had been right about one thing: there wasn't much else to do around here.

Closing the bedroom door behind her and leaning against it, she admitted silently that it wasn't so much the house she yearned to domesticate, as the man. What would it take to turn him into a real husband, even if only a temporary one?

She had a few ideas she might try, beginning tomorrow.

KIERAN COULDN'T BELIEVE he'd let himself slip so far. Another few minutes and he couldn't have stopped for all the good judgment in the world.

He could still feel the yielding softness of her breasts beneath his lips, and the tautness of her nipples. How natural it had felt, slipping between her legs in the flowing current; how easily her body fitted against his.

How the hell was he going to get any sleep tonight?

He stripped off his trunks in the bathroom and, hating the cliché, took a cold shower. It didn't help.

Neither did a beer in the drab kitchen, nor an attempt to read a book on hotel management that a friend had recommended. Even the dull phrasing couldn't obscure the fact that he was reading about hotel rooms.

He could picture what a room at the Hidden Springs Resort would look like. It would be lush and low-key, secluded amid greenery, equipped with a whirlpool bath and, on request, a water bed.

As he stretched out on the couch and draped his feet over the end, Kieran visualized a woman on the water bed. Her cinnamon hair lay spread across the pillow and her black lace nightgown was slit to the thigh. As he watched, a deep breath redefined her breasts. The silken fabric clung to the inner curve of her hips.

He could feel himself moving toward her, and then, by the grace of his fantasy, levitating over her. His body covered hers, demanding satisfaction, and she seized his hips and pulled him into sweet ecstasy.

He groaned, rolled over and crashed to the floor.

"Damn!" Kieran snarled between clenched teeth. He stalked back into the bathroom and took another cold shower.

It still didn't help.

SAMANTHA WOKE LATE. She could tell by the slant of sunlight through the shades that it was well past her usual time to rise. But then, it wasn't as if she had to go to work.

She lay dozing, letting her mind review the unexpected events of these past few days. Images played like a movie: Hank's sudden reappearance, the dance in the rec hall, the tango with Kieran.

And then last night. An unwilling groan escaped as she remembered the hardness of his body against hers, the insistence of his mouth, the moment when she'd thought all barriers would fall between them.

Samantha sat up, reminding herself that once Hank's trial was over, she could return to her usual devil-may-care life. If she didn't get the job on the cruise ship, she'd find something else to do, she told herself, padding toward the kitchen to get coffee. She'd saved enough money during her months in San Diego to go to Japan, or maybe India—she'd never visited the subcontinent.

But no, India would be too hot this time of year. As for the Japanese, well, they had a beautiful country, but did it have to be so crowded?

Samantha realized she couldn't think of anywhere she wanted to go, which seemed odd. Well, she felt confident she'd land the cruise job. How many applicants spoke several languages, and had worked in travel-related businesses across the globe?

Lost in thought, Samantha stood for several minutes in the middle of the kitchen before she gathered her wits enough to look around. It was the first time she'd been in here, and she could see why Kieran had wanted to spare her the experience.

Long and narrow, the kitchen resembled a hallway, which it was, since it led directly to a tiny utility room and the back door. The linoleum had been scuffed right down to the rubber backing, and the small window was bare except for a grimy ruffle.

Samantha eyed the aged stove and the tiny oven beneath it. If she ever decided to bake a cake, she'd have to make it one layer at a time. But cake wasn't the item on her mind this morning.

Even Kieran French had to keep coffee around somewhere.

The high shelves revealed a sparse supply of plastic plates, a jar of peanut butter and a few cans of beans. Bending to examine the lower cabinets, she observed a couple of thin aluminum pots and a bottle of all-purpose cleanser.

Samantha prowled through the refrigerator, finding a six-pack of beer, four diet sodas, a stale half-loaf of bread and an almost empty jar of grape jelly.

This guy would not win the "Good Housekeeping Seal of Approval," not by a long shot.

Samantha noticed a wall clock pointing to half past ten. The dining hall would have cleared away breakfast long ago, and she had no intention of waiting another hour and a half for her morning potion.

If Kieran didn't keep coffee here, there must be some at his office. Samantha hadn't intended to intrude this morning, but some things couldn't be helped.

KIERAN SPENT MOST of the morning helping fix a broken forklift. One thing about running your own operation was that everyone pitched in, according to his skills.

He was scrubbing the grease off his hands in the trailer bathroom when the front door banged open. Peering out, Kieran was startled to see Samantha studying the scale-model of the hotel that sat on a large table.

She didn't seem aware of his presence, and he took a moment to observe her.

This morning, she'd worn a short halter top, shorts and sandals. From the side, he noticed the brightness of her hair and the clarity of her skin. The pink halter emphasized the tempting fullness of her breasts and her low-slung shorts revealed a slender waistline that cried out for a man's hands to encircle it.

Then Samantha swung around to face him, and Kieran saw a gleam of challenge in her eyes. She must have selected the outfit deliberately.

"Guess I promised to show you the office, didn't I?" he said with all the coolness he could muster.

"The truth is, I'm trying to score some coffee." Samantha spied the pot in one corner. "Great!" As she poured herself a cup, she added, "Where's your desk?"

Kieran nodded toward the hallway. "I have a private office."

"How private?" she said.

"You have something in mind?"

Amber eyes pierced him. "You know I like exotic locales."

He was tempted to show her exactly how exotic his office could be. But even if his good sense hadn't stopped him, Kieran knew the men treated his trailer like their home away from home.

"It's not as private as all that," he said mildly.

Samantha leaned against the doorframe, sipping her coffee. She looked perfectly at home, but then, she had the knack of making herself at home anywhere she went.

She wrinkled her nose. "Who brewed this stuff? It's terrible."

"I did," he said.

"Ever clean the coffeepot?"

"No. Should I?"

"The manufacturer recommends it."

As far as he was concerned, dumping out the paper filter was as much cleaning as an office pot needed. If she wanted anything more, she'd have to do it herself. "There's a project you could tackle in your spare time."

"I'll take it under consideration." She set the cup aside. "Does your general store sell coffeemakers? Not to mention food?"

"Probably." Kieran couldn't believe Samantha was actually considering cooking. He wondered what she would do next, fix up the cabin? The lady changed her mind more often than he changed his sheets.

The outer door swung open and Lew marched in. He caught sight of Samantha and gave a low whistle of appreciation. "The bride looks radiant," he said.

"Did you make that?" Samantha indicated the model, and Lew nodded. "I'd have loved to have a dollhouse like that when I was a kid. Not to mention that the design is breathtaking."

"I'm looking forward to showing it to Beth. She's coming up next weekend," the architect said.

Kieran was surprised to see Samantha's broad smile. Apparently the women had really hit it off.

"You know, I have an idea I want to discuss with her," Samantha said. "The Fourth of July is coming up, and I think Hidden Hot Springs ought to celebrate."

"Great. I'll order a keg of beer and some sparklers," Kieran said, and then remembered that the Fourth would mark the last weekend of Samantha's stay here. That would really give him something to celebrate, he supposed, and wondered why he didn't find the prospect cheering.

She glared at him. "That wasn't what I had in mind. I mean something special—food and games, a real country festival. Something to bring people together. Besides, you were talking about another mixer. Why not schedule it that weekend as well?"

Kieran sighed. She'd never get around to fixing up his cabin now. And he didn't want her to feel she had a real bond to Hidden Hot Springs that might justify hanging on to her portion.

"You know," Lew said, "she may have something there. Think about it, Kier. Our slowest season will be summer, with all the heat. Suppose we build up the Fourth of July as a special holiday? We're not in any city's jurisdiction, so we're free to stage fireworks—if we take the proper precautions. We wouldn't want to start a brushfire."

"And some kind of regional food or favorite dish," Samantha said. "Like some towns have a corn festival or a strawberry festival. There's even a garlic festival."

"I've heard of chili competitions," Lew offered.

"I know!" she said. "Pizza! We could have a pizza festival."

Kieran had to draw the line somewhere. "Nobody's going to drive two hours to a pizza festival, not with a pizza parlor on every corner in Southern California. How about cheesecake?"

"Cheesecake?" Samantha said dubiously.

"Sure!" Lew seized on the idea. "I'd drive even farther than this for cheesecake! Who wouldn't?"

Samantha chewed on her lip. "I suppose it makes sense. Besides, it's the only kind of cake small enough to fit in Kieran's oven."

Lew chuckled, and Kieran felt the skepticism melt from his soul. If he had a weak spot, it was for cheesecake. Besides, he knew enough about promotions to recognize a good idea when he heard one. "It might work."

"I'll tell Beth next time we talk," Lew said. "She's great at organizing things. This summer, the festival will be just for us townies, but then it could become an annual event for tourists."

He and Samantha left the trailer together, each trying to top the other with ideas. Kieran had a stack of work to do, but he remained standing in the middle of the room.

The Hidden Hot Springs Fourth of July Cheesecake Festival. It could turn into a popular event, year after year. He could picture Lew and Beth organizing things as families returned, first with babies, then toddlers, then growing youngsters.

But Samantha wouldn't be there.

Of course she wouldn't be there. Damn it, he didn't want her there. She was like—well, like a burst of fireworks, bright colors that shoot through the sky and then they're gone.

Somehow he didn't find the prospect of Samantha shooting out of his life nearly as appealing as he should.

By DINNERTIME, SAMANTHA could feel an attack of grumpiness coming on. One thing after another had gone wrong, all day.

First, when she and Lew tried to discuss the festival idea with Pete, he'd shown little interest, finally admitting he doubted Mary Anne would be joining them. Samantha had to fight back the instinct to argue. *Didn't the man re-alize what a jewel that girl was? How could he discard her so callously?*

She realized she'd been counting on Beth and Mary Anne to keep her company for the rest of her stay, and she'd been looking forward to watching their romances blossom. She'd especially wanted a happy outcome for Mary Anne.

Then, still mulling over ways to bring Pete to his senses, she'd called the district attorney's office to complain about Hank's harassment on Friday. Instead of sympathizing, the secretary had scolded her for leaving the area and in-sisted they needed to know her whereabouts. Samantha had slammed down the phone.

The third thing that had gone wrong was that she'd ar-rived for lunch just as Kieran was departing. He'd given her a distracted wave, half-eaten sandwich still in hand, and bolted out the door. She'd wondered whether he was really that busy or just afraid she'd try to seduce him over French dip and julienne carrots?

It wasn't that she wanted to spend any more time than necessary in his domineering company, but this town re-ally was devoid of entertainment. Even an argument with Kieran had its advantages for breaking up the monotony.

With the afternoon stretching ahead, Samantha had made her way to the abandoned cabin by the highway. Determined to put her time to good use, she'd conducted a top-to-bottom search for the missing diary, letters, or anything that might attest to Albert French's state of mind.

She'd found nothing in the rickety dresser or the kitchen drawers. There were only dust mice under the sofa, and a world-class collection of roaches in the bathroom.

The proof *had* to be here, but she just couldn't find it.

When she'd emerged with the vague idea of exploring the surrounding brush, a mountain lion cub had padded into view around the back corner of the cabin. Its kittenish face bared very unkittenish teeth, and she'd beat a hasty retreat across the highway and up the hill.

Banging open the door to Kieran's cabin, Samantha had stared around in dismay. In daylight, it looked even shabbier than at night. If she were going to live here, she'd decided then and there, she really would need to clean the place up.

The more she'd thought about it, the more playing house sounded like fun. If there was one thing Samantha had never done, it was to act domestic.

She was going to give Kieran the surprise of his life, and had spent the afternoon washing away the grime and then lugging groceries from the general store.

After calling in a message for Kieran to come home before dinner, Samantha had set out to broil a steak. Then she'd gotten busy cooking scalloped potatoes and making salad.

But now, a few minutes later, the smoke pouring from the broiler reminded her that she'd forgotten the steak. No sooner did she set the blackened thing on the counter then she realized she hadn't stirred the potatoes in a while, either. They turned out to be stuck to the bottom.

At least the salad looked decent, Samantha reflected. Anyway, the guy had nothing to complain about. Steak was steak, even burned, and the potatoes were only slightly charred.

She hadn't thought about how the house must smell until the door slammed open and Kieran burst in. Before she realized what he was doing, he'd seized a fire extinguisher from the wall and foamed the bride's first dinner.

"Sorry," he said at her shocked expression. "I thought the cabin was on fire."

Samantha knew she should laugh the whole thing off, but she couldn't. "I'd like to see *you* cook dinner!"

"I do appreciate the effort," Kieran said, and started to laugh. "And I thought I was getting a month with Betty Crocker!"

"I never said I could cook!" Pride made her add, "But I do bake a terrific cheesecake."

"Oh, sure." He began scraping the mess into the trash. "Don't worry. There's always the dining hall."

She really *could* bake a cheesecake, Samantha told herself angrily. And in due time, she was going to prove it.

At the dining hall, they found Mack, one of the construction workers, regaling the men with tales he'd picked up from a passing rock hunter.

"Seems back in the gold-rush days, a fellow named Pegleg Smith found a fortune out in one of the canyons," said the stocky man, wolfing down a double helping of roast beef and gravy. "Then he lost it. That was out in the Borrego Badlands, I reckon."

"How'd he lose it?" Kieran leaned forward.

"Probably filed it under *F* in one of our filing cabinets," said Pete, and everyone chuckled.

"The fellow I talked to didn't rightly know," Mack answered. "But he did know that either Pegleg Smith or somebody else died out there, looking for it, and ever since there's been a skeleton running around chasing miners. Real scary looking thing with a lantern flickering through its ribs."

"Sounds like he's been reading too much Stephen King," Lew observed.

"Wait'll you hear the other story he told," Mack said.

Samantha didn't stick around to find out what it was. She decided it was better to make an early retreat and avoid the inevitable awkward moment with Kieran at bedtime.

He didn't look up when she returned her tray and slipped out the door. She didn't think he even noticed she was gone.

The evening air smelled fresh and tangy. She paused on the steps to gaze down the main street of Hidden Hot Springs.

It hadn't grown any larger or any fancier since she'd first arrived, but it was funny how it no longer looked so shabby. She could hear the showers running in the bathhouse and the hoots and joking from inside the dining hall. The place had come alive for her; its coarse surface, like the rough faces of the men, couldn't disguise the vigorous life of the community.

It was a life, she realized, as deep and rich as the life of any city. And unlike most cities, it opened itself readily to a newcomer.

Except that she could never be a part of it. Not the way Kieran was. Not even the way Beth, with her boundless enthusiasm and warmth, would become when she married Lew.

What kind of pioneer woman couldn't even cook her husband dinner? Samantha grumped silently as she paced along the path. The rocks dug into her thin-soled sandals, and she reminded herself that what she needed around here were hiking boots.

What about her suitcase full of strappy high heels? What about the filmy dresses perfect for dining in Rome or celebrating Carnival in Rio? Why was she even thinking about broiling a steak when her tastes ran to aromatic Chinese shrimp?

As Samantha passed the hotel turnoff, she became aware of the night sounds. An unidentified bird called insistently for a mate; the springs burbled as they boiled to the surface; and far off a coyote howled.

She shivered. Maybe it hadn't been so smart, venturing out here alone. She didn't think Hank could have traced her, but there might be other dangers.

Samantha never allowed potential perils to intimidate her while traveling, but she also didn't take foolish chances. Usually she joined forces with a fellow tourist or friendly resident when she went exploring the nightlife.

But now there was no one around to break the silence, and clouds covered the stars. In the heavy darkness, she felt very much alone.

The cabin lay just ahead. Samantha resisted the instinct to quicken her pace, aware that she faced more likelihood of a twisted ankle than of meeting the skeleton of an ancient prospector.

With a twinge of relief, she turned onto the lane leading up to the cabin. In a few feet, she would step inside and close the door behind her.

As she reached the clearing, Samantha noticed something glittering to one side. She hesitated, puzzled. The thing moved, and with a surge of unreality she found herself staring into two huge yellow eyes.

Samantha screamed.

Chapter Nine

Afterward, Kieran could never be sure whether he heard the scream or felt it in his bones. He was sitting in the dining hall, listening raptly to Mack, when a shiver ran up his spine.

He'd never before felt a primal sense of danger, but he recognized it instantly.

Shoving back his chair, he leapt up, gazing around for Samantha. "Where'd she go?" he demanded of his startled companions.

"She left," someone answered. "About ten minutes ago."

With half-a-dozen men on his heels, Kieran ran into the street. To his dismay, he saw no sign of Samantha. Where the hell was she?

Another scream pierced the air, from the direction of the cabin.

Kieran lit out at full speed down the highway. With adrenaline pumping through his limbs, he cleared the half-mile distance in a matter of minutes.

Why hadn't he taken her concerns more seriously? She always seemed so damn sure of herself that he hadn't considered that she might really be in danger.

He spotted no unfamiliar vehicle that might belong to her former fiancé. But Kieran had heard real terror in Samantha's voice, and she wasn't the type of woman to panic easily.

He flew up the hill, the men trailing behind. A burst of energy powered Kieran right into the clearing.

The scene that greeted him sent his heart hammering into his throat. Samantha stood near the pump, her back to him. Not ten feet beyond her, a female mountain lion crouched ready to spring.

The lady might be a spitfire, but she looked tiny and vulnerable standing alone beside the cat. He estimated its weight at one-hundred-fifty pounds, a good fifty pounds less than his own, but it was all muscle, teeth and claws. Nature's perfect killing machine.

At least it looked well-fed. It hadn't come in search of prey; it must be seeking its stray cub.

Kieran remembered Uncle Albert's instructions. "You ever come up against a mountain lion, boy, you jump around and yell and wave your arms so you look bigger'n you are. That'll give 'em pause."

He strode toward Samantha. She cast him a grateful glance over her shoulder, but didn't turn her back to the cat. He felt a wave of admiration for her courage. If she'd tried to run, the creature would have attacked at once.

"Hey!" Kieran yelled, and the cat flinched. He stepped forward, and the lion bared its fangs but didn't retreat.

This beast wasn't easily intimidated.

Branches cracked behind him, and he realized the men had arrived. The cat drew back by inches but showed no sign of leaving, and he thought he recognized desperation in its eyes.

"We don't have your kitten," Kieran said. "Now beat it. Hey!" He shouted the syllable over and over, waving his arms threateningly. *Why the hell didn't anybody else join him? What did they think this was, performance art?*

He could sense the frozen shock of his men, and prayed it would thaw in time. But it wasn't Lew or Pete or any of the others who began shouting with him; it was Samantha.

"Get out! Go on!" Waving her arms and yelling, she moved up beside Kieran.

The lion gave her a dubious look, as if considering whether to refer her to the nearest psychiatrist, then loped off into the brush.

Someone behind Kieran let out a low whistle. "That was a close one."

Samantha sagged against him. Kieran scooped her into his arms, still so wired that he hardly noticed her weight.

"You know, on balance, I think I'd rather come up against Hank," she muttered. "By the way, there's something wrong with my knees."

"Weak with relief," said Kieran. He swung around to face his men. "Well, boys, thanks for the moral support."

If there'd been more light, he was sure he would have seen plenty of red faces.

"Sorry."

"Don't know what came over me."

"It won't happen again," the men mumbled as they scuffled off. He noticed they stayed in a clump as they proceeded down the hill, as if worried that the big cat might return.

Samantha nestled closer. She looked exhausted.

"Guess I should get you to bed," said Kieran. As he carried her over the threshold, he added, "You know, this is getting to be a habit."

She wrapped her arms tighter around him and pressed her cheek to his chest.

RELIEF WAS TOO MILD a word for what Samantha felt as Kieran lowered her to the bed. Fear had fallen over her with crushing force, and she could scarcely believe the danger was gone.

She tried not to let herself think about what might have happened. It wasn't in Samantha's nature to dwell on life's terrors, but tonight's experience had challenged everything she thought she knew about herself.

She raised herself on her elbows. "Kieran?"

He paused in the doorway. "What is it?"

"Thank you."

He nodded slowly. "Just doing my job." He turned away.

"Kieran?"

After a beat, he swung toward her. "You don't have to keep thanking me."

"I didn't plan to. It's just... your job's not finished."

"Excuse me?"

How was she going to phrase this? "It might not be safe. To leave me alone, I mean," she said. "What if the lion comes back?"

"I'll lock the door," he said. "And I'll be right out here. On the couch. You know, the one with the lumps."

Did he have to make this difficult? "The truth is, I'm a little nervous."

His jaw worked as if he found this momentary weakness amusing. "The woman who shoved me out of my own bedroom two nights ago, and is single-handedly organizing the town's Fourth of July festival, is afraid to go to sleep alone?"

"Of course not," Samantha said. "I'll be all right." Her teeth chattered on the last few words.

Kieran moved toward her and sat on the edge of the bed. "It's all right. You've had a shock. I can stick around for a little while."

Samantha tried to salvage at least a little of her pride. "If you insist."

A gust of laughter burst from him. "I've got a good mind to make you beg, but I won't. Only don't push your luck."

He left the room briefly, to let her change into her nightgown. By the time he came back, Samantha was already dozing, snug beneath the covers.

The last thing she noticed was that Kieran was wearing Superman pajamas still creased from the package. He filled them out exactly the way a superhero should, she noted sleepily, but he'd forgotten the cape....

Kieran had left the window open, but the room still felt hot. After a moment's internal debate, he slipped his shirt off over his head.

He usually slept nude, but the last two nights he'd worn his robe. The Superman pajamas, a gag gift from Pete and Lew last Christmas, were the only ones he possessed.

Beside him, Samantha stirred, muttered something about a cape and then subsided. He'd just stick around until she fell into a deep sleep, Kieran decided.

Her usually animated features had taken on a deceptive air of innocence. In the dappled moonlight, he studied the sweep of eyelashes against her cheek and the gentle parting of her lips. He knew how soft they would feel against his....

Kieran tore his thoughts away, forcing them back to the lioness. Arrangements would have to be made for the state Department of Fish and Game to move her and the cub to a remote area.

But even more pressing than that was tomorrow's meeting in San Diego with his lawyer and Beatrice. There was a lioness of truly awe-inspiring ferocity.

Showing up with Samantha might help his case, but Kieran doubted it. Beatrice's main contention, that her father hadn't been of sound mind, remained impossible to disprove.

Knowing she would never voluntarily step aside, he planned to offer her a share of the property in order to avoid years of litigation. Any reasonable person would accept, but he had never known his cousin to be reasonable.

Well, he had one more ace in the hole that might help his case. Kieran hated shooting blind, but sometimes a man had to use the weapons at hand.

He shifted on the bed, wishing it were larger. He knew he ought to move to the front room, now that Samantha had fallen asleep, but his eyelids felt heavy.

Kieran lay back, finally detecting a faint breeze from the window. In its soothing caress, he fell asleep.

HE WAS NEVER SURE when the dream ended and the reality began. In the dream, Kieran and Samantha had been bathing in the hot springs. He wore his pajama bottoms, which mysteriously avoided getting wet, and she was lounging in a black nightgown.

Like a figure from mythology, she climbed onto the rocks and lifted her arms to the sky. Then, slowly, she pulled up the negligee, baring slender legs and a tapered waist. The nightgown continued rising of its own accord, revealing the orbs of her breasts and finally flying off into the night. In the strange light of an alien moon, her skin glowed.

She held out her arms to Kieran, and he joined her on the rock. His hands rested on her hips; she cupped his face in her palms, and their lips met.

Afterward, he could almost swear that it was at that moment that he awakened to find Samantha leaning over him, her mouth against his, her fingers exploring the stubbled expanse of his jaw.

"What?" he murmured. It began as a protest, but Kieran was too foggy to remember why he shouldn't enjoy the tantalizing pressure of her tongue against his teeth.

Samantha's body matched his, the firm peaks of her breasts pressing against his chest through silken cloth, her hips grazing his, her legs entwined with his thighs.

Raw primitive desire roared through Kieran. An urgent masculine need made him roll Samantha over and hoist himself above her, poised for the moment of union.

But first he needed to claim every inch of her and make her his own.

He heard Samantha gasp as his tongue traced her throat. He pushed up the filmy cloth and bared her inviting breasts, framing them with his hands and biting at the peaks until she moaned and moved against him.

Not yet, he thought. First she must want him beyond endurance. She must belong to him in every sense.

As his knee parted Samantha's thighs, she stroked the pajamas down from his hips. Nothing lay between them; he felt her open to his arousal.

Reveling in her spontaneous response, he drew his tongue over Samantha's stomach. She arched against him, demanding fulfillment. Kieran could hardly contain himself, hardly postpone that moment of domination and surrender, yet he forced himself to elongate this moment of perfect anticipation.

He tasted the most private recesses of her body and felt her shudder with unbearable passion. He had become a lion, and Samantha was his savage accomplice. Both huntress and prey, she stalked him with the insistent rhythm of her movements until he could no longer fight his instincts.

The moment he drove into her, heat transformed him. His body ceased to belong to Kieran French, civilized man, and became a ravaging flame.

Samantha cried out in ecstasy, but he could no longer distinguish her response from his own. They had become a force of nature, merging and parting, her heat tempering and honing his hardness.

He plunged into her with the mounting rhythm of a blaze racing across the landscape. In the pure white-hot fusing of two souls, they melted together. Samantha's great shudder of satisfaction rocketed through Kieran's body, echoed and magnified in his climactic cry.

His arms closed around her and they lay in shallow waters, drifting, slowly sinking once more into the dream.

SAMANTHA AWOKE with the sense of having overslept. Vaguely, she felt that something had happened, but it was a moment before the truth came clear.

That hadn't been a dream. She'd known it, of course, but had allowed herself to take what she wanted, buoyed by her half-dazed state.

She gazed at Kieran, who slept beside her with one arm thrown over his eyes. He wore neither covers nor pajamas, his bronze body unapologetic in its power. The muscles lay dormant, but she could feel the tension just beneath the surface, ready to thrust against her and claim her.

Samantha sat up and rested her chin on her knees. If there was anything she hated thinking about, it was consequences. She'd decided long ago that it was useless to worry about things you couldn't change.

They'd agreed to keep things temporary. *Becoming lovers hadn't really changed that, had it?* she mused.

At least they wouldn't have to endure the next few weeks in an agony of frustration, she decided. It might even be fun.

KIERAN HARDLY SPOKE during breakfast. He was having trouble sorting out his thoughts.

His body radiated the heat of last night's encounter. He didn't want to drive to San Diego today, he wanted to throw Samantha across the bed and ravish her again.

But he wasn't going to.

He glanced up from his cereal at Samantha, who sat across the breakfast table leafing through a magazine. He was grateful that she'd picked up supplies yesterday and they didn't have to eat in the dining hall. At least they could talk freely here.

Kieran cleared his throat. "Well," he said. *That seemed like a good beginning, but what came next?* "We'd better get this over with."

"Over with?" Amber eyes peered at him over the top of the magazine. The front cover featured a woman in a tiny bikini and the legend read, How To Drive Your Man Crazy This Summer. "Well, shoot."

"Okay, here it is: from now on, I go back to sleeping on the couch."

She lowered the magazine and stared at him in disbelief. "If you're still worried that I'm going to refuse to sign the quitclaim, let me set your mind at ease."

Kieran was determined to run damage control. "My mind will be set at ease when the next few weeks are over and we part as friends."

She heaved an exaggerated sigh. "Kieran, Hidden Hot Springs is a great place but I wouldn't try to cheat you out of it."

"Let's just say that you've been known to change your mind," he pointed out.

"The way you did last night?" she teased.

"Who was it that asked me to stick around?"

"You're supposed to be immune to my feminine wiles," she shot back.

"Hey," he said. "You knew I was a man when you married me."

They both laughed, and Kieran realized with a start that the dynamics had shifted between them. It wasn't only the union of their bodies, but a sense of being on the same side of the joke, of looking at the world through the same window.

Dangerous ground, he thought. It was time to bring things back to reality. "But the point is, I never actually changed my mind."

"Oh?" said Samantha. "I thought you were determined not to consummate our marriage."

"We didn't," he said.

"We didn't?" Her amusement faded.

"We didn't because we had no intent to consummate our marriage," Kieran explained. "We were both half-asleep and recovering from a shock."

Samantha stood up so abruptly she jolted the table, which clunked back into place amid the rattle and chink of dishware. "Well, fine. We didn't really sleep together last night because both of us are mentally incompetent, especially you. Does that satisfy you, Mr. French?"

"It will do," he said.

She stalked into the bedroom, the hem of her nightgown flapping angrily in her wake.

Kieran cleared the dishes and then gathered the papers for his lawyer that detailed the progress of construction, the status of loans and the agreements made to the men. And one more sheet of paper, the one that might do the trick if all else failed.

When Samantha returned, he noticed that her camp shirt was tied at the waist, leaving bare a tempting stretch of skin. At least she'd worn jeans instead of shorts this morning. This must be her idea of dressing up for the city.

It was going to be a long few weeks.

Chapter Ten

"This marriage business isn't going to help much, I'm afraid," Joel Phillips said after he finished congratulating them.

The lawyer was a slim, quick man with an office on the third floor of a five-story building. Samantha gathered that he was an old friend of Kieran's who, like the other associates, was working for a share of the project.

"I've got something else I want to show you," Kieran told Joel.

Samantha regarded him quizzically but, when he didn't explain, she let the matter drop.

He'd made it clear this morning that he didn't want her getting too involved in his business or his life. Not that she planned to, but she didn't understand why the guy had to be so stubborn.

Samantha didn't know whether, technically, they'd consummated their marriage or not. But they'd sure as heck made love.

In a few weeks she'd be off to the Caribbean, or wherever. She planned to put Kieran out of her life and out of her plans permanently.

He seemed to relax after she signed the quitclaim, but Samantha could see that he wanted to talk to Joel alone. That was fine with her.

"When is Beatrice showing up?" she asked.

Joel glanced at his watch. "In about fifteen minutes."

"Then if you guys want to talk, I've got a few calls to make. Is there a phone I could use?"

"For a long conversation?" Joel asked and, when she nodded, directed her to a bank of pay phones in the lobby.

En route, she looked around in vain for a vending machine. They'd left early this morning, and it was getting close to lunchtime. Samantha was tempted to retrieve some of the groceries she'd stashed in her car, but she wanted to make her calls first.

They'd brought the red sports car this morning, after finding one of Kieran's tires flat. Arriving over an hour early, they'd stopped at her post-office box—no response, yet, to her job application—and then at a shopping center.

While Kieran bought himself an air mattress at a sporting-goods store, Samantha had loaded up on nonperishable foods, a few pots and pans, and some ready-made kitchen curtains. It was hard to figure out why she felt this urge to improve the cabin; she decided she didn't want to leave feeling in Kieran's debt.

Locating the phones, Samantha dialed the district attorney's office. Mrs. Gray informed her that Hank still hadn't been locked up.

"Aren't you guys going to do anything about it?" Samantha demanded.

"I'll give Mr. Enright another note," the secretary said, "but don't expect any immediate action. He's a very busy man. You wouldn't believe the number of cases on his desk."

"How long does it take to ask a judge to revoke bail?" Samantha tried to keep her tone polite, but it wasn't easy. "If Hank catches up with me, there won't *be* any case."

"We're working on it," said Mrs. Gray. "And the police have some leads to that accomplice. But we need to know where to contact you if anything comes up."

"Just a minute." Samantha fumbled in her purse for the card she'd taken from the lawyer's office. "You can leave a message for me here."

Mrs. Gray wrote down the number. "Is this where you're staying?"

"No, I'm only here for the day, but just ask for Joel Phillips. He'll know where to reach me."

Samantha hung up in frustration. No wonder the criminal justice system was such a mess, when jerks like Hank were free to roam the streets.

Her next call was to the office at SpeedWest Airlines. When she reached Mary Anne, Samantha noticed immediately that her friend's voice had lost its customary lilt.

"What's going on?" she said. "What's wrong between you and Pete? He didn't seem to think you'd be visiting again."

Mary Anne sighed. "I don't think he really likes me."

"Come on, tell all."

There wasn't much to tell. Pete had promised to call every day, but he'd only called once. Granted, he'd urged her to visit the next weekend, but Mary Anne didn't believe he meant it.

"Why shouldn't he mean it?" Samantha said. "Men get busy and forget to call. What's the big deal?"

"Well, think about it. He didn't exactly choose me. By the time he got to the dance, I was practically the only girl left. Come on, Samantha, he doesn't really want me, he's just desperate for female companionship."

"You'll never know unless you give him a chance," Samantha said. "What's one weekend? I think Pete likes you, but you can't expect him to fall madly in love unless he gets to know you better."

"We're not like you and Kieran, or Beth and Lew," said Mary Anne. "You guys seem to fit together naturally. With Pete, I felt like I was tagging along. He's so outgoing and friendly, and, you know me, I can hardly put two words together."

"You're doing pretty well today," Samantha pressed. "Come on, Mary Anne. You've got to pay at least one more visit."

"I'll think about it," said her friend. "Gotta go. I hear Alice in the hallway, and she's not supposed to know I'm in touch with you."

"Take care of yourself." Samantha hung up wondering if Mary Anne's fears were grounded, or if her friend was simply afraid of taking a risk. Either way, Mary Anne was going to return to Hidden Hot Springs if Samantha had to drag her there.

It was a few minutes past twelve, she discovered when she glanced up at a wall clock. The appointment with Beatrice must already have started.

As soon as the elevator doors opened on the third floor, she discovered that the conference was indeed under way. A brittle female voice echoed down the corridor, loud enough for the whole world to hear.

"You must be joking!" the voice snapped. "Do you think I care about your loans or your buddies? That's *my* land you're developing without *my* permission. You have no right to any of it. And as for your getting married, it's obvious my uncle didn't mean some wife you picked up five years after he died!"

The persuasive tenor of the lawyer intervened, but Samantha couldn't make out the words. She sighed, wishing she had a magic wand that could make the woman disappear.

Much as Kieran's occasional high-handedness annoyed her, Samantha respected the way he'd developed this project. Maybe Beatrice was legitimately entitled to a share, but certainly not to the whole thing.

She walked quietly into the outer office, which stood empty with the door ajar. The secretary must have gone to lunch.

Peering into Joel's office, she could make out the tall figure of a woman in a black suit. The woman tossed her head, her dark hair cutting the air like a scythe. Samantha caught an impression of sharp bones and sallow skin but didn't get a direct look. "I don't care how long it takes or how much it costs. What's mine is mine."

"It's not yours and you know it." Kieran's reply came low and angry. "You abandoned your father and you didn't give a damn about Hidden Hot Springs until I developed it."

"Prove it!" jeered his cousin.

"Please," said the lawyer. "It isn't in anyone's best interest..."

Through the half-open door, Kieran caught sight of Samantha. Tight-lipped, he shook his head in a warning to stay out.

She slipped from the room. Apparently Joel had been right; the marriage hadn't made a difference. But she'd gotten the impression Kieran had some other trick up his sleeve. *Hadn't that worked, either, or hadn't he played it, yet?*

A hollowness in her stomach reminded Samantha that she had dried fruit and Sun Chips in her car. No point in starving herself.

As she descended on the elevator, she wondered why the thought of Beatrice taking Hidden Hot Springs annoyed her so much. It just didn't seem fair, she supposed. Besides, the woman would probably ruin the place. From what Kieran had said, his cousin lacked the exact qualities needed to make it a success: management skills, patience, dedication and a capacity for hard work.

The woman was going to destroy everything Kieran had struggled for. Somebody ought to stop her. Samantha hoped Joel Phillips was up to the task.

She hurried through the lobby into the parking area. The modern black-glass building had been landscaped with tall tufts of pampa grass and palm trees to provide a sense of privacy amid the parking bays.

The effect was charming but not very safe, Samantha thought as she strolled around a clump of pampa grass. Then she stopped in dismay.

Two bays ahead, someone was bending over the red sports car. *Should she run inside and call for help? Or stand here and scream?*

Maybe she'd made a mistake. It would prove horribly embarrassing if she started yelling her head off and it turned out the fellow was innocent. After all, she couldn't see him clearly.

Samantha moved past a minivan and a station wagon to get a closer look. Her shoe scuffed the sidewalk and the man's head jerked up. She found herself staring into Hank's narrow eyes.

Samantha's mouth dropped. *How on earth had he found her?*

Hank's jaw worked for a moment, and then he leapt toward her. It was a scenario out of Samantha's worst nightmare.

Oddly, she didn't feel as frightened as she would have expected. Unlike a mountain lion, he could be defeated, although not necessarily by her.

Still, she hadn't taken a self-defense class for nothing, Samantha reflected as she tossed her purse aside and crouched in a fighting stance.

Hank stopped a few scant feet away. "Give me your keys," he said.

"Come get 'em."

"You don't know what's good for you, do you?" The words emerged in a snarl.

"I'm not giving you my car or anything else. Why don't you just leave me alone?" She couldn't believe how steady her voice sounded. Her knees were knocking like woodpeckers.

"I offered to share my life with you. Lots of women would have begged for the chance." Those thin lips, once so quick to utter compliments, curled into a sneer.

Seen in broad daylight, sans toupee, Hank reminded Samantha of a weasel, from his thin face to his skinny chest. "I don't see anyone kneeling in the street, do you?" she retorted.

Samantha thought she saw his eyes dart toward her purse. What was he planning to do, anyway? Surely he wasn't going to all this trouble merely to steal the car. San Diego, like every other city, was full of vehicles with the windows rolled down and a key hidden under the floor mat. Whatever Hank was up to, it could prove dangerous, even deadly, for Samantha.

"How did you find me?" she asked.

"Shut up." Fists clenched, he advanced on her. "Shut up now, like you should have shut up the day you saw the ring. I never met a woman with such a big mouth. From now on, you'll do what I tell you. Got that?"

Samantha waited until precisely the right moment, as she'd been taught. Then she thrust her shoulder into Hank's midsection, prepared to hoist him and toss him to the pavement.

That was the way it was supposed to work. That was the way it *had* worked with her self-defense instructor. But that wasn't the way it worked with Hank.

She got stuck somewhere around his solar plexus. The air whooshed out and he staggered against her, but she couldn't lift him. His center of gravity was in the wrong place. Samantha couldn't remember where it was supposed to be, but definitely not around his ankles. What was he wearing, lead weights in his shoes?

Struggling to straighten, she felt Hank rise a few inches off the sidewalk. How could such a skinny guy feel so heavy?

Attacking had been a tactical mistake, she realized as his hands gripped her throat. She should have screamed while she could.

Samantha opened her mouth. The only thing that came out was a croak.

"Put me down," Hank whined in her ear. "Now!"

She would have, but with his weight on her shoulders she couldn't shift position without falling. "Gak," choked Samantha.

"You think I'm kidding?" His grip tightened.

She couldn't keep her balance. She just wanted to take a deep breath. Samantha felt herself stumbling, and then they both fell with a crunch across the hood of the station wagon.

A string of fiery curses burst from Hank's throat. Gasping for breath, Samantha noticed that he was wearing only shorts and a T-shirt and that his bare limbs lay across the scorching metal of the car.

She removed herself from the bumper, sucked in several deep gulps of air and screamed like a banshee from hell.

And, miraculously, Kieran heard.

He came flying out of the lobby, looking even larger and more muscular than she remembered. Behind her, Hank continued cursing as he wriggled snakelike off the car.

"Samantha! Get away from him!" Kieran thrust her across the sidewalk as he confronted Hank.

"Who the hell are you?" Alarm wiped the sneer from Hank's face.

"Her husband," Kieran ground out.

"Try again." Hank rubbed his burned arm.

"We got married Saturday." Kieran stood protectively in front of Samantha, so she couldn't get a clear look at Hank, but she could sense his disbelief.

"She works fast. A month ago, she nearly married *me*."

"Amazing what a difference a few weeks can make, isn't it?" Kieran braced himself, legs apart. "Let's shake hands and call it even, shall we?"

"Right after she gives me her keys." Stepping into Samantha's view, Hank pulled something metallic from his pocket. Sunlight flashed off the thin blade as it snapped open. "I wouldn't want to spoil your honeymoon."

Tension gripped Kieran's body as he weighed how to respond. She knew him well enough to realize his instincts called out to attack. But it wouldn't be a fair fight, and no car was worth getting killed for.

"It's all right." She reached for her purse.

"No, it isn't. I want him to leave you alone, permanently," Kieran said.

Hank favored them with a menacing smile. "Scout's honor," he sneered.

Samantha scooped up her purse and pulled out the keys. "I hope a truck runs over you."

Hank snorted. "And your car with me?"

"It would be worth it."

"Did I forget to mention one little thing?" He tossed the knife from right to left hand and back again, as if to emphasize the threat. "You're coming, too. That way, hubby keeps his mouth shut to the police until he hears from me."

"No." Kieran circled in front of Samantha.

"Then you're dead, buddy—"

Behind them, high heels beat a tattoo on the sidewalk. A voice like the bray of a donkey blurted, "And what the hell is this? Did you really think you could get away with it?"

They swung around to see the tall figure of Beatrice French Bartholomew storming toward them. With her black suit and sleek hair, she reminded Samantha of Morticia from "The Addams Family."

"Beatrice—" Kieran began in warning, but she cut him off.

"I don't know where you got this, but it's a lie!" She waved a sheet of paper. "I did *not* owe my father ten-thousand dollars! And I certainly don't owe it to his estate!"

"I found the signed IOU in his cabin," Kieran said. "Look, Beatrice—"

About to rage at him, Beatrice caught sight of the knife. Surprise and outrage flashed across her face as she glared at Hank.

"You little creep." From her purse, she snatched a pistol so tiny it resembled a toy. "I hate muggers."

"Just trying to settle matters with my ex-, er, with her." Hank indicated Samantha as he sheathed the knife and sidled away, crablike.

"I've always wanted to shoot somebody," Beatrice snapped, "and I'm in the mood to do it today."

Hank took one more look at the gun, then turned tail and fled. As he vanished around the building, Kieran started after him.

A gunshot cracked. Kieran turned abruptly. "What the hell are you doing?"

"You aren't going anywhere." Beatrice pointed the gun at him.

"I need to follow that man."

Out of sight, an engine roared, followed by the screech of overstressed tires. "You're too late." Beatrice tucked the gun into her purse. "Don't worry, I'm not going to shoot you. The only thing I hurt was that tree over there." A dozen feet away, bark littered the grass around a palm. "This is about as low as a man can sink, Kieran, trying to steal not only my land but my money. I'm not only going to stop you, I'm going to ruin you."

She strode away, and Samantha didn't know whether to thank her or despise her. "She's awful, but she did save my life."

"Not intentionally." Kieran wrapped his arms around Samantha and pulled her against him. "But I'm glad she showed up, all the same. Damn, I wish I had caught that bastard."

"I can't figure out how he found me," she said.

"Who did you call this morning?" Kieran eased Samantha toward her car.

"The D.A.'s office and Mary Anne. But I didn't tell them where I was. Well, I did give Joel's number to the D.A.'s office, but I hardly think he managed to sneak in and steal it. Or maybe he had my post-office box staked out."

As she unlocked the car, Kieran helped her into the passenger seat. "You can't be in any shape to drive, after what you just went through."

"What about you?"

"I'm a man," he said.

"Now wait a minute!"

"And I spent a few years in the Marines," he added. "I didn't see combat, but I was trained for it. Now, listen. Did you call your friend at your old office number?"

Samantha nodded.

"He might have a tap on the phone." Kieran powered up the motor. "I'm not familiar with all the surveillance devices they've got these days. I wasn't aware a phone number could be traced that easily, but he must have managed it. No more calls to that office. Or to Mary Anne at home, either. And no more trips to your post-office box."

Reluctantly, Samantha agreed.

She hated to admit it, but he'd been right: she wasn't in any shape to drive. As they edged toward the freeway, her lungs still felt constricted and her heart pounded.

During the encounter with Hank, she'd been thinking more about overcoming him than about her danger, but in retrospect the incident scared the wits out of her.

She leaned back, her gaze falling on Kieran as he swung the car onto the freeway. He looked so solid and strong. She could almost forgive him for that nonsense he'd spouted this morning about not having consummated their marriage.

It wasn't as if she cared. It was simply a matter of principle.

Samantha's thoughts returned to what had happened last night. The pressure of Kieran's body against hers had awakened her several times but, at first, in her exhaustion, she'd simply drifted back to sleep.

Then gradually she'd become aware of the desire building inside. Each accidental touch of his leg, each whisper of his breath across her neck had aroused an almost unbearable yearning.

Her hand had reached out to trace the sculpted contours of Kieran's chest. He had muttered and tossed in response. As his lips parted, she had realized he was dreaming about the same thing she was.

What harm could come of spurring his dream a little by leaning over and kissing him? And then, before she knew it, firm hands had seized her hips and his mouth claimed hers with a fire she'd never experienced before.

She could hardly sort out the impressions, the overwhelming longing to be possessed mingled with the delicious agony of delay. How had he known exactly where to touch her, how to stroke her, how to stimulate her breasts until she reached the bursting point?

Startled, Samantha realized she was becoming aroused all over again. She glanced at Kieran, but he was frowning at a large truck ahead of them. Thank goodness he couldn't read her thoughts.

It occurred to Samantha that this was the second time in less than twenty-four hours that Kieran had come to her rescue. And their marriage hadn't even helped his case with Beatrice.

If there was one thing she didn't want, it was to leave Hidden Hot Springs feeling in his debt. If she could find some evidence to substantiate Uncle Albert's will, she could leave with her head held high.

Uncle Albert's papers might be as lost as Pegleg Smith's fabled treasure. But unlike the treasure, the existence of which was questionable, Kieran had actually seen his uncle writing in a diary. It had to be lying around somewhere.

It would be fun playing detective, Samantha thought, not at all dissuaded by her lack of success when she'd explored the old shack. She'd have to dig deeper, take a creative approach and overcome the odds. She was looking forward to it.

It would give her something to do during those long days at Hidden Hot Springs while Kieran was working.

Chapter Eleven

Kieran hated the heat waves that swept through Southern California in late summer. He hated this one even more because it had arrived early, in June.

He pushed up his yellow hard hat as he trudged across the construction site, but it promptly slid back down. Sweat trickled along his forehead and threatened to obscure his vision.

A breath of wind cooled his neck, but it also raised a cloud of dust that tickled his throat into a cough. Kieran ached to retreat into the air-conditioned trailer, but if his men could endure this hundred-and-ten degree misery, so could he.

From all around came the rap of hammers and whine of saws, echoing off the canyon walls. The hotel structure was beginning to put flesh on the skeleton.

They might actually meet their goal of opening the first phase this fall. Was it possible that five years of struggle were about to bear fruit?

A whistle sounded, and the hammering stopped as the men headed for a rest break in the shade. At Kieran's request, the kitchen staff had opened an outdoor bar to provide fruit juices and ice cream. He was afraid the men would suffer heatstroke if they took in insufficient liquids, or made the mistake of drinking alcoholic or caffeinated beverages.

Watching them, Kieran felt his heart squeeze. He'd received a call from Joel Phillips this morning to tell him Beatrice was seeking a court order blocking further work on the project. Her motive could only be pure spite.

It had been a mistake, slapping her with that paper showing she owed her father ten-thousand dollars. Kieran bit back the urge to kick himself. The debt was legitimate; the paper was one of the few documents his uncle hadn't managed to hide or lose.

Actually, he had to concede, Albert might have intended to discard it, since the paper had been tossed in a corner with a stack of old magazines, but that didn't make it any less authentic.

Kieran had been afraid Beatrice might have paid the damn thing off, but she hadn't produced any evidence of that. At their confrontation last week, she'd simply claimed that the estate rightfully belonged to her, and she could hardly owe herself money, could she?

Seeing the paper had made her angry, not fearful. That was why she was seeking an injunction, and, knowing how unpredictable judges could be, Kieran feared she might prevail.

He couldn't let himself dwell on the possibility. It was too painful and counterproductive. He intended to keep working to the last possible minute, and so did his men.

He'd broken the news to them this past weekend about Beatrice's suit. Their response had been the same as his, an urge to fight back. Still, he'd noticed the men talking seriously among themselves, conversations that sometimes broke off as he approached.

They had to keep their spirits up. Especially Kieran, Lew and Pete; the others looked to them.

He headed for the trailer. Since the others were taking a break, he supposed he could afford to, also.

En route, he nearly collided with Pete, as the foreman emerged from a portable toilet. Pete merely nodded, instead of stopping for a chat as he usually would.

Kieran put a hand on his friend's shoulder. "You feeling okay?"

"Yeah, sure." Pete didn't meet his eyes. "Just on my way to have some juice."

"The heat getting to you?" Kieran realized he must sound like a substitute mother, but he'd never seen Pete this downhearted. "Or is it my cousin that's got you worried?"

"I'm not worried," Pete said. "Just thirsty."

Kieran lifted his hand and let his friend go. *What the hell was the matter, anyway?*

He reached the trailer and, with a sigh of relief, stepped into its cool interior. His first instinct had been to conserve energy and rely on fans, but Lew had pointed out that their computers weren't going to suffer in silence. Apparently they only functioned in a narrow temperature range, thank goodness, so the air-conditioning stayed on.

Kieran poured some water from the cooler and took a swig. As cold air blasted at him from a vent, he could feel the sweat chilling his face and chest. Was there anything on earth as pleasurable as cooling off in a California heat wave?

The answer to that question struck Kieran thirty seconds later when he opened the door to his office.

The first sight that met his eyes was a pair of perfectly shaped bare legs crossed at the ankle and angled rakishly atop his desk. The most delicate sandals he'd ever seen displayed slender feet with the toenails polished pink.

It was a sight worth walking through the Sahara Desert to see. But why was it making itself at home in his office?

"Excuse me," Kieran said to the back of a two-day-old copy of the *Los Angeles Times*.

The paper rustled aside and Samantha peered at him from his swivel chair. "Is this your seat?"

"As if you didn't know." He sat on the edge of the desk. "What brings you here?"

"Progress report," she said.

In the past week, since their trip to San Diego, the two of them had by unspoken agreement fallen into an arm's-length relationship. Kieran made a point of walking Samantha safely to the cabin after dinner, but then he either buried himself in a trade journal or returned to play cards with his buddies.

He had to admit that she'd been cooperative about keeping her distance. She'd also proven a valuable aid in working with his men as she helped organize the upcoming Fourth of July celebration.

Samantha had placed an ad for a mixer, made plans for the cheesecake competition, hired a fireworks company and helped divide the men into teams for a softball tournament. She'd worked smoothly with Lew and his new girlfriend, who'd come to visit last weekend.

If Kieran had any complaint, it was Samantha's clothing. She managed to look presentable enough in public, wearing shorts and a camp shirt, but in private the shirt always managed to fall open, revealing a bikini bra underneath.

Samantha claimed it was her way of dealing with the heat. Kieran wondered which kind of heat she was referring to.

Right now, his position gave him a Class A view of her thighs leading into the cutoff shorts. At hip height emerged a nipped waistline and two generous breasts inadequately restrained by a flowered bikini top. The Hawaiian print clung for its life to two volcanic peaks, and if *he* weren't careful, Kieran feared there might be an eruption one of these days.

Nope. He wasn't going to dwell on that tempestuous night when they'd made love, even though it reverberated through his dreams. Now that Samantha had signed the quitclaim, Kieran doubted she would try to rescind it. Nevertheless, their plans still called for the marriage to be annulled, and the last thing he needed were any more complications in his life.

He wished he could control what his subconscious did while he was sleeping; morning after morning, he awakened restless with longing on the air mattress he'd picked up in San Diego. But he didn't have to entertain such thoughts during the day, and he didn't appreciate being tempted.

"I wish you'd cover up," he said.

Samantha glanced down. "There's nothing here you wouldn't see at the beach."

"In case you hadn't noticed, we're nowhere near the beach."

"I noticed." She tossed him a steno pad. "Take a look."

"What's this?" Kieran flipped open the cardboard cover. Page after page was covered with chicken scratches.

"My progress report."

"On what?"

"The Fourth of July festival, among other things. Don't you want to read it?"

He peered at the scrawl, able to decipher only a few words here and there. One of them looked like "bake," another might be "dick" and a third, he could almost swear, read "ZZZZ-ouch!"

"Well?" Samantha prompted.

Kieran dropped the pad on the desk. "Are you trying to scare the hell out of me?"

"Huh?" She blinked. "Scare you?"

"According to this, you're going to bake my dick while I'm sleeping," Kieran said. "I'd say 'ouch!' is inadequate."

Samantha grabbed the pad. "Let me see that."

Kieran chuckled. He'd discovered long ago that Samantha's handwriting was almost unreadable. The problem wasn't a lack of hand-eye coordination, but with the fact that her thoughts ran at warp speed and she was too impatient to restrain them. She needed to master touch-typing, preferably on a computer. Make that a Cray Supercomputer.

"This is perfectly clear," Samantha snapped. "We need to make some practice runs at the cheesecake. Just in case nobody else brings any, I'm planning to bake three or four myself."

"I'm sure our chef can provide backup," Kieran offered.

"Yes, but it's not the same." She glared at him over the spiral pad. "He's a professional. Besides, he's one of the judges, so he can't enter the contest. I want to try out an idea I've got for using chocolate chips. We need to experiment!"

"We?" Kieran said.

"You wouldn't trust me alone with an oven, would you?" In the past week, Samantha had managed to burn a soufflé and whip up a dish of rice and lentils so enormous and so tasteless that Kieran wished he had a horse to feed it to.

"I'll help with the cheesecakes," he offered. "What's this dick business?"

"We'll get to that later." She hurried down the page. " 'Zzzz-ouch!' Well, that couldn't be plainer."

"It couldn't?"

"Beth and some of the other women are coming up this weekend to help get organized for the following week," Samantha said. "You can't expect them to sleep out in tents, not when the place is swarming with mountain lions."

"Two isn't swarming, but you're right." Kieran had called the state Department of Fish and Game last Wednesday, and they'd promised to send someone out— but not for another week. Along with the heat wave had come brushfires in half-a-dozen areas of the state, threatening wildlife and driving bears and big cats into suburban neighborhoods. The rangers were spread thin. "It's okay with me if they pitch their sleeping bags in the rec hall."

Samantha made a note on a clean page. "Excellent idea."

"Now what's this business about the dick?" he said.

Samantha chewed on the end of her pen. "Like Dick Tracy," she said.

"A detective? To do what?"

She favored him with a "how dumb can you get?" look. "To get the dirt on Beatrice. Just in case we can't find the diary, and heaven knows, I've looked."

He had to admit, Samantha had been a trooper, poring over not only every inch of Albert's cabin but also of the three others. With Lew and Pete's permission, she'd crawled into sweltering attic spaces and poked behind the furniture, to no avail.

"I'd love to discover something devastating about my cousin, but it won't work," Kieran said. "Joel has asked me to leave any investigating up to him. He knows how to handle these matters."

"He's a stick-in-the-mud." Samantha flung the pen onto the desk so hard it bounced. "You know he'll play everything by the book."

"He's a lawyer. He's supposed to."

"She's a rotten person, and she's probably wanted in six states and the Republic of Panama," Samantha protested. "Maybe she's not even Beatrice but some imposter."

"I know what my cousin looks like," Kieran said. "You've been watching too many old movies."

"We can't let Hidden Hot Springs go down the tubes!" Her chin rose in the air. "I'm surprised at you, Kieran French!"

He shared the sentiment, but he'd seen how heavy-handed tactics could backfire. Thanks to Beatrice's outrage over the ten-thousand-dollar debt, she was now trying to stop construction altogether.

Kieran leaned across the desk and skewered Samantha with his gaze. "Let's get one thing straight. There will be no detective unless Joel Phillips hires one."

Her lips clamped shut.

"Samantha? I want your word on it."

"My word is useless," she said. "I lie all the time."

"Like when?"

She bit her lip and arched her shoulders, deepening the cleavage between her tantalizing breasts. "Like telling you I go around with my shirt open because of the heat."

Kieran threw back his head and laughed. "You little minx."

She grabbed the steno pad and swung her feet to the floor. "I'll see you later. There's work to be done around here, in case you hadn't noticed."

"In case I hadn't what?" he challenged.

She breezed past him in a scented cloud of suntan lotion and herbal shampoo. "Rest break is over, Kieran. Get to work."

She vanished out the door. He wondered what would have happened if he'd stuck out his arm and caught her by the waist.

She would have kissed him, that's what. Kieran closed his eyes, momentarily trapped in fantasy. Kissed him and come to him....

And then he would have pulled off that damn bra and made her regret every one of her lies.

He went to the window and watched her sultry shape undulate across the driveway. She was buttoning her shirt as she went.

MEN WAVED GREETINGS as Samantha passed the juice bar, and she waved back. She was getting to know them by name, and they seemed to have accepted her as a pleasant fact of life around the town.

All but Pete.

She knew he was Kieran's best friend, and she wanted very much to feel accepted by him, although she wasn't sure why, since she'd be leaving in two weeks.

But since Mary Anne failed to show up last weekend, Pete had avoided meeting Samantha's eyes. Obviously, the sight of her reminded him of her absent friend.

She wished she dared call and scold that silly woman. Mary Anne's low self-esteem was making her miss the chance of a lifetime. If she'd only spend time with Pete, she might find out that he really cared about her.

Was it possible Samantha might be mistaken? Well, she thought, this was one risk worth taking. It might be a long time before her shy friend met another such promising fellow.

But how was Samantha going to persuade Mary Anne to come when she couldn't even contact her? She didn't dare call Mary Anne at work *or* at home. And she certainly couldn't drive into San Diego to get her, not after the way Hank had materialized out of nowhere last Tuesday.

She'd just have to figure something out, and the sooner the better.

Before she realized where she was headed, Samantha found herself at Uncle Albert's cabin. She no longer worried about walking around alone, despite her close encounter with the mountain lion.

It had only ever been spotted early in the morning or late in the evening. Besides, the animal appeared well-fed.

As she pushed open the ramshackle door, Samantha wished she felt as optimistic about finding Albert's diaries and papers as she felt about escaping any more mountain lion face-offs.

She couldn't even turn up any witnesses to his mental health; which was hard to believe in this age, when everybody seemed to know everybody else's business.

During the past week, Samantha had telephoned every organization that came to mind for someone who might have met Albert. She'd tried all the senior citizen centers she could locate from miles around, but no one had heard of Albert French. In vain, she'd contacted historical societies and the Sierra Club. She had driven nearby roads in search of residents who might remember him, and had even checked his aging magazines in case he'd written letters to the editor.

There was no sign of a computer, so he hadn't been interfacing with the world via the Internet, either. For all she'd turned up, Albert French might as well have lived out his later years on Mars.

Samantha stepped into the shady interior, noticing how the temperature dropped by ten degrees. In this dry climate, the air cooled easily.

Not like the Caribbean. She tried to picture herself strolling into a café in Kingston, Jamaica, blissfully ignoring the steaming atmosphere as she ordered a piña colada.

The fantasy refused to gel. Her eyes searched the imaginary bar for a good-looking man, one with, say, shaggy blond hair and eyes the color of robin's eggs. Nowhere in sight.

Okay, maybe she'd spend her shore leave diving among coral reefs, swimming among the incredible colors that nature saves for those who live life to the fullest: those who dare, those who risk, those who give up friends and loved ones and air-conditioned trailers where men built like Adonis perch on the corner of a desk....

This was getting her nowhere.

As she had half-a-dozen times before, Samantha inspected the cabin, trying to figure out where Uncle Albert might have found a hiding place that had so far escaped her. The place was even smaller and simpler than Kieran's house: a single living-and-sleeping room, with a kitchenette along the back wall, a utility room and a bathroom.

She tried moving to the back of the room to inspect it from a different angle, looking for cracks in the wall or a trapdoor. Surely the man wouldn't have wrapped up his papers and hidden them outside; even with waterproofing, they wouldn't have lasted long.

The first question she'd put to herself was, why had he hidden the papers in the first place? The answer had come swiftly: in case Beatrice showed up and tried to destroy them.

Following a logical course of reasoning, she'd deduced he might have stashed the material in one of the other cabins, but that hadn't panned out. The only other buildings still standing from the old days were the bathhouse, which had been gutted and remodeled, and the church-turned-rec hall, which Kieran and Lew had gone over last weekend with a fine-tooth comb.

What could she be missing?

The approaching rumble of a motor drew Samantha to the door. Not many cars found their way to Hidden Hot Springs.

An aging minivan zipped toward her, primer-gray showing in patches through the green paint. Madonna sang lustily from the radio.

The van screeched to a halt and a window hummed down. "Need a lift?" called Beth.

Samantha hurried over, smiling. "Thanks but what are you doing here in the middle of the week?"

"Moving in," said her friend.

"Then you'd better park right over there. This is as close as you can get to Lew's cabin."

"Okay." The dark head disappeared into the van's interior, and the vehicle rattled a few feet down the road, executed a U-turn and stopped.

Beth hopped out. "I'm glad I ran into you. I don't want to disturb Lew while he's working."

"Doesn't he know you're coming?" Samantha brushed off her hands, which always felt dusty after visiting Albert's cabin.

"Sure. But not exactly what time." Beth slid open a side door and pulled out a couple of suitcases. "I just figured, this is crazy, we're always on the phone, and I'm not working this summer, so why am I in Chula Vista while he's here?"

Samantha picked up a suitcase and led the way up the path. "Are you planning to stay long?"

"I'll have to make a decision about going back to work." Beth strode behind her, not even breathing hard as they lugged the heavy cases up the slope. "But I've got some time, yet."

Pausing for breath, Samantha set down the suitcase and glanced back over the highway. A tan shape flicked across the periphery of her vision, near Uncle Albert's cabin, but when she looked again it was gone. It might have been a deer, or the lion cub or a sheet of brown paper blown from the construction site.

Beth hummed restlessly. Samantha picked up the suitcase and resumed her climb.

Like most buildings around Hidden Hot Springs, Lew's cabin was never locked. Samantha helped her friend unload, grateful to see an array of appliances that she might be able to borrow.

Even more, she was glad to have someone to talk to during the day, someone she could trust for an objective opinion. There was one subject she particularly needed advice on.

"I'm trying to figure out what to do about Mary Anne," she explained.

Beth listened thoughtfully to her account. "What about that other friend of yours?"

"Alice?"

"Isn't there some way to contact her? She might be able to light a fire under Mary Anne." Beth arranged an armful of stuffed animals around the living room. "Samantha, meet Bowling Alley, Mop, Toast, Sky and Wind Boy."

"Those are their names?" Samantha eyed the well-worn bears dubiously.

"I use them in my teaching. The kids get to take them home and write diaries for them. They provided the names, as well."

"Maybe I should contact Uncle Albert's second-grade teacher," grumbled Samantha. "Maybe *she's* got his diary."

They made another trip to the van, returning with a vacuum cleaner and a sewing machine. "I've got a lot of work to do," Beth explained. "If I end up staying, my mother will want to visit, and she's a real neatness fanatic."

Samantha tried to picture Beth's mother, or anyone's mother, trotting around the town's paths. The poor woman would have to spend most of her time soaking away the aches at the hot springs.

Something about the image of a mother tickled the back of her memory. "What day is this?" she asked, sliding the sewing machine onto the cabin's only table.

"Wednesday, last time I checked."

"Oh, Beth, that's perfect!" Samantha hugged her friend and ran out the door.

"What's perfect?" called her bemused friend.

"I'll tell you later. I promise!"

At Kieran's house, Samantha dug through her dresser drawer until she found her address book. First she looked under *J* for James and then *M* for Mother. She finally found the number she wanted under *A* for Alice's Mother.

Wednesday was Alice's day off, since she worked the Saturday shift, and she always went to visit her mother in Oceanside. Samantha had gone with her once, enjoying the clean beach and small, picturesque house.

To her delight, Alice answered the phone. It took a few minutes to calm her excited friend and explain why she was calling, but Alice readily agreed to drag Mary Anne to Hidden Hot Springs after work on Saturday.

"Not that I'm a big fan of marriage, as you know, but Mary Anne needs a good man," Alice said. "Besides, I'm dying to see you. And a town full of single men with big muscles? This I've got to experience."

"Speaking of marriage," Samantha began, "I sort of got married again."

"You did what?"

That explanation took even longer, and Samantha's ear ached by the time she got off the line. But she felt a sense of accomplishment. She'd made real progress on one of her goals.

Now to get the goods on Beatrice.

She hadn't actually promised Kieran that she wouldn't hire a detective. In Samantha's opinion, she had finessed that point rather nicely.

But where was she going to find one?

There was no point in calling Joel Phillips. Alice wouldn't be much better; she could check a San Diego phone book, but a personal recommendation would be preferable.

Samantha wondered if she dared call the D.A.'s office. So far, she hadn't contacted them directly from Hidden Hot Springs. Could they trace the call? And what difference would it make if they did?

Just to be on the safe side, when Mrs. Gray answered, Samantha identified herself and said, "I'm calling from a pay phone, out in the middle of nowhere. I have to keep moving around until you get Hank locked up. Have you?"

No, the secretary admitted, Hank's bail hadn't been revoked, yet, but Mr. Enright would be submitting the request later in the week.

"What I'm really looking for is a detective," Samantha said. "It's a personal matter, nothing to do with Hank. Could you recommend someone?"

"We're not in the business of referring people to detectives," the secretary replied.

"I'm not asking for anything official." Samantha hated to request a favor, but she didn't know who else to turn to. "Surely there's someone you've worked with, or heard about, who's reputable."

Mrs. Gray clicked her tongue. "I'll tell you what. I feel bad about all the delays in this case, so I'll make some inquiries. I'm not promising anything, but give me your number and I'll call you back in a few days."

"I told you, I'm calling from a pay phone," Samantha said. "And I don't know where I'll be in a few days. I'll call you back, okay? Thanks so much. I really appreciate this."

"I don't understand why you're being so secretive," the woman complained.

A noise outside made Samantha jump. With a start, she realized it was after five o'clock. If Kieran overheard this conversation, there'd be hell to pay.

"Gotta go. I'll call you in a few days," she said, and hung up.

As she went to the door, Samantha realized the sound she had heard was the rhythmic creak-creak of the water pump. She still hadn't gotten used to using it, preferring to put up with the thin trickle of water from the faucet, but Kieran swore by the thing.

Stepping onto the porch, Samantha paused abruptly. Kieran had tossed his shirt, shoes and socks onto the glider and stood splattering himself with water.

Sunlight sparkled off the rivulets that ran along his shoulders. His skin gleamed as he threw back his head and splashed his chest and neck. As she watched, she sensed an elemental masculine presence that made Samantha's breath catch in her throat.

She'd spent the past week teasing Kieran, just to keep life interesting, and trying to divert her thoughts from that night when they'd made love. Samantha had almost managed to convince herself it was a fluke and that she'd worked out her sexual feelings toward Kieran.

Observing him in this spontaneous moment, half-naked and dripping, she ached to tear off her clothes and run into the water with him. It took all her strength to shove her emotions under control.

Pinching herself sharply on the arm helped Samantha calm down. With luck, Kieran wouldn't have a clue what she'd been feeling.

Then he swung toward her, a grin lighting his face, and made no secret of inspecting her figure. Samantha was glad she still wore the camp shirt, but she could feel his eyes unbuttoning it.

"Well?" she demanded.

Instead of answering, Kieran bounded up beside her, showering her with droplets. He smelled of honest sweat and a trace of after-shave lotion as he towered over her on the porch. "Are you ready?" he asked.

"For what?" Samantha wished she didn't sound so breathless.

"For me."

Chapter Twelve

"Ready for you?" Samantha repeated. "To do what?"

"To help you bake cheesecakes, of course," Kieran said. "What did you think I meant?"

Samantha tried her best to act nonchalant. "I thought you meant ready to go to dinner. But you aren't even dressed."

"Let's skip dinner," Kieran suggested. "Let's pig out on cheesecake."

The hint of a smirk on his face told her he knew exactly what she'd been thinking. Samantha knew she had to change the subject, fast. "Did you know Beth moved in with Lew?"

It worked. "She did? When?"

"A couple of hours ago." She walked calmly into the house, hearing the floorboards yield as Kieran followed. "How come guys never tell each other important things like that?"

"Because we have even more important matters to discuss," he said.

"Like who's going to win the World Series?"

"Well, yes. For starters." With that, Kieran disappeared into the bedroom.

He emerged a few minutes later, drier but not much more covered up. He wore the torn cutoffs she'd seen during their first encounter on the highway, the same sandals and a tank top that left little to the imagination. Not that you needed much imagination, with a body like that to admire.

Samantha sneaked a look at Kieran from where she bent by the refrigerator, removing bars of cream cheese. From this angle, she got an Academy Award-winning view of his muscular thighs.

As she stood up and swung the refrigerator door shut with her hip, she caught sight of a little smile playing around the corners of Kieran's mouth. He had definitely dressed that way on purpose.

Two could play at this game. Without a word of explanation, Samantha took off her shirt and tossed it over the back of a chair. Catching Kieran's startled look, she said, "Something wrong?"

He cocked one eyebrow. "I like your bikini bra, but is there a point? Are we playing a chef's version of strip poker?"

"In case you hadn't noticed, it's hot in here." She nodded at the bowls and the hand mixer. "The recipe book is right there. Why don't you try the chocolate version and I'll try the lemon?"

"You'll have to show me what to do," he said. "I'm more of an eater than a baker."

Samantha assembled all the ingredients on the chipped counter. "We won't need to soften the cream cheese. Thirty seconds at this room temperature and it will liquefy."

"It's your call," said Kieran.

She wished he would stop regarding her as if she were the tastiest item on the menu. Maybe she shouldn't have pulled that stunt with her shirt. Maybe she ought to go change into a caftan, just to be on the safe side.

But Samantha refused to let him see she was intimidated. She was going to tough this one out.

KIERAN WONDERED if the little minx had any idea what effect she was having on his libido.

She only had to slant that mischievous gaze at him to get his heart beating faster. Her throaty chuckle, her pouty lips, the way her hips swayed when she walked, all heated his long-suppressed desires to the boiling point.

Their night together, rather than relieving his tensions, had reawakened needs long held in check. Once freed, they had no intention of returning to the dormant state.

Kieran knew he'd pushed her a bit, taking off his clothes outside and then coming out of the bedroom in nothing but a tank top and shorts. But women didn't get aroused by the mere sight of a man, did they?

Once she pulled off her shirt, he'd felt himself skid along the delicious, tantalizing, scary edge of losing control. Damn if her skin didn't look like silk, every bare inch of it. He loved the way her waistline creased when she turned, he relished the vulnerable curve of her throat and what kind of man could tear his eyes away from those orbs rising above the horizon of her bra?

Kieran didn't have a clue how to make cheesecake, but he followed Samantha's example as she measured sugar, eggs and almond extract into her bowl. Catching her prompting nod, he studied his recipe and tossed in a handful of chocolate chips.

A stupid recipe if he'd ever seen one. In Kieran's view, cheesecake was best left pure and simple. Besides, he didn't want to learn about the effect of heat on eggs, cream cheese and sugar. He preferred a different kind of physics experiment, namely to teach that bra a lesson in aerodynamics that would leave it dangling from the highest shelf.

As he watched Samantha deftly whipping the hand mixer about, it struck Kieran as surprising that such a nondomestic person knew this much about baking.

"Where'd you learn to bake?" he asked.

"My landlady taught me, when I lived in Paris," she said.

"You've lived in a lot of places. Don't you get tired of being on the move?"

Her amber eyes widened in surprise. "Not really. I suppose I would if I traveled all the time, but I don't. I go to one place and stay there for six months or a year."

Leaning on the counter, Kieran tried to focus on what bothered him about that life-style. "Doesn't that leave you unsatisfied?" He thought about the closeness that had developed between his men over the years. "It takes time to get to know people."

"Depends on your personality." Samantha scraped the rim of the bowl with a spatula. "I've only known Mary Anne for a few months and she's one of my best friends. I've only known Beth for a week and a half, and we get along great."

She was having trouble pouring the mixture into the graham-cracker crust, so Kieran reached over and held the bowl for her. Their hands bumped, and a tiny thrill of desire ran through him at the contact. But he stood motionless, watching the quick efficiency of her movements.

Samantha worked more rapidly and with less wasted motion than anyone he'd ever met. With a start, Kieran realized that was how she approached everything in life.

In the short time he'd known her, she'd reorganized the town's social life, learned most of the men's names and thrown his thoughts into turmoil. Of course, she didn't know that—or did she?

"Let's do yours," Samantha said. "Kieran?"

Realizing she meant his cheesecake, he obligingly tilted his bowl and let her scrape it into the prepared crust. "So you breeze into people's lives like Mary Poppins, solve their problems and float away when the wind changes, is that it?"

"More or less." Samantha licked a drop of filling that had landed on the back of her hand. "Now we stick these in the oven for twenty-five minutes while we make the topping."

Kieran held the oven door for her, then forced his attention onto the recipe. Despite a light breeze from the open back door, the kitchen was heating up. It was a crazy idea, baking cheesecakes on such a hot day.

Well, soon enough, he'd have peace and quiet in his own cabin. Not to mention a good night's sleep.

It was something to look forward to, he supposed.

BETH AND LEW joined them a short time later. They smelled the cheesecakes on their way to dinner, stopped in and didn't leave until bedtime.

Already, Samantha noticed, the two of them finished sentences for each other. Lew appeared more relaxed than she'd ever seen him, and Beth positively glowed.

From beneath her lashes, Samantha peered at Kieran, who was listening to Beth's tale of how one of her students insisted on bringing a dog to class. A rumpled forelock gave Kieran a boyish air, and his strong features softened as Beth described the boy's insistence that his pooch needed an education, too.

She wondered how it would feel if, like Beth, she were prepared to spend the rest of her life with one man. The thought made Samantha's head ache, and she returned her attention to the conversation.

"I finally convinced him to take the dog to a weekend obedience class," Beth said. "Not only did it solve my problem, but his mother wrote me a thank-you note."

Lew draped an arm around her shoulders. "You really know how to handle kids."

Beth beamed at him. "You seem like you'd be good with children, too."

"I've always wanted to be a father."

"I can tell," she said.

They were talking about having children together, Samantha reflected, while she, herself, was leaving in a little over two weeks. Why had the prospect suddenly begun to bother her? She wasn't ready for children. And if her experiences of the past month had taught her anything, it was that she certainly wasn't ready for marriage.

Maybe her biological clock was starting to tick. If that were the case, she needed to figure out how to use the snooze alarm, and fast.

EARLY THURSDAY MORNING, Kieran awakened to hear the scrape of the front door opening.

He got his bearings immediately. He knew it must be about five-thirty, from the paleness of the light filtering through the windows. What he didn't know was why Samantha had gone out at this hour, when she usually slept later.

Pushing back his light blanket, Kieran sat up on the inflated mattress. The air felt cool against his chest; he'd taken to wearing pajama bottoms, a reluctant concession to nighttime decency.

Stretching, he moved to the doorway.

Samantha stood at the edge of the clearing with her back to him, the dawn light silhouetting her body through a gauzy nightgown. Her short hair formed a reddish brown halo.

From her position, Kieran knew, she could see for quite a distance over the valley floor. At this hour she would have a view of a land almost primeval in its wildness.

From the start, he'd pegged Samantha as a city girl. He wondered what she was staring at so avidly.

Despite his curiosity, Kieran found himself planted to the floor, watching the morning breeze ruffle her hair and turn her nightgown to billowing mist. He remembered an image of her from a dream, posing atop a rock at the hot springs. This morning more than ever, she resembled a naiad, a nymph that ruled over brooks and streams.

Without turning, Samantha said, "I wonder what he's doing down there."

Kieran shoved his feet into a pair of huaraches and stepped forward. Reaching Samantha, he followed her gaze down the hill, across the highway to Uncle Albert's cabin.

The lion cub was frolicking in the bushes, pouncing like a kitten on some unseen prey, a chipmunk or a mouse. It kept escaping, and the cub kept pouncing, until finally the little cat lifted its head triumphantly with breakfast dangling from its mouth.

"Guess he was just rustling up some food." Samantha didn't move from her lookout post. "I'm surprised his mama hasn't found him by now."

"He must have a hiding place," Kieran said. "I wish Fish and Game would hurry up."

Samantha sighed. "I'll kind of miss the little guy." She shot a wry look at Kieran. "But not his mother."

They stood for a moment longer, observing the quiet valley. The road lay silent, and the town couldn't be seen around the bend. Kieran couldn't even make out the hotel site to their left, although he observed steam rising from the hot springs.

What would Beatrice do with Hidden Hot Springs, if she won? It didn't bear thinking about.

"Starting to appreciate nature?" he asked Samantha.

For once, she didn't rip back with a clever answer. "Actually, I am," she said. "You have to slow down your rhythms and get in sync before you can observe what's going on. I never tuned in to butterflies and wildflowers before. I guess I'm not used to focusing on things that aren't moving fast."

"Next thing you know, you'll take up bird-watching," Kieran teased.

To his surprise, her expression was wistful as she turned back toward the house. "I won't be here long enough," she said.

IT WAS FRIDAY before Samantha called the D.A.'s office again. Mrs. Gray had two pieces of news for her.

"First of all, Hank's back behind bars," she said. "So you can stop lying low."

"If he got out once, he can get out again." Samantha had come to believe that Hank had almost magical powers to manipulate the system. "I'm happy where I am, thank you." Just to be on the safe side, she added, "Which means I'll keep moving around."

"I had a feeling you'd say that." The secretary clicked her tongue. "I hate to say this, Ms. Avery, but I'm beginning to think you're paranoid."

"Paranoid but alive," Samantha said.

"As to this business about a detective. . . ." The older woman hesitated. "I could get in trouble for this. It's not my place to go recommending investigators."

Samantha reassured her quickly. "I understand that it's not a formal recommendation, just the name of someone reputable."

"Well, several people have spoken highly of a Mr. James Dunaway," said Mrs. Gray. "He works out of his home in La Jolla." She gave the seaside community its correct Spanish pronunciation, *la hoya*. "I've spoken with him, and he's agreed to discuss the case with you. I don't know how much he charges."

Samantha wrote down the number. "Thanks, Mrs. Gray. You don't know how much I appreciate this."

"Think nothing of it."

She didn't follow up immediately, because Beth dropped by and they went to bring the men lunch. The heat wave had cooled by a good twenty degrees, making a shady picnic outing a pleasure.

The conversation at lunch remained general. Work was proceeding ahead of schedule on the hotel; the news about Beatrice's lawsuit had galvanized the men, who took out their anger by working even harder than usual.

The four of them talked about the coming weekend. A barbecue and softball play-offs were planned, and some of the women from the last mixer would be visiting. Samantha kept her fingers crossed, hoping Alice would deliver on her promise to bring Mary Anne.

Kieran seemed distracted, and excused himself early to get back to work.

"It's that cousin of his," Lew advised the women. "She's got a court date next Friday on her preliminary injunction to stop our work. It's the day before the Fourth of July holiday—how's that for rotten timing?"

Samantha made a mental note to call the detective as soon as possible. They needed the evidence fast.

"I hate that woman," Beth said.

"You've never met her," Samantha said.

"I hate her, anyway." Beth glanced at Lew. "I can see what she's doing to these guys, how stressed out they are. It's rotten."

Beth insisted Samantha return to Lew's cabin to help her plan the decorations for the cheesecake festival. They mixed and matched colors until they settled on red, white, blue and forest green.

"That makes it a little more subtle than just red, white and blue," Beth noted. "The green can stand for Hidden Hot Springs itself. You know, how the high water table makes the desert bloom."

"Great." Samantha stood up. She wanted to call the detective before it got too late.

"I thought we'd start lettering directional signs," Beth suggested.

Samantha glanced at her watch. It was after two, and with the weekend coming up, James Dunaway could be leaving soon for a weekend getaway. The fact that he worked at home might mean he was still within reach, assuming the guy didn't spend all his spare time on a surfboard. That couldn't be—didn't detectives have to go on stakeouts?

"I've got a phone call to make," she said. "I'll come back later."

"Don't be long," said her friend. "This is a lot more fun when I have someone to talk to."

"It sure is," Samantha agreed.

On her way to Kieran's place next door, she thought about Beth and Lew getting married and tried to picture life here after she left. *Would Mary Anne and Pete get together? Would Beatrice win her suit? If Kieran succeeded, how would the hotel and the town look in another year or two?*

Samantha had never worried about such things in any of the other places she'd lived, so why was she starting now?

Annoyed, she hurried into the cabin and dialed the number Mrs. Gray had given her. A man answered on the second ring.

He had a gruff voice and a slight Southern accent. "Dunaway Detective Agency."

"Mr. Dunaway? My name is Samantha Avery." She explained the situation involving Beatrice. "Given her unsavory past, I'm sure she must be in trouble somewhere. There might even be a warrant out for her arrest. We need to stop her and I've only got a week to do it."

He asked a few questions, then said, "I think I can help you."

"What do you charge?" Samantha asked.

"A hundred dollars an hour," he said.

She gulped. "Do you take credit cards?"

"Yes," he said, to her vast relief.

"Any idea—I mean, how many hours do you usually put in?" she asked.

"I'll mostly be working by telephone and computer in a case like this," said James Dunaway. "Six to eight hours, maybe."

Six-hundred to eight-hundred dollars. It would be hard to spare, but Kieran deserved no less. "When do you think you'll have any results?"

"Not before the middle of next week," he said. "Where can I reach you?"

"I'll call you," Samantha said. "Thanks, Mr. Dunaway. This is important."

"All my cases are important. Talk to you next week," he said.

That would only give her a few days before Beatrice's court date, but it would have to do.

IT WAS MIDAFTERNOON on Saturday before Kieran quit working. He finally admitted to himself that he was just shuffling papers and double-checking accounting figures to keep his mind off next Friday's showdown in court.

Joel Phillips had said Kieran didn't need to be there. In fact, the lawyer preferred for him to stay away. Joel believed Beatrice's strategy would be to portray herself as a victimized woman. Kieran's muscular build and strong presence might help build sympathy for his cousin.

If there were only something he could do! Kieran's fists clenched, frustrated by his inability to take action. But he had to trust Joel's assessment of the situation.

As he emerged from his office into the trailer lobby, Kieran spotted Pete pouring himself some coffee. "Going to the cookout tonight?"

His friend shook his head. "Not much point."

Kieran wanted to ask what had gone wrong with Mary Anne, but some matters were too personal to broach.

"Don't brood on it," he said. "Drop by and eat with us. It won't be the same without you."

Pete shrugged, and Kieran walked out of the trailer unsure what his friend planned to do.

He'd heard the men knocking off work at noon. They'd been buzzing with excitement about the cookout tonight, even though there wouldn't be very many women. The fact that another mixer was scheduled in a week had soothed hurt feelings.

Except for Pete's. He'd apparently fallen for one woman, hard, and her rejection had hurt him. *What was wrong with her, anyway?* Samantha's explanation that Mary Anne couldn't believe a guy like Pete really cared for her didn't make sense. *Why did women have to be so difficult?*

As Kieran strolled down the hill toward town, the sound of cheerful shouting rose to meet him. *What on earth were all those people up to?*

Descending the path, he got his first clear view of the main street. Someone had strung a volleyball net across the middle of it, and ragged teams of men and women fanned out on either side.

As he watched, Lew popped the ball to Beth, who knocked it over the net. Mack fell to his knees and smashed the thing with his wrists, but it was clearly going to fall short.

With a whoop, Samantha raced forward, flinging herself at the ball and whacking it over. In her headlong rush, however, she lost her balance and fell onto the net.

It tipped over and down it went. The ball landed unattended while everyone rushed to her aid.

Kieran quickened his pace, but before he could arrive, Samantha scrambled to her feet. "Our point!" she yelled, and her team cheered.

Beth and Lew's team shouted a good-natured protest, but soon the net was righted and the play resumed.

Kieran remained where he stood, unnoticed on the sidelines. He was amazed how Samantha had become part of the community so fast. She seemed to fit in naturally. But then, he remembered, Samantha had a lot of experience at fitting in, all over the globe.

As he watched, she jumped up and down, hollering encouragement while Ernie lumbered toward the ball. When the worker stumbled and knocked the ball sideways, sending it plunging earthward, she called, "Way to fake them out!" Everyone laughed, including Ernie.

Kieran could hardly believe that Hidden Hot Springs meant no more to her than the other places she'd lived, Paris and Costa Rica and—well, wherever. He supposed her response would be that all of them meant a lot.

And he supposed that that would be the truth. But he didn't have to like it.

Chapter Thirteen

The sun was sinking and the tantalizing aroma of the barbecue had set Samantha's stomach growling before she finally gave up on Alice and Mary Anne.

She'd calculated they would arrive around six o'clock, and it was nearly seven. The other women, about two dozen in all, had showed up between early morning and midafternoon, and cheered enthusiastically for the softball play-offs. Four teams had been whittled to two for next weekend's championship.

Alice's shift usually ended at four. Had she been forced to work overtime? Had Mary Anne refused to come?

Samantha didn't dare call them at the office. Even if Hank was in jail, his accomplice hadn't been caught.

With a sigh, she abandoned her lookout post on the slope by the trailers and trudged up the hill to the picnic area. Her muscles ached from the volleyball game, and she flexed her shoulders as she walked.

It was amazing how quickly these past few weeks had flown. She'd never imagined that living in a small town could keep a person so busy.

Of course, she wouldn't normally be searching high and low for missing papers, but she'd also been helping Beth create banners and a schedule of events for the holiday. It was the first time Samantha had helped organize such a large event, and she enjoyed imagining how much fun people would have.

The Fourth of July. For many years she hadn't celebrated it at all, being overseas. It had certainly never been an important holiday like Christmas.

But everything seemed to be coming together—the town's burgeoning romances, the work on the hotel, the lawsuit, even her relationship with Kieran. Not coming together, she reminded herself—coming to an end. Just one more week to go.

Samantha paused to watch the workers and their guests queue up for hamburgers. Good-natured banter floated through the air, mixing with the delicious smells of grilled food. This camaraderie was one of the things she would miss, even if she had the Caribbean to keep her busy.

There had been no opportunity to check her post office box in San Diego for over a week, but oddly, she didn't feel any compulsion to drive into the city just to find out what mail had arrived. The cruise job would have to wait until after Hank's trial, in any event.

She spotted Kieran by the relish table, deep in conversation with Pete. The foreman stood with hands thrust in pockets, not bothering to brush back the wayward bangs that had fallen across his forehead.

Samantha got in line. A moment later, Kieran joined her.

"No luck with your friends?" he asked.

She made a wry face. "Not even a smoke signal. I guess they're not coming."

"It's not that late."

"It'll be dark soon."

He stood sideways to the line, facing her, legs braced like a cowboy. "I hate to admit it, but you women do civilize things. The guys are having a great time."

"Pete isn't."

"Would you stop worrying about Pete?" he said. "He's a big boy. If I didn't know you better, Samantha, I'd say you were an old-fashioned matchmaker."

"I like to see people happy," she admitted, "and I hate loose ends."

"You mean you plan to wrap us all up in fancy paper before you fly off to realms of adventure?" The words were light, but Kieran's tone had a serious edge. "We're capable of managing our own lives, you know."

"Something bothering you?" she challenged. "A minute ago, you were saying how great it was to have women around. Now suddenly you don't like my meddling."

"Some of us prefer flying solo." Kieran fixed his gaze on a distant crow circling above the woods. "We don't need some copilot mucking up the controls."

"Well, Pete's not you," she said.

Before he could respond, Samantha grabbed a plate and took her turn at the serving table. Soon her plate was piled with pickles and potato salad, baked beans and a loaded hamburger. She poured herself some lemonade and gazed around for a place to sit.

That's when she saw the two figures huffing up the hill. Mary Anne wore an embroidered smock and sensible flat shoes, but Alice had tortured her bottle-blond hair into an explosion of split ends, tucked her womanly frame into a black sheath dress and crammed her feet—Samantha couldn't believe it—into four-inch heels.

"Didn't anybody tell her this was a picnic?" Kieran murmured close to Samantha's ear.

"I did. I swear it." She waved to her friends, nearly spilling her lemonade. "I guess it was the prospect of meeting a whole townful of eligible men that ripped her loose from reality."

"Isn't she the one who doesn't like men?" Kieran steered the way to a spare blanket.

Samantha put down her plate and drink. "It's marriage she dislikes, not men. Alice! Mary Anne! Over here!"

She met her friends halfway across the clearing. They all tried to hug each other at once, which must have looked as if they were performing an impromptu version of a folk dance.

"I'd almost given up on you!" said Samantha.

Even in the fading light, she could see the pink staining Mary Anne's cheeks. "It was Alice. She had to go home and change after work."

"I thought this was a dance." Alice glared around the pastoral setting. "Isn't that what you said?"

"Barbecue and softball play-offs." Samantha grinned. "But if you come back next weekend, we can accommodate you."

In a few minutes, she had her friends' plates filled. Samantha noticed Mary Anne kept sneaking glances around the area, but Pete had disappeared.

"He was here a few minutes ago," Samantha said as they all sat down.

"That's okay." Mary Anne toyed with a pickle. "We really came to see you."

"Like fun we did. You're the boss, right?" Alice gave Kieran a friendly nudge. "How about lining up the boys so I can take a look?"

He chuckled. "You won't be left unattended long."

He was right. In short order, men began drifting their way. The guys pretended to want to talk to Kieran, or to have a joke for Samantha, but their eyes never left Alice.

She seemed right at home, exchanging greetings and laughing at their jokes. But no one provoked Alice's sharp tongue, which meant she hadn't met a worthy sparring partner yet.

Mary Anne watched her friend with only a flicker of interest. She seemed to be drooping by the minute. Samantha wished she knew where Pete had gone to. It was starting to get dark, and she hoped he hadn't retreated to his cabin.

Kieran dumped his paper plate in the trash and wandered off, presumably to locate his friend. It was a kind thing to do, she thought.

Mack plopped down nearby. The burly workman had filled a small plate with slices of apple and cherry pie. "So," he said, "anybody want a beer?"

He'd brought three bottles, Samantha noticed. "With dessert? Doesn't that taste funny?"

"His taste buds got shot off in the war," called Ernie.

"Which war was that?" Alice joined in.

"Anywhere Mack goes, there's a war," someone sniped, and was greeted with general laughter.

"Don't let him bore you with stories about lost gold mines." Ernie was trying hard to catch Alice's attention, without success.

"They're jealous." Mack handed Alice one of the bottles of beer and kept the other two for himself. "I talk with the prospectors who come through here. Sometimes I pick up good stories. They're the truth, too."

"Like what?" asked Alice.

"Don't you believe him," Ernie said. "He makes things up. Or else those prospectors do. Heck, half of 'em claim their mules can talk."

Mack shook his head. "I found this one in a book in the rec hall, so you know it's true."

Alice was regarding the self-assured newcomer with interest. "I'll listen to a good lie any time," she said.

The men hooted.

"She's got his number." Ernie gave a nod of satisfaction.

The workman didn't know Alice, Samantha reflected. The harder she ribbed a man, the more that meant she liked him.

"Now, this happened in the thirties. In nineteen thirty-three, to be exact." Mack leaned back, enjoying the attention. "A couple of local folks were camping out at Agua Caliente Springs, not too far from here, and were looking for wildflowers in the canyons. They were some sort of amateur botanists, according to this book."

As the story unfolded, Samantha realized Pete had sat down near Mary Anne. The two of them exchanged shy smiles, and she felt an unexpected tightness in her chest. She wanted so much for her friend to be happy.

But if Pete was here, where had Kieran gone?

The amateur botanists, according to Mack, had met a prospector who told of seeing a fantastic sight: an old ship jutting from a sheer mountain wall. He also claimed to have found Pegleg Smith's lost mine, so the couple cheerfully dismissed his account.

But the next day as the couple was hiking through a canyon, they saw exactly what the miner had described. A curved prow that looked for all the world like the front of a Viking ship was sticking out of a cliff high above them.

"Ridiculous," snapped Ernie.

"Kind of farfetched," Pete agreed.

To Samantha's surprise, it was Alice who spoke next. "Not really," she said. "The sea level used to be a lot higher and these canyons were all under water once. Haven't you guys heard of whale skeletons being dug up around here? And people say Chinese sailors discovered the California coast a thousand years ago, so why not the Vikings?"

"Then why haven't we heard about this before?" someone protested. "A Viking ship half-buried in a mountain? You'd have a theme park built around it, at least."

"Well, if you guys are done exercising your jaws, I'll tell you what happened," Mack said, and they fell silent.

The couple made a note of the landmarks and went back to their camp, intending to return later with witnesses, Mack told them. But only minutes after they left the canyon, the historic earthquake of 1933 shook the ground with tremendous force.

A rockslide blocked the trail back into the canyon. The landmarks vanished. Either the ship had been crushed, or buried or blocked off so completely that it was never found again.

As soon as Mack finished speaking, the group began debating the plausibility of the story. Alice took Mack's side, while he sat silent. But when he began arguing on his own behalf, she led the crowd in teasing him.

Alice had found her man.

Suddenly the friendly quarreling broke off. The insistent harmony of a guitar penetrated the night, and conversation hushed.

Samantha couldn't see who was singing, but she recognized the baritone voice the moment she heard the opening line of "Wind Beneath My Wings." It was Kieran.

The bittersweet words touched Samantha's heart as his fingers roved over the guitar strings, summoning up a gentle but insistent rhythm. And what a voice he had, ragged around the edges but rich and resonant at the center. In the growing darkness, the canyon walls intensified his rounded tones.

Samantha's throat closed tight as she listened to the plaintive melody and poetic words. Earlier, he'd said that he liked to fly solo. She wondered why he had picked this song.

All too soon, the ballad ended. At the crowd's urging, Kieran segued into some hits by Elton John, and even Samantha couldn't resist joining in.

She had endured sing-alongs during her one sorry summer at camp, especially despising the stupid ditty about a big ship going down. During her miserable sojourn at boarding school, the girls had performed torture en masse on Christmas favorites, an experience from which "Silent Night" had never recovered.

Until now, Samantha hadn't realized that singing together was a form of bonding. People shared their emotions, their dreams and their memories through songs they'd grown to love.

Kieran was the perfect leader, his baritone soaring above the others, yet never dominating them. He knew when to pause and let the others catch up, and when to push them to a faster tempo. And he knew when to quit and leave them wanting more.

"Encore!" people called as Kieran abandoned his post atop a rock. "You can't quit now!"

"It's somebody else's turn," he said, slipping the guitar strap over his head. "Mack?"

"Why the hell not?" With a wink at Alice, the construction worker made his way forward and took the instrument. He launched into a medley of toe-tapping country songs.

Kieran slid into place on the blanket next to Samantha. Around them, their friends whispered compliments.

He accepted with a trace of embarrassment. "I haven't sung in years," he murmured to Samantha. "It took me forever to tune the guitar."

"I'm glad you did," she said.

A few minutes later, Samantha's eyes drooped, and she rested her head against Kieran's shoulder. It was just the right height to support her, she noticed in surprise.

The man was full of surprises tonight.

KIERAN AWOKE on his air mattress sometime after midnight. As usual, he came fully alert, taking in the calls of night birds and, from far off, the soprano yips of frightened coyotes.

What had startled them? He put on his sandals and went out to check.

From the edge of the clearing, moonlight revealed a tableau of silver and mist. Fog had laid its mysterious blanket across the valley, muffling sound and sight. Nothing moved in the stillness, and then the yapping and whining came again.

The mountain lion must be on the prowl. Nothing else could have disturbed the coyotes that way.

Kieran felt a twinge of sympathy for the big cat. She still hadn't found her cub, and the weeks were passing. Surely she must be picking up the little guy's scent, but the fact that it appeared to be hiding near the old cabin meant its scent would be confused by the comings and goings of humans.

Some of the men had taken to leaving food scraps near the cabin, despite a warning that they were only making the situation worse. The food always disappeared. Apparently the cub, well-fed and curious, was enjoying his game of hooky.

The Fish and Game officials planned to arrive the following week, but Kieran had heard on the radio of two new fires burning in one of the national forests. He hoped the rescuers wouldn't be delayed, yet again.

As he inhaled the scents of night-blooming flowers, Kieran felt again the odd mixture of sadness and joy that had stolen over him tonight at the picnic. It had been a special evening.

Behind him on the porch, he heard the whisper of bare feet. He turned to see Samantha leaning sleepily against a post, rumpled hair framing her delicate face and a low-cut, sleeveless gown tumbling to midthigh.

He wanted to cover the distance between them and take her in his arms. But he remained where he stood, safely distant.

"You sing pretty well for a wild man," Samantha said. "Where did you hide the guitar? Even Pete didn't know you had it."

The real question, Kieran thought, was why had he chosen to break his long silence tonight? Instead, he said, "I stashed it in the office storeroom. I guess it has some painful memories attached but I didn't quite want to get rid of it."

"Memories of your fiancée?" murmured Samantha.

He nodded. "She used to play several instruments and sing. For a while, I was really into it, too."

"What happened?"

Kieran gazed over the canyon he had once dreamed of showing to Michele. "We made a lot of plans. After we were married, I was going to put her through graduate school. Michele was working as a music teacher, but she wanted to be a composer.

"Then my construction business ran into trouble. I guess I wasn't the easiest guy to put up with those days; I was short-tempered, and working long hours. And it became obvious I could hardly support myself, let alone a graduate student. I don't know which was worse, my moodiness or my poverty. We didn't really quarrel as Michele didn't like to talk about her feelings. She just told me one day it was over, and that was that."

Samantha's sleepy eyes grew troubled.

"That was a long time ago," Kieran added. "More than five years."

The mist muted the lines of Samantha's body so that she seemed to blend into the night. "I know people's feelings change. But I can't understand her leaving you just because times got hard. It wasn't as if you robbed a jewelry store."

"Were you in love with that guy? The one you nearly married?"

"No."

"Then why did you agree to marry him?"

"Impulse, I suppose," Samantha said. "I'm very impulsive, in case you hadn't noticed."

"I've noticed."

"And we spent a wonderful weekend in Acapulco. He said all the right things. I guess I convinced myself that my dream man had come at last. Looking back, I can't believe I was so stupid."

"Ever been married before?"

"Never."

"Think you'll ever get married again? For real, I mean?" Kieran wasn't sure why he had asked the question. He didn't want to hear her say that yes, someday she would find the man of her dreams.

"I don't know," Samantha said slowly.

The wistfulness in her tone touched Kieran's heart. Looking at her there, waiflike in the moonlight, he wanted her so much he couldn't even think about the future.

For five years, he'd lived for a tomorrow that might never come. Tonight, nothing existed but the moment.

Samantha was watching him, her face a study in conflicting emotions. Kieran walked toward her, ready to stop if she pulled back.

Instead, she stepped to the edge of the porch. At this height, she was eye-to-eye with him. Their arms slipped around each other and their mouths met without the slightest hesitation.

He stroked her, wanting to stretch each moment. Through the thin nightgown, he could feel the fullness of her breasts, the inlet of her waist, the thrust of her hips.

After a moment, she stepped back, only to catch his hands and pull him after her.

In the bedroom, it was Samantha's turn to explore him. Kieran relaxed beneath the ministrations of her mouth and hands, his misgivings checked by the rush of desire she awoke. He wondered if it had really been the haircut that sapped Samson's resistance, or his awakening desire for Delilah.

Then Kieran caught Samantha's wrists as she moved above him and held her at full length, feeling warm femininity bring his hardness to life. He rolled her over and made them one, shuddering when she shuddered, gasping when she gasped, amazed at the synthesis between them, and then losing all awareness of self as sensations stormed through him.

When they were finished, he cradled Samantha in his arms. Her hair fluffed across his chest as she lay there, her breathing gradually quieting into the rhythm of sleep.

Away in the night, the coyotes were howling, no longer frightened but staking their claim to the land. It was a tentative claim that they held, but then, Kieran thought, all claims were tentative.

Chapter Fourteen

Kieran couldn't figure Samantha out. First thing Sunday morning, she jumped up and called, "Last one to the dining hall is a scrambled egg!"

He barely had time to notice that she was dressing with unaccustomed restraint, a colorful blouse topping a denim skirt. Then she scurried out the door before Kieran had even brushed his teeth.

By the time he sat down to breakfast, she was popping up to put her tray on the conveyer belt. Since then, she hadn't stood still long enough for him to talk to her.

Not that she avoided him; in fact, she seemed to touch his cheek or stroke his shoulder every time she passed. Then she would dart away, galvanized with energy as she and the other women prepared for the upcoming festival.

What had last night meant to her? Kieran wasn't even sure what it had meant to him. They needed to talk about it, but Samantha wouldn't hold still long enough.

It wasn't like him to agonize over matters like this. Yet he'd felt last night as if matters had changed between them. He could have sworn Samantha had opened up to him in a new way, but she gave no sign of it today.

He thought he might get a clue to her feelings at lunch, when Beth and Lew announced over glasses of wine that they'd set a wedding date for September. He turned to study Samantha for any hint that she might have changed her mind about leaving.

All she said was, "Too bad she's so tall. My wedding dress would never fit."

Then she hugged Mary Anne, who managed to look pleased for Beth and wistful at the same time.

Women didn't make sense to Kieran today, and it wasn't only Samantha. There was Mary Anne, who clung to Alice and avoided making eye contact with Pete. *What was the woman afraid of?*

And that Alice! Kieran liked her forthright manner, but the way she and Mack argued all day, he expected to have to cart them both off to the infirmary. Why Samantha regarded the two of them with a knowing smile was a complete mystery to him.

It came as a relief when the women started heading for their cars. At last the town would return to normal. Maybe now he'd find the right moment to talk to Samantha.

Teary-eyed, the women were hugging each other, as if Alice and Mary Anne were setting sail for some far shore instead of driving two hours to San Diego. Mack helped Kieran haul Alice and Mary Anne's suitcases from the rec hall to their car.

"She's quite a pistol, ain't she?" Mack said, and there was no mistaking to whom he referred.

"I'd say that's a good description," Kieran agreed.

"She's coming back next weekend for the Fourth of July." Mack broke off as they neared the car, and Kieran was left to imagine what might happen when the two were reunited. Maybe he should invest in bulletproof vests all around.

Samantha was handing something to Alice, and Kieran saw the sunlight glint off a key. "That's to my post-office box," he heard her say. After giving the location, she added "I'm expecting to hear about a cruise job. Could you bring my mail next weekend?"

"Sure." Alice gave Samantha another hug.

Kieran felt as if someone had punched him in the stomach. Was that all that mattered to her, a damn cruise job?

He felt like a fool. Samantha had never pretended to be anything other than what she was—a woman who loved 'em and left 'em. Last night hadn't changed a damn thing.

For him, either, he told himself grimly. Not a damn thing.

SAMANTHA CALLED James Dunaway a couple of times during the week but only reached his answering machine. She was beginning to despair of ever getting hold of him.

She had to leave Hidden Hot Springs right after the long weekend. Unlike the lengthy celebrity cases on television, Hank's trial might only last a day or less, and the prosecution was relying on Samantha.

Until now, she'd tried not to think about what might happen, but there was no getting away from the fact that her testimony didn't amount to much. Without the accomplice or new evidence, he'd get convicted at most of possessing circumstantial evidence.

Deputy District Attorney Enright had said that due to a previous robbery conviction, Hank would get jail time, but it might be short.

Like it or not, Samantha would have to make herself scarce. The farther she went from Hidden Hot Springs, the better.

But she felt less and less like leaving. Saturday night, when Kieran had asked whether she would ever marry again, it had struck Samantha that she doubted she'd ever meet anyone who compared to him.

Then when they had made love, she'd felt herself opening up and letting him inside her usual protective veneer. This was danger of a new and treacherous kind, and she had beat a quick retreat.

To make matters worse, as the week progressed, Kieran transformed himself from a grumpy workaholic into a charming lover. On Monday, Samantha found wildflowers beside the bed when she awoke. At dinner, Kieran swept her off to a private table for an intimate tête-à-tête, and that night he proved that Saturday had only been a warm-up.

Tuesday evening, he serenaded her with "Are You Lonesome Tonight?" On Wednesday, after Samantha lost one of her favorite earrings, he presented her with a beautiful pair made of silver and turquoise.

On Thursday afternoon Kieran left work early to help Samantha and Beth complete the decorations for the holiday. For him to knock off before five was the most meaningful tribute of all.

As the men hung banners and set up tables, everyone pointedly avoided any reference to Beatrice or the injunction she would be seeking tomorrow. Joel Phillips had as much at stake as any of them, since he was one of the shareholders, and even Kieran had to concede the attorney would do his best.

After dinner, while it was still light, Kieran and Samantha walked to Uncle Albert's old cabin. They didn't speak, but Samantha knew they shared the feeling that they might have missed something and this was their last chance to find it.

Inside the cottage, Kieran climbed on the rickety table and inspected the rafters for the umpteenth time. Samantha turned over the mattress on the bed and checked it to make sure nothing had been stashed inside.

They prowled through the cabinets, thumping the sides for a hidden compartment. Finally Kieran pounded on the wall in frustration.

"The worst part about not finding it is that it's got to be here," he said. "Uncle Albert liked to write in his journal whenever he observed something interesting. I'm sure he would keep it close by." He whacked the wall again, so hard it made Samantha jump.

"Sorry," he said.

"That's all right. My nerves needed the exercise." She felt like pounding on something herself.

"I wish this weren't happening on your last week here." Kieran's mouth twisted wryly. "You're not having a very good time, are you?"

"I'm having a wonderful time," she said, and wiped a spiderweb off her forehead.

He reached over and plucked a dust mouse from her hair. "Every woman's dream vacation."

They both started to laugh. "Well, it is," Samantha insisted. "This resort has the best-looking men on the entire West Coast."

"We aren't on the coast," he pointed out.

"Don't split hairs." She ruffled her messy locks ruefully. "I've got enough of those already."

He sat on the bed and pulled her onto his lap. "Let me check that for you."

Samantha dutifully lowered her head and let Kieran pretend to examine her. "How did you pick up so much dust?" he demanded. "What did you do, sweep the floor with your head?"

"I just turned over the mattress." She let herself relax against him. "It's hard to imagine your uncle living here alone for so long."

"I wonder if Uncle Albert ever made love on this bed," Kieran mused.

"Wasn't he married?" Samantha asked. "He did have a daughter."

"Aunt Lou never lived here," Kieran said. "She died a long time ago."

They stretched out on the mattress, both so dusty they no longer cared about its dilapidated state. "Who built this cabin?" she asked.

"My uncle used to claim he bought it from a former general in the French Foreign Legion, and his wife, who was a courtesan," Kieran said. "I think he made that up. I think he bought it from a corporation."

Samantha chuckled. "I like the part about the French Foreign Legion."

"I like the part about the courtesan," teased Kieran.

In the narrow space, their bodies pressed against each other. She could hear his breathing speed up and feel the tension of his muscles through his jeans.

When he kissed her, their surroundings vanished. They lay in a tent in North Africa, two renegades risking their lives for a passionate liaison.

She slid her hands under Kieran's shirt, enjoying the smooth expanse of skin. Her skirt lay loose around her and his denim-clad thighs moved against her bare legs. A great sigh escaped Samantha as she shifted beneath him, feeling their bodies beginning to melt together.

A knock at the door made them both jump. Kieran sat up, waiting while Samantha rearranged her clothes. Then he called, "Who is it?"

"Sorry to disturb you. It's Lew."

Kieran admitted his friend. "I'm amazed you found us."

"It must be my Sherlock Holmes instinct. Also the fact that you mentioned you were going to search the cabin one more time." The architect must have noticed Samantha slipping on her shoes, but he discreetly said nothing. "Joel Phillips just called. He has to go out of town on a family emergency but his partner will represent us tomorrow and call you as soon as it's over."

Kieran glowered. "His partner's a wimp compared to Joel. Maybe I should drive in."

"He specifically asked you not to," cautioned Lew. "He went over the strategy with me. Here, I made some notes."

Seeing the two men deep in conversation, Samantha slipped away. She'd called the detective earlier, with no luck, and this might be her last chance.

She hurried up the hill toward home, her thoughts in a tangle. Kieran's attentiveness this week, the instinctive rightness of their lovemaking forced her to face a possibility she'd been fighting tooth and nail.

Maybe she belonged here. Maybe she ought to consider staying.

Samantha felt part of the community in a way she'd never experienced before. And making love to Kieran had awakened instincts and passions she'd never suspected she possessed. If she left, his intensity and his laughter would echo through her heart for the rest of her life.

Yet—what would it feel like to give up traveling? To never again fly alone to an unknown city, filled with the spirit of adventure? She knew she'd miss it terribly.

She hadn't told Kieran, yet, that there was a slim chance she might stay. There was still time to reconsider.

At the cabin, Samantha dialed the detective's number. After so many futile attempts, she was startled when he answered with a gruff, "Yes?"

"Mr. Dunaway?" she said. "It's Samantha Avery."

For a moment, she wondered if he'd forgotten her, but then he said, "I've been working on your case."

"Have you found anything? It's very important. Our lawyer is due in court tomorrow."

"I've come across some documents but I'm not sure they're relevant to your case," he said. "Is there any way you can drop by here?"

Drop by La Jolla? Samantha stifled the instinct to laugh. "No. I'm afraid I can't." She hated to ask him to fax the information to Kieran's office, but what choice did she have? "I'll tell you what, Mr. Dunaway. Whatever documents you've found, I need them tonight, so—"

The front door crashed open. Kieran stood there, glaring.

From his dark glower to the fists clenched at his sides, she knew he'd overheard part of the conversation.

"Hang up," Kieran said.

"But—"

He strode over, grabbed the phone and slammed it down. "You lied to me. You went behind my back, didn't you?" The words ground out from between clenched teeth. "You hired a detective even though I specifically told you not to."

Samantha tried to ignore the sense of guilt that squirmed in her chest. "But I had to. And he's found something. Well, he's not sure if it's relevant, but it might be."

"God knows what damage you've done." Kieran smashed his fist onto the table so hard the phone jangled. "If Beatrice finds out, she'll try to sue us for invasion of privacy. It'll help her make her case, that I'm a domineering jerk who'll sink to any depths to cheat her of her inheritance. Don't you have enough respect for me to trust my judgment?"

"I'm sorry." The apology dropped uselessly into the void. "But Kieran, I couldn't sit here and do nothing. We've got to stop her. I thought at least we should try."

"I am trying!" He stalked the length of the room, his fury too intense for the small space. "Give me a little credit, Samantha. I'm a businessman. I know how the system works. If Joel says a detective won't help, then he knows what he's talking about."

Listening to him, Samantha knew she'd been wrong to meddle. But she cared about Hidden Hot Springs, and him. "I didn't see what harm it could do."

"It could backfire in any number of ways," Kieran raged. "You don't get it, do you? This isn't a game. This isn't some challenge for your skills, a puzzle you can solve before you move on. This is my life, and you have no right to interfere against my express wishes."

"I thought—" Samantha started to say that this could be her life, too, but the words stuck in her throat. She had betrayed his trust. She hadn't meant to, but that wouldn't smooth things over.

"What does this place mean to you—just one more fun vacation spot on your way to somewhere more interesting?" Kieran snapped. "Well, maybe it's a good thing."

"What is?"

"That you're leaving." She wished he were shouting and out of control, but now he sounded deadly calm. "We're like oil and water, the two of us."

Samantha had to try to break through this wall of coldness. "Kieran, I'm sorry I went behind your back. I don't always think before I leap. Heck, I hardly ever do."

"That's what I mean." Kieran gazed out the front window. "I play by the rules. Sometimes I may lose, but I do my best. I don't run away and I don't try for a quick fix."

"We have different styles," she agreed. "That doesn't mean—"

Kieran's tone was sad but it carried a heavy note of finality. "Let's just get through this weekend, shall we?"

Samantha wanted to swing him around to face her, and argue that one mistake shouldn't spoil their future together. But she knew he wasn't just referring to her error in hiring a detective.

Oil and water. More like fire and water, she thought. A lot of heat, a lot of steam and then nothing.

She had almost been led astray by her emotions. She realized now that she loved Kieran in a way she would never experience again. But that didn't mean they could be happy together.

"I'll do my best to behave through the holiday," she said. "That much, I can promise."

Kieran turned, and for a painful moment she thought he was going to shake her hand on the bargain. Then he shrugged. "I think I'll go catch a movie at the rec hall," he said, and went out the door.

KIERAN SPENT FRIDAY afternoon going over proposals for the interior design of the hotel. He'd spent too much time this week playing; his work needed his attention.

He refused to let himself dwell on the scene last night with Samantha. But he couldn't stop picturing her amber eyes glistening with regret as she watched him leave.

His actions this week had surprised even him. *Where had it come from, that urge to pick flowers and sing love songs?* He'd actually begun to hope that the two of them might be able to create a future together. They experienced magic in bed, so why not in the rest of their lives?

Last night had taught him why not. Samantha was a loose cannon. She might fit into his world for a while, but sooner or later she'd do as she pleased.

Two people couldn't build a home that way. They had to work as a team; they had to be able to trust each other.

Resolutely, Kieran turned to the portfolios in front of him. He needed to make a decision if the hotel were to be finished on time.

Before this mess with Beatrice started, he'd combed his list of designers he knew until he came up with two who might be willing to work for shares. Both had toured the property and the designs had arrived this week.

Having a designer as a partner wouldn't alleviate the need to pay for carpeting and window coverings, not to mention furniture. But Kieran was already fielding inquiries from organizations seeking convention facilities, and he hoped to get a loan on the strength of advance reservations.

Or was he just spinning his wheels? Were all his hopes and plans about to come crashing around his head?

He needed to know what was happening in a San Diego courtroom at two o'clock, and he had no way to find out.

He could see now that he should have sent an observer. If Joel didn't want Kieran himself there, why not send Lew or Pete? The problem was, no one had thought of it in time, and now they'd never be able to get there.

If only he'd known earlier that Joel wouldn't be representing them personally. If only he hadn't been so upset last night by his confrontation with Samantha to think straight.

Kieran glanced at his watch. Nearly three o'clock. *Didn't Joel's partner realize the importance of this event? Why hadn't he called?*

Kieran knew court cases were often delayed, and judges took long lunch breaks. Possibly the injunction hadn't even been considered, yet. But couldn't the representative call to say what was happening?

The man's name, Kieran recalled, was Laird Baird. He'd laughed the first time he heard it. He wasn't laughing now.

An injunction blocking further work on the resort didn't necessarily mean Beatrice would win her suit. But if they couldn't complete the first stage of the hotel by fall, there would be no income to pay off their loans. The resort would be forced into bankruptcy.

Kieran had never imagined his project might reach such an impasse. As he'd told Samantha, he played by the rules. Right now, he felt as if the rules were strangling him.

Maybe she had the right idea. If you never committed yourself, you limited your losses. But you never built anything worth keeping, either.

Grimly, he forced his attention onto the first set of sketches and fabric samples. The designer, a sometimes flaky but always entertaining old pal by the name of Joshua Jerome, had gone with a Wild West theme. Lots of sunset colors, murals of cowboys, railings in the style of hitching posts.

It was a bit rustic for Kieran's taste, but he supposed he could fly it by Lew. The architect had impeccable judgment.

He turned to the second set of designs, submitted by a friend named Eva Humphrey. Divorced in middle age, she'd gone back to school and shown a flare for design, but her staid appearance and low-key manner held her back. Clients expected her to be conventional and dull, when she was exactly the opposite.

Kieran could see from her designs that she'd taken Hidden Hot Springs to heart. Her theme was less rooted in a locale than in the concept of something hidden and secluded. She used curved lines and subtle blendings of color that captured exactly the right image.

He would consult Lew, of course, but he already knew that Eva had found her showpiece and Hidden Hot Springs had found its designer . . . if that judge in San Diego didn't halt their work and force them out of business.

Stretching his legs, Kieran pushed back from the desk. His muscles were stiff in unfamiliar places and his eyes burned.

He'd hardly slept last night. He'd regretted yelling at Samantha, and had felt even worse because she'd been so apologetic.

When he'd overheard her talking to the detective, Kieran's temper had ignited in a white flash. In its incandescent light, he'd imagined he saw Samantha clearly for the first time.

Now, he admitted silently, he wasn't so sure. He couldn't blame her for being the person she'd always been. He could only blame himself for wishing she were different.

Kieran glanced at his watch. The hands were edging past four.

He picked up the phone and dialed the number for the courthouse. It rang twice and then a recording said "The court is now closed for the holiday weekend" and gave the hours for the following week. He couldn't believe it. They'd closed early!

Kieran tried Joel's office. He got another recording.

Had the injunction been granted? Denied? Postponed? Damn that idiot Baird! Why hadn't he called?

He'll call soon, Kieran told himself. The jerk will remember that we're waiting, and he'll call.

Meanwhile, the men were holding a mixer tonight, with a festive dinner at the dining hall beforehand. There was no point in sitting around waiting for a phone call. Laird Baird knew how to leave a message.

Kieran switched on his answering machine and went to have dinner.

Chapter Fifteen

Samantha awoke with a start, disoriented to see dim light filtering through the blinds. Was it morning already? Which morning? Hadn't she just lain down for an afternoon nap?

The digital clock clicked to 7:03, and the little red dot was lighted indicating that it was evening. She'd slept for three hours. No wonder, considering all the tossing and turning she'd done last night.

It had been the slowest Friday in memory. She didn't want to pester Kieran to find out about Beatrice's injunction, but she was burning to know what had happened. Beth and Lew had taken the day off to go hiking, and the only Fourth of July preparations left were being handled by the kitchen staff. Samantha had spent most of the day wandering around like a lost soul, finally giving in to her weariness and taking a nap.

Now she stumbled to the bathroom, brain in a fog. She wished she'd slept all the way until tomorrow morning, when Alice and Mary Anne would arrive and there'd be plenty of activities to keep her busy.

She didn't want to think about the dark spaces between her and Kieran. Even though she hadn't left, yet, she already missed him so much her ribs ached. Well, not her ribs, but something in that area. Her heart, maybe.

Splashing cold water on her face, Samantha began to feel hungry. She'd missed dinner; even the salad dishes would be cleared away by now.

Half asleep, she slogged into the kitchen and peered into the refrigerator. The shelves were packed with cheese-cakes she'd baked for tomorrow's contest: chocolate and vanilla and raspberry and, to use the leftover ingredients, a chocolate-raspberry-vanilla blend. They were definitely off-limits tonight.

Nothing else whispered "eat me," so Samantha opened the cupboard and found chicken chili and fruit salad. She ate them out of the cans.

Domesticity had never been her strong point, but it felt odd to eat like this. In the last few weeks, Samantha realized, she'd become accustomed to companionship at a meal.

What would she do on the cruise ship, assuming she got the job? Probably snarf down leftovers between stints of shepherding passengers around, she supposed glumly.

She plopped the cans into the trash. Why had she imagined working on a cruise ship would be so much fun? Samantha had taken a cruise once and she knew the staff members worked from morning till night.

Hidden Hot Springs had spoiled her. Kieran had spoiled her. Well, she told herself, she would just have to get un-spoiled.

Dinner over, she debated what to do next. The prospect of sitting around the cabin filled her with gloom. Besides, she'd helped the men plan the mixer, and she wanted to see how many women showed up and how many matches were made.

Half an hour and her entire wardrobe later, Samantha decided on something completely inappropriate, a short, frothy pink dress with a plunging neckline, worn with a black velvet choker and glittery earrings. She slipped her feet into the highest heels she owned and examined herself in the mirror on the bedroom door.

She looked sexy, sophisticated and completely out of place in Hidden Hot Springs. Just the image she wanted.

Eat your heart out, Kieran.

Samantha strode onto the porch and almost immediately ran into trouble. One heel caught between two planks and only a quick hop in midair saved both her balance and the shoe.

No way was she walking half a mile without a man to catch her when she stumbled. After a moment's consideration, she fetched her keys, made her way cautiously down to the road and drove to town.

The downtown area was cluttered with vehicles. As she rolled past, Samantha was startled to see from the volume of cars that this mixer had attracted even more women than the first one.

She had to drive nearly to the end of town to find a space. Grumbling, she thrust open the door.

Music filled the air, blasting from the recreation hall. The current tune was a hard-rocking number, and Samantha's body began swaying in time.

The street was surprisingly empty. Apparently everyone had gone inside.

Starting down the uneven walkway, Samantha remembered her first visit to Hidden Hot Springs. Had she really sneered at the ramshackle buildings? It seemed odd that she hadn't realized the dining hall rocked with laughter during meals. Even the general store offered something you couldn't find anywhere else: postcards with I Found Hidden Hot Springs printed over a faded photograph of a girl in a 1930s bathing suit. Real old-time stuff.

This was a town. A community. The kind of place she'd never believed existed outside old movies.

The rock song ended, followed by silence. Samantha could picture the men arguing over what to play next.

None of them ever agreed on anything, yet they always managed to get things done. She still hadn't figured it out.

She had nearly reached the rec hall when a tall figure strolled out, silhouetted by the light from the doorway. The man paused on the steps as if lost in thought.

Samantha knew every inch of that powerful frame by heart. Even before he heard her footsteps and swung around, she could picture the angle of his head, the involuntary flexing of his shoulder muscles, the clean line of his tailored jacket swinging over slim, jean-clad hips.

"Didn't think you'd make it," he said.

Samantha could feel his eyes raking her body. His gaze made her keenly aware of the frothy skirt shifting around her thighs, and she changed course abruptly, striding into the middle of the street.

"I challenge you to a duel," she said.

Kieran cocked an eyebrow. "Showdown in the Hot Springs corral?"

"You could put it that way."

Inside, a decision had been reached. Music sounded once more. In an abrupt change of pace, someone had selected Frank Sinatra crooning "Strangers in the Night."

"Well?" Samantha challenged.

Kieran's mouth crooked in an unwilling smile. "Can't turn down a dare like that."

He strolled out to meet her. His arm encircled her waist while his free hand caught hers. She rested the other hand on his shoulder.

Before she was ready, Kieran twirled her around. Samantha stumbled, but she refused to let herself fall. This was a duel to the death.

She regained her balance. "I'll be ready for you next time."

"I'm ready for you now," he murmured, and Samantha felt her heartbeat speed up.

This wasn't foreplay, darn it. It was a contest of wills. There would be no compromise and no retreat.

Kieran struck again, dominating her with a series of swirling steps that Samantha could barely match. Her shoes put her at a serious disadvantage, but at least they elevated her enough to reach his shoulder.

After a few awkward moments, she fell into the rhythm, as if her body had simply needed a warm-up. Her legs felt fluid, her hips quick to swivel, her shoulders attuned to Kieran's least movement. Soon she was able to predict which way he would turn, and to follow so closely that she might almost have been leading.

The air between them crackled with unspoken longing. Like steam rising from the hot springs, the music surrounded and isolated them. She felt as if the pool currents were floating and curling around them.

Then Kieran seized her waist and lifted her to his shoulders. Samantha willed herself to relax as he twirled her around his neck in an acrobatic lift. As if warmed by champagne, a lightness invaded her bloodstream, and her marrow had turned to liquid by the time he set her down again, close against his body.

Samantha melted into Kieran as they finished the waltz, no longer aware of his physical signals but simply a part of him as they covered the width of the street. They had never been closer than this, and yet, she reflected wildly, they had never been farther apart.

When the music faded, Kieran stood motionless, holding Samantha, lost in the world they had created together. The spell lasted until the music resumed with a series of thumps and screeches.

"I hate punk rock," Kieran grumbled, his arm around Samantha's waist as they walked home.

"So who won?" she asked.

"Won?"

"Our duel," she reminded him.

Kieran's grip helped Samantha keep her balance on the narrow path. "I don't know. I guess we'll have to have a rematch," he said.

"Ready when you are."

They staged the rematch as soon as they reached home. It filled the bedroom with the kind of rhythm two people could share only in private.

WHEN KIERAN AWOKE to find Samantha halfway out the door en route to breakfast, it didn't surprise him. In response to his call that he'd see her later, she simply replied, "Count on it."

As if they were casual friends. Or a husband and wife who could expect a thousand such mornings, and didn't need to make the most of this one.

On the other hand, since she'd pulled this kind of stunt before, he guessed that maybe Samantha didn't feel any more comfortable with mornings-after than he did.

Reluctantly returning to reality, Kieran dressed and made his way to his office. His throat clamped shut as he let himself into the trailer and went to his private quarters.

There was no light blinking on the answering machine. That jerk Baird hadn't called!

Kieran knew he could either stand here fuming or he could go and enjoy what might be the first and last big celebration this community would ever have.

Positive thoughts create positive results, he told himself as he marched out of the trailer, but he wasn't sure he believed it.

He paused outside to regard the construction site. The buildings were rapidly taking on finished form; even in the past two weeks, he could see a dramatic change. Hidden Hot Springs had existed for five years in his mind's eye, but at last it was reaching the stage where anyone's eye could see it.

It was hard to believe how many lives had been affected by this project, Kieran thought. He wished Uncle Albert were here to share his sense of accomplishment.

Kieran strolled across the picnic grounds, where red, white, blue and green balloons punctuated the sky. Ribbons marked off game areas and a huge banner proclaimed the greatest cheesecake festival in the world. Beth and Samantha had done a hell of a job.

As he reached the road, he saw most of the cars from last night still jamming the parking spaces. He hoped the new guests hadn't been too crowded, camping in the rec hall. He doubted any of them had minded. They'd been a lively bunch, just what his men needed.

Everything was on course. He had to believe the injunction had been denied. He couldn't accept any other possibility.

Besides, if they'd lost, Baird would have been obligated to call to prevent Kieran from continuing work on the resort, right?

Inside the dining hall, he found Lew, Beth, Pete and Samantha sitting with Mack, some other men and two women Kieran hadn't seen before. They were introduced as Betty and Suzanne.

Helping himself to bacon and scrambled eggs, he let the conversation fly by. With a start, Kieran realized he'd grown used to having women in Hidden Hot Springs. Especially one woman.

She looked fresh as a fawn this morning. What had happened last night apparently hadn't interfered with Samantha's getting a good rest.

Her short hair had grown these last weeks, and she kept sweeping the bangs from her eyes. Her skin had taken on a bronze glow, and as usual, her quick movements and even quicker retorts energized everyone around her.

It was hard to picture the tantalizing pink dress from last night decorating this athletic body. Today, Samantha wore a white T-shirt tucked into blue shorts, with a red bandanna around her neck.

Pete kept glancing at the door, and Kieran realized he was waiting for Mary Anne to arrive from San Diego. He hoped his friend would work things out with her. It wasn't like Pete to mope around.

Love did funny things to otherwise rational people, Kieran mused.

It wasn't Pete but Mack, however, who jumped up a moment later and announced, "They're here!" As soon as he said it, Kieran became aware of a motor rumbling and then dying outside the dining hall.

"How can he tell?" asked Beth as the workman and Pete headed for the door. "Some of my girlfriends are coming today. Doesn't one car sound like another to you, Samantha?"

"Alice's car pings like crazy," Samantha said. "She told me she was waiting until she got a new boyfriend. The number one requirement was that he know how to fix cars."

"That's awfully cold-blooded," Lew observed. He caught a dubious look from Beth and amended, "There are more important qualities, don't you think?"

"I like a man who can fix things," she answered. "Or build things." She smiled.

"Besides," Samantha pointed out, "people fall in love for all sorts of reasons, and usually they fall right out again. So why not pick somebody practical?"

Like you did? Kieran reflected. But there had been nothing practical about how they felt last night.

As predicted, Alice and Mary Anne appeared a moment later and, with Pete and Mack in tow, joined the group at Kieran's table.

Mary Anne, he noticed, kept sneaking peeks at the foreman. After the general greetings had abated, he heard her say, "You didn't meet anyone last night?"

"Meet anyone?" Pete queried.

"At the mixer."

"Why would I go to a mixer?" he said. "I was waiting for you."

The wariness vanished from her eyes. "Oh," Mary Anne said. That was all, just a small "oh," but her face lit up with happiness.

Kieran wished his problems could be solved as easily. But he refused to worry. The injunction must have been denied; that was the logical and inescapable conclusion. Otherwise, he would have to drive to San Diego and punch Laird Baird in the jaw.

Alice handed an envelope to Samantha. "This was the only thing in your mailbox."

The crisp white paper bore the logo of a cruise line. Samantha took it hesitantly. "I'm afraid to open it."

To the queries of the table mates, she explained, "It's about a job."

There were a few puzzled glances, but Kieran had explained to Pete, Lew and the men about his arrangement with Samantha. He didn't like keeping secrets, and, besides, he'd wanted them on the lookout for Hank.

Well, that was one thing they apparently wouldn't have to worry about. According to Samantha, Hank was behind bars, with the trial set to start in a few days.

She sliced open the envelope with a table knife and pulled out a letter. "'Dear Miss Avery,'" she read aloud, "'We're pleased to inform you'—I got the job!"

Congratulations poured in, but, Kieran noticed, they sounded subdued. No one else wants her to leave, either, he thought.

"I have to be in Miami in two weeks," Samantha informed them. "That's a bit tight, but I guess I can manage."

Miami. Two weeks. The finality of it hit Kieran like a thunderclap.

He forced himself to focus on the excited flush rising in Samantha's cheeks. She loved traveling. This job was the right thing for her, and he had to let her go as they'd agreed.

Sometimes he hated acting like a gentleman.

The festival didn't officially start until eleven, and people broke into small groups after breakfast. There was a dip-in-the-springs group, and a poker-playing group, and a number of twosomes wandering off in search of privacy.

Kieran went back to his office and checked for a message. Still nothing.

He was standing in the outer office, trying to decide whether to hound Information for Laird Baird's home phone number, when Samantha popped in.

"There you are," she said. "Heard anything?"

He shook his head.

She perched on a spare desk. She'd put on green socks, he noticed, so she'd match the colors of the festival.

"What are you going to do on the cruise ship, anyway?" Kieran had to change the subject or he'd sweep her into his arms and kiss her.

"Guest relations," she said.

"What's that?"

"Meeting and greeting. Problem-solving. Emergency baby-sitting. Handing out discount coupons for souvenirs. You name it." Samantha tugged up one of her socks. "I wish we'd hear from that lawyer. I wish that stupid detective had come up with something. Well, he did, kind of. He wasn't sure—"

"Let's not mention him again, shall we?" Kieran half wished he'd gone along with hiring a detective, but he wasn't going to admit now that he might have made a mistake. The problem was, he'd put his faith in Joel, but after Baird's negligence in reporting to them, Kieran wasn't so sure he trusted his friend's judgment anymore.

It was too late to change matters now. Whatever had been decided was writ large in the annals of the court.

And outside, people were laughing and shouting, and a glorious canyon setting called them to enjoy its splendor.

"Let's go have fun," Kieran said suddenly.

Samantha hesitated. "You're sure?"

"I changed my mind. Let's go have a miserable time."

She laughed. "In other words, end of conversation."

He held out his arm. She slipped her hand through it. They went out into the sunshine.

SAMANTHA HAD FOUND herself wanting to linger in the office with Kieran. Actually, it had taken all her resolve to get out of the cabin this morning while he was still lying there naked in bed.

She had to keep reminding herself that she was leaving. Soon, her customary itch would take over. A few days before departing, she always began to feel restless and cranky. Her mind would dance ahead to new thrills and new friends. Everyday chitchat would begin to bore her, and familiar settings would pale before the magnificent scenery of the travel brochures.

So why did she feel like sticking her toes into the dirt and holding fast? Why had she enjoyed every minute of the banter at breakfast? Why did she cling to Kieran's arm as if it were the only thing keeping her upright?

Maybe she was coming down with one of those pesty summer colds, Samantha thought. She almost wished her sinuses would run, just to prove it.

As soon as she and Kieran rejoined the others, they were swallowed up in a flurry of activity. With so many people on hand, events took on a momentum of their own.

Even before the scheduled eleven o'clock start time, people began gathering at the front of the hotel building where a softball field had been marked off.

The two teams that had survived the play-offs warmed up, with plenty of catcalls at each other. The onlookers divided into cheering sections, some of them waving bits of colored paper as if they were banners.

The championship game surged ahead with more enthusiasm and brute strength than skill. Even the world's best umpire would have been challenged to call a play in which an onlooker caught a fly ball, and another in which the third baseman flung his shoe at a runner, felling him as he approached home plate.

That one nearly precipitated a fistfight, but eventually tempers were soothed and one team was declared the winner.

Afterward, the kitchen staff served lunch outdoors—lasagna and garlic bread and three kinds of salad. Samantha heard several women comment that they would love to move here just for the food.

Pete took over a microphone set up on a small stage to announce it was almost time for the cheesecake competition. Nearby, Mary Anne handed out entry cards.

"I need help!" Samantha said, and was inundated with offers. Kieran, Lew, Alice and Mack trouped to the cabin with her to carry pies.

Alice beat them all to the refrigerator, lifting out a chocolate specimen and inhaling deeply. "If this tastes as good as it smells, you've got my vote."

"Where's Beth?" Samantha gazed around suspiciously. "I knew it! I'll bet she's entering, too."

"She wouldn't dare!" said Alice. "We're all going to vote for you."

"No, you're not." Samantha held the door for them. "This is a fair competition. If Beth can bake a better cheesecake, she'll even get *my* vote."

Kieran gave her a shadowed look as he went out carrying the chocolate-vanilla-raspberry blend. "Not mine," he said.

She wanted to kiss him. The truth was, much as Samantha wanted to root for Beth, she'd put a lot of love into these cheesecakes. She hoped one of them was good enough to win.

Of course, none of them would actually get to vote. The chef and two members of his staff made up the expert judging panel. Samantha hoped there wouldn't be too much competition.

As soon as they turned onto the path, she saw Lew and Beth ahead of them, each carrying a pie. Curiosity overwhelmed her. Where had Beth gotten her recipe? What were her ingredients? Teachers probably had all kinds of secret sources of information, Samantha reflected, and then couldn't believe she was getting so worked up over a silly contest.

As she followed the others, she realized that this weekend marked her farewell to Hidden Hot Springs. Could she help it if she wanted to go out with a bang?

Beth, it turned out, was far from the only entrant. The pie table was filled to the edges with cheesecakes. Samantha's heart sank.

She filled out entry cards while her friends wedged her pies into a few spare spaces. Then she strolled along the table, reading the names on the other entrants. Kieran started to follow, then seemed to think better of it and went to talk to Lew.

Some of the entrants were workmen; two were women Samantha had met at the first mixer; but quite a few names she didn't recognize. Elizabeth McMillan and Maria Perez and Lee Huang and Shaunita Washington. A whole universe of new people had come to Hidden Hot Springs, lured by the ads Samantha herself had placed. Now she knew how it felt to be a victim of her own success.

Over the microphone, Pete introduced the judging panel, and the onlookers cheered. There must be several hundred people here today. Samantha had never imagined her idea would blossom so.

With a pang, she realized many of these people would still be around after she left. And it wasn't fair to expect Kieran to put his heart on ice. He deserved a good woman, the right woman, Samantha told herself.

She hoped the right woman took a wrong turn and never made it to Hidden Hot Springs.

Then the chef cried, "Let the judging begin!" And he and his two assistants hurried to the dessert table. As if by herd instinct, hundreds of people pushed forward at the same time to get a better view.

Samantha found herself surrounded, jostled, shut in and stifled. Being shorter than most people made it impossible for her to see, and then a heavy purse banged into her ribs, knocking the wind out of her.

She tried to grab hold of something, but the shifting crush of bodies turned into an amorphous mass. Samantha tried to scream, but her throat clamped shut. Her head swam and heat flushed her skin. She needed to find a safe place to sit down, but she couldn't budge the bodies jammed around her.

"Samantha?" Like a breath of cool air, Kieran's voice soothed from behind her left shoulder. "Are you all right?"

Two strong hands caught her waist, and Samantha found herself lifted onto Kieran's shoulders.

"You okay?" he asked from below. All she could see of him was the top of his shaggy mane.

"Yes," she managed. "Yes, I—" She took one deep breath, then another. "I'm fine now."

The judges were sampling tiny slices of each pie, clearing their palates in between with nibbles of cracker and sips of water. They made notations on a checklist, which she knew—because she'd helped draw it up—rated the entries on texture, freshness, flavor and originality.

Kieran strolled to a clear space uphill and lowered her to the ground. "What happened? You had a glazed expression when I spotted you."

"I got trapped," Samantha admitted. "I hate getting trapped."

"I know." His aqua eyes regarded her with a depth of sadness she'd never seen before.

"It's something I can't explain," she admitted.

"We all have our inner demons." Kieran turned back toward the judges, sparing her a response.

The panel finished their tasting and retreated into a huddle. Samantha reminded herself that first prize was a certificate suitable for posting on a wall she wouldn't have and a set of pie pans she wouldn't need on a cruise ship.

But it also meant having one's name and recipe inscribed in the *Book of Cheesecake Festivals*. That had been Beth's idea. The teacher had decorated a notebook herself in red, white, blue and green. The idea was to publish the recipes at some future date.

Samantha would probably never even see the publication. *Why should she care whether her name or someone else's was posted? But she did,* she conceded silently.

What seemed like eons later, the chef mounted the podium. He was a tall, pink-faced man with an engaging Australian accent.

"Well, mates, we've got our winner," he announced. Samantha felt her heartbeat speed up. "And her name is— Beth Bonning!"

Samantha applauded by rote, telling herself that at least the winner wasn't some stranger. After all, Beth had helped organize the festival, too.

That didn't dispel the disappointment weighing down Samantha's stomach. She'd tried so hard. Now there'd be nothing left to remind anyone that she'd ever been a part of Hidden Hot Springs.

The chef held up his hand. "Did I mention she wins first prize in the Low-fat Category? Mates, let me tell you, your diet never had it so good! Nonfat sour cream topping, low-fat cream cheese and egg substitute, a real treat for you health enthusiasts. And for the rest of us, too!"

More applause followed as Beth climbed up to take a bow and accept her certificate and pans. Samantha wondered if the low-fat category had been Beth's idea in the first place, but it didn't matter. She could hardly wait to hear who had won the other first prize.

"And now," the chef said when Beth had descended, "the moment you've all been waiting for. Let me tell you, it was a hard decision. We really suffered over this one, mates."

Men called good-natured jeers. "I'd like to suffer like that, too!"

"My heart bleeds for you!"

"We never knew cheesecake came in so many varieties," the chef continued. "We'd like to give special mention to the oatmeal-raisin cookie crust developed by Lee Huang!"

A dark-haired woman with a shy smile waved from the audience and everyone clapped.

"And now," the chef said, "I have to say, for me personally, I like to keep things simple. Basic ingredients, perfect execution."

Samantha's heart dropped. Her pies each featured some novelty twist. This didn't sound promising.

"But sometimes I'm proved wrong," the chef said. "And in this case, first prize goes to the chocolate-vanilla-raspberry pie baked by our own Samantha!"

A huge roar went up. Propelled toward the stage by Kieran's hand on her back, Samantha wondered why everyone seemed so excited. The crowd hadn't even had a chance to taste her pie, yet.

Then, as she mounted the stage, she realized the cheers weren't for the cheesecake but for her. Samantha Avery, the woman who considered herself a perpetual short-timer, had a lot of friends in this audience.

She stumbled up, overwhelmed by the sight of so many people who cared about her. Even the newcomers joined the ovation as if they'd heard of her and were glad for her success.

Tears pricked her eyes. No group of people had ever welcomed Samantha this way before.

She faced the microphone, and the noise rippled away. "I guess—I mean—I'm just glad you've all come today—"

A popping noise echoed against the hills. Samantha paused. Was someone setting off fireworks early?

The sound reverberated again, a clear ringing shot. People turned in alarm, trying to see where the noise came from.

Pete jumped up beside Samantha. "Everyone keep calm," he said. "Sounds like someone's got hold of a few firecrackers. You folks sit tight while we investigate."

At the foot of the stage, Kieran and Lew joined Pete. The three of them started toward the highway.

Kieran called back to Samantha, "You stay here."

She loped alongside. "Why? What's going on?"

He kept his voice down. "That wasn't a firecracker, it was a gunshot."

Chapter Sixteen

Kieran reached the downtown first, but it sat silent and deserted. Then another shot jolted his ears, due west. Near Uncle Albert's cabin.

As he sprinted down the highway ahead of Lew and Pete, Kieran remembered the night when he'd confronted the mountain lion. Now, as then, he wished he had a weapon.

Although he kept a rifle at the office in case a rabid animal menaced the site, there was no time to go for it. Kieran would have to rely on his wits—and trust to luck.

With the mountain lion, that had worked out for the best. He wasn't so sure that would be the case if he came face-to-face with Hank.

What the hell was the guy shooting at, anyway?

Kieran rounded the bend, startled to see a shiny Cadillac sitting in front of the cabin. It wasn't the kind of car he pictured Hank driving.

Then a bony figure in a bloodred skirt and jacket stalked into sight around the cabin. Beatrice.

Kieran got a dark chill in the pit of his stomach. Her arrival could mean only one thing.

When she spotted him, the triumphant sneer on her face confirmed it. Damn Laird Baird. Damn the stupid judge who couldn't see that he was condemning the innocent. Damn—well, damn everything.

"What's going on?" Kieran waited at the edge of the blacktop.

Beatrice stuffed her handgun into her oversize purse, then glanced nervously behind her. "I stopped to look for you. Don't you live here?"

"You were trying to shoot me?" he said.

"No. That—cat thing. The lynx or the puma or whatever it is. Unfortunately, I missed."

"You tried to shoot the cub?" Kieran couldn't believe the woman's cruelty, not to mention ignorance. "Don't you know they're a protected species? You can't just shoot them."

"You may call it a cub, but it was big enough to do more than snag my panty hose," Beatrice snapped. "This is my property and I'll shoot anything I want to."

"It's not yours, yet."

Lew and Pete came puffing up as Beatrice pulled a sheaf of papers from her purse. "Here's the injunction, in case you didn't know. You're to stop all work until the claim is resolved."

"Then you stand to inherit nothing but vacant land," Kieran said. "If we can't work, we can't pay our bills."

"That isn't my problem." Beatrice shrugged as Lew examined the papers. "Besides, I'm sure you're making things sound worse than they are. Well, it won't do you any good. I don't scare easily."

Lew handed the papers to Pete, so the foreman could read them for himself. "She's right. We can't drive in another nail until we get this thing lifted."

"Which you won't," Beatrice said. "By the way, who are these people?"

"Lew Jolson, project architect. And this is my foreman, Pete Zuniga."

The bony woman regarded Lew with interest. "The architect? Well, now. I've heard it's dangerous to change horses in midstream. I might have a job for you."

Lew shot her a level gaze. "Not if hell freezes over."

"You'll regret those words." Beatrice's anger mutated into confusion as a band of people trotted into view on the highway. "What's this, some kind of jogathon?"

"We're having a Fourth of July festival," Kieran said. "Everyone heard the gunshots."

Beatrice gave the crowd a disdainful look. "I might as well get something to eat, then. Tell them to clear the road. If they want to gawk, they'll have to do it somewhere else."

As she climbed into her car and slammed the door, Kieran waved the new arrivals back. Spotting Samantha, he pulled her aside to the path.

"What's going on?" she asked. "Was that your cousin?"

Kieran grimaced. "She got the injunction. The project is dead."

Samantha planted herself in front of him. "Kieran, we can't let this happen."

"We have no choice," he said.

Her lips pressed into a thin line. "I won't accept it."

His anger boiled over. "It doesn't matter whether you accept it! This isn't your problem!"

"Maybe there's still something we can do."

"Sure there is," Kieran said. "We can finish entertaining all these people and then I can clean out my office. And next week I'll call my creditors and try to figure out how to avoid dragging my friends down with me."

He spun around and stalked toward the picnic area, not even checking to see whether she was following.

SOMETIMES YOU HAD TO save a man from his own bull-headedness, Samantha reflected as she sped toward Kieran's cabin.

She supposed that, from his perspective, he'd done everything he could to save Hidden Hot Springs. And he had, if you played by the rules.

But Beatrice was manipulating the rules to hurt good people. Sometimes, Samantha reflected as she went inside, an honest person had to play things a little fast and loose.

Just a little.

Her fingers shook as she dialed the detective's number. She got it wrong the first time and had to apologize to a grumpy young man whom she'd awakened. He sounded as if he'd done too much celebrating the night before.

She glanced at her watch. Two o'clock in the afternoon. Her wrong number may have been sleeping in, but James Dunaway was probably either out on a case or enjoying a weekend at the beach.

Steadying her hand, she punched in the number again. The phone rang five times. She was on the point of giving up when someone lifted it from the cradle.

"Yeah?" The gruff voice sounded familiar. A wave of relief washed over Samantha.

"It's me," she said. "Samantha Avery. You said you had some documents."

"That's right. I'd be happy to show them to you if you can drop by." She couldn't place his Southern accent. It seemed different from the last time they'd spoken, but that was probably the result of her nerves.

"I'm afraid I'm several hours' drive from La Jolla," Samantha said. "Could you fax them?" She figured she could sneak into Kieran's office and turn the thing on before anyone noticed.

There was a pause at the other end of the line. "I—uh—my fax is broken."

"Surely there's a mailbox place open on a Saturday. Or one of those office supply stores. They usually have a fax."

Couldn't he hear how desperate she was? "This is urgent. I'll pay extra."

Dunaway grunted. "Where are you? Up the coast somewhere?"

"Inland. A place called Hidden Hot Springs," she said.

"Aren't they running some kind of ad?" She heard paper crackle in the background. "I saw it in the paper somewhere."

"It's a Fourth of July Cheesecake Festival." Samantha was amazed that her ad had drawn so much attention.

"Here it is." Dunaway cleared his throat. She wondered if he smoked; he sounded terribly congested. "Okay, I see the directions."

"You mean you'll come here?" She couldn't believe it.

"I'm a fiend for cheesecake," he said. "Didn't have much to do today so I was thinking of checking it out. They got any of that pie left?"

"I'll bake one special for you if they don't!" Samantha said. "Oh, Mr. Dunaway, that would be wonderful!"

"There some place private we could meet?" he said. "I'd rather not have people around when I give you these documents. They're confidential."

She thought quickly. The most secluded place would be Kieran's cabin, but she would feel like a traitor inviting the detective here. "On the highway, the first place you'll see is a ramshackle cabin. It's out of sight of the town. I could meet you there."

"Good enough," the man growled. "In about two hours?"

"I'll be there," she said. Only after he hung up did she realize she'd forgotten to warn him about the cub. But he wasn't likely to panic the way Beatrice had.

Now came the hardest part, Samantha thought. She had to go back to the festival and pretend she wasn't waiting for the most important information of her life. If they gave

Academy Awards for real-life performances, she was going to earn one today.

MARY ANNE KNEW something was wrong the minute Pete came slogging up the hill.

His sturdy shoulders drooped and his mouth was set with unaccustomed fury. At least he hadn't gotten shot, which was what she'd been afraid of.

"It's the injunction," he said as soon as he reached her. "She got it."

Mary Anne tried to figure out what that meant. She didn't know much about business, or the law, either. But she knew Pete was hurting in a bad way.

"Does this mean you lose your job?" she asked.

His head made a sharp, decisive movement that meant yes. She checked the impulse to tell him there'd be other jobs. This one, she knew, was special.

"I'm one of the partners," Pete said. "I don't just lose a salary. I lose my time, my investment and worst of all, I'm on the hook for some of the debt."

Mary Anne wanted to help. She wished she had bright ideas like Samantha. She gazed around, willing her friend to appear, but Samantha was nowhere in sight.

"Aren't debts usually secured?" she ventured.

"Our security was the land," Pete answered. "If it turns out Kieran doesn't own it, we're all screwed."

Since the first time she met him, Mary Anne had felt a sense of security with Pete that she'd never experienced with anyone else. It seemed impossible that he could truly care for her, but today she'd begun to believe that he might.

Now he looked so far away. Mary Anne wanted to put her arms around him, but she didn't dare. Pete had always taken charge, but right now he needed help, and she didn't know how to give it to him.

Hearing the buzz of conversation die, she looked toward the food table. There stood a woman as thin as an exclamation point, surveying the picnic area with a grimace of distaste.

This must be Beatrice. Everything about her had sharp edges, from her pointed chin to her bony ankles. With her scarlet suit, she stood out among the townspeople like a bloodstain.

Something about Beatrice French Bartholomew frightened Mary Anne. The coldness in the woman's eyes and the sneer on her mouth made her look as if she could kill without remorse.

Mary Anne scolded herself for her uncharitable thoughts. *How could she hate someone she didn't know?* From what Samantha had told her, Beatrice must be miserable and bitter. She had no friends and no children, and probably never would.

To Mary Anne's surprise, Beatrice climbed up onto the podium and tapped at the microphone. Pete's head jerked up in surprise.

"What the hell is she doing?" he muttered.

"Hello there." The woman had a tight, brittle voice. "I'm Beatrice French Bartholomew. As most of you know, I've won the first step in my battle to reclaim my father's property."

Angry grumbling arose from the crowd. Beatrice raised her hand.

"Don't misunderstand," she said. "My quarrel is with my cousin, not the rest of you."

"What's the point?" Pete growled.

"Maybe she's having second thoughts," Mary Anne whispered hopefully.

"More likely she didn't visualize how big this project is. Now she needs our help." Pete's words carried a certain satisfaction.

"I understand some of you are partners in this resort," Beatrice went on, "and the rest of you are working for low wages in return for shares. I'll have to have my lawyer look over your contracts. I'm willing to come to a reasonable arrangement with you."

She stopped, and Mary Anne saw that Kieran had stepped onto the stage next to her. Beatrice glowered at him but moved aside.

Sunlight beat down on Kieran's tanned face as he spoke. "A judge has granted my cousin an injunction stopping all work on Hidden Hot Springs until trial, which won't be for months. You guys know what that means. I'm ruined, but you don't have to be. I don't want anyone throwing his investment away out of a sense of loyalty to me. I want each man to do what's best for him. Don't make a snap judgment out of anger."

As he walked away, Beatrice wore the smuggest expression Mary Anne had ever seen. She wanted to shake the woman.

Where was Samantha? Surely she'd have something helpful to say.

Mack approached Pete, with Alice at his side. "I don't want to work for her." He laid one arm around Alice's waist. "I'd just as soon cut my losses and move to San Diego."

"That lady is pure poison," Alice added. "Might as well inject yourself with bile as sign up with her. She'll cheat you in the long run, anyway."

Other men drifted by, a few at a time. They all seemed to agree with Mack and Alice.

When he and Mary Anne were alone, Pete said, "I know how they feel, but I hate to see them lose years of work. And their dreams. We'll never find an opportunity like this again."

"Is that what you want?" Mary Anne struggled to keep her tone neutral. She couldn't believe Pete would turn away from Kieran, but it wasn't her place to lecture him. "To stay on?"

Pete's brown eyes met hers. "I'm thinking about you. About us, and the future. Here we could have a nice home in a good community. If I leave, I'll have to start from scratch. I wouldn't have much to offer a wife."

The words slipped out as if spending their lives together were a foregone conclusion. *Wife,* he'd said. *And we. And the future.*

"I want you to respect yourself," Mary Anne said. "Lots of couples start with nothing. I have a job, and you'll get one soon enough. So what if things are rough? We'll build a future together."

She stopped, unable to believe her boldness. Pete hadn't actually said he wanted to marry her. Maybe he'd been talking in the abstract.

Lost in thought, he stood motionless for a moment and then strode over to the stage. *Had she offended him? Or had he even noticed what she'd said?*

Pete took the microphone. "Some of us have been talking, Ms. Bartholomew. I don't know how many of the men I speak for, but I'm the foreman on this project, and I'm packing my bags and getting out of here first thing tomorrow."

A man shouted "You tell 'em!" and someone else called "That goes double for me!" Slowly other voices joined in, until the hills shook with the roar.

When the noise abated, Pete said, "And by the way, Mary Anne and I are getting married. You're all invited to our wedding. Except for you, Ms. Bartholomew."

He flew down the steps amid a burst of cheers, and caught Mary Anne in his arms.

For once in her life, she thought giddily, she must have said the right thing. And she hadn't even had Samantha to help her.

SAMANTHA WAS SURPRISED to find the crowd's mood defiant and almost exuberant when she returned.

"She may win in court, but she'll lose, too," Beth explained after describing how the men had reacted to Beatrice's offer. "There'll be nothing much worth having. Lew says they'll take all the building supplies and trailers and the architect's plans."

"Revenge is sweet, but outright victory is better." Samantha tried to spot Kieran, but her height prevented her from locating him among all the people.

"And Pete announced that he and Mary Anne are engaged," Beth added. "Maybe we can have a double wedding." In a more subdued tone, she said, "But not here, I guess."

The one person Samantha couldn't help seeing was Beatrice. Not at all fazed by the animosity around her, the spiky figure helped herself to cheesecake as if she hadn't eaten in weeks.

Or as if she owned the place. Which she almost did.

Samantha remembered that Kieran's former fiancée had left him when times got tough. Although Samantha's own departure had been arranged weeks ago, she hated to think about the timing.

No, it wasn't the timing that bothered her. It was the idea of leaving Kieran alone, stripped of his work and his dreams. She had to help. And with James Dunaway's assistance, she would.

Samantha tried to imagine what documents the detective had uncovered. In the best of all possible worlds, it would turn out that Beatrice was an imposter, but surely Kieran would have noticed.

What else could it be? What if the documents turned out to be useless, after all?

They couldn't. Fate wouldn't be that cruel.

From the podium, Beth announced the Hidden Hot Springs's "Silly Olympics" were starting with a one-foot hopping relay. The people got organized with surprisingly good spirit, and the games began.

By the third zany contest, Samantha had located Kieran sitting on a rock overlooking the picnic area. She took a seat beside him, trying obliquely to read his expression. His skin had darkened beneath his eyes, and his jaw was set tightly.

Below them, burly workmen zigged and zagged as they tried to scurry to the finish line with water balloons clenched between chin and chest. The women had a definite advantage in holding the balloons in place, and it was a rare man who wasn't penalized by a loud *pop!* and a huge slosh of water over his feet.

Kieran didn't crack a smile.

Words, usually so quick to spring to Samantha's tongue, failed her now. What could she say? That life was unfair, that Kieran shouldn't have invested so much of himself in a dream, that sometimes the grasshopper won and the ant lost?

She wanted to trace the line of his cheekbone and smooth the anger from his soul. But all she could think of to say was, "I'm sorry. About everything."

"I'm not giving up," he said.

"But the court case won't be for months," she said, puzzled. "I thought by then you'd be bankrupt."

"Sooner or later I'll win the suit," Kieran said. "The banks will take the land, but at least that will clear our debts. Besides, Uncle Albert would want me to keep fighting."

Below, the race had given way to a "shoe mix-up." Divided into groups of ten, the participants tossed their shoes into the middle of a circle, then competed to see who could get his or her feet into the right pair first.

No one was trying very hard to win. Men minced around in ladies' sandals and women clomped cheerfully in oversize boots.

Samantha reached out and played her fingers through Kieran's hair, feeling the hard curve of his head beneath the softness. He turned his attention to her as if waking from a bad dream. "I wish—" Kieran stopped, and she saw Alice and Mack marching toward them.

"Treasure hunt!" Alice explained as she poked around the rock. From a crevice, she produced a small plastic Donald Duck. "One for us!"

There would be no peace for a while, Samantha realized. Beth had planted baubles all over the picnic area, and first prize for the person finding the most items was dinner for two at a San Diego restaurant.

"Might as well join them," she said. Kieran nodded slowly and got up.

HE'D NEARLY SAID the one thing he'd sworn never to say. He'd nearly asked her to stay.

He wasn't afraid of rejection. Hell, nobody liked getting turned down by the woman they loved, but if he didn't ask, he'd lose her for sure.

Ever since they'd made love last night, Kieran had been weighing asking Samantha to stay. As he retrieved a tiger's-eye marble from a clump of bushes, he reflected that he should have asked her first thing this morning. He shouldn't have let her bound out the door without pinning her down.

But he'd been preoccupied with the injunction. Not until he found himself staring his bleak future dead in the face had it occurred to Kieran that time was slipping away.

Pocketing the marble, he kicked a rock out of his path and was surprised to find a silver star underneath. He stuck that in his pocket, too.

The only thing that really mattered wasn't the town but the people in it and the love that bound them together. Especially the love that had grown between him and Samantha, whether she recognized it or not, Kieran thought.

On the other hand, maybe he was being selfish.

Once Beatrice had arrived with her devastating news, the whole balance of his life had changed. What did he have to offer Samantha now besides debt, hard work and a court battle that could drag on for years?

With a start, he realized the other treasure-seekers were gathering near the dessert table. The hunt must be over.

How long had he wandered around lost in thought? He had nothing to show for it, unless you counted a marble, a cardboard doll, a paper-clip chain, an eraser shaped like a dinosaur, the silver star and a tongue depressor covered with glitter.

Approaching the group, Kieran spotted Alice and Mack arguing over whether a pigeon feather counted. Mary Anne and Pete were examining a rock crystal as if they'd made a spectacular find. Even Lew, who must be almost as upset as Kieran, watched with pride as Beth calmly brought order out of chaos, tallying up the discoveries on a "magic slate."

Kieran surveyed the area, trying to ignore his cousin standing haughtily near a technician setting up for to-night's fireworks. At first he couldn't spot Samantha, and then a slim figure in red, white and blue caught his eye. She was heading downhill, toward town.

Puzzled, Kieran walked after her. She moved quickly, as if with some definite purpose in mind.

He was emerging from behind the rest rooms when he spotted a red sports car whipping down the highway with Samantha at the wheel. Did he imagine it, or was there a furtive air to her movements?

Maybe she'd forgotten something at the cabin. In any case, she was a grown woman and entitled to freedom of movement.

He would just have to trust that she knew what she was doing.

Chapter Seventeen

As she sped toward the cabin, Samantha hoped Kieran hadn't noticed her departure. If she came back empty-handed, she didn't want to have to explain where she'd gone. He got so angry whenever she mentioned the detective.

She rounded the bend, disappointed to see no one had yet arrived. She'd allowed a little under two hours, to be on the safe side.

Pulling over, she drummed her fingers against the steering wheel. James Dunaway had to show up. He was her only hope.

What kind of man was he? From his accent, she thought he might be Southern, but in her travels Samantha had learned that each state had a distinctive accent. He wasn't from Texas or Georgia or Tennessee. In fact, the way his accent wavered, she suspected he'd lived in several states.

Or maybe he was faking.

The suspicion jolted through her, sending her heart thudding into her throat. Why would he fake an accent?

Mrs. Gray at the district attorney's office had recommended James Dunaway. He was well-established, not some fly-by-night picked out of an advertising circular.

Gradually Samantha's breathing slowed to normal. She was acting paranoid, that was all.

In the heat of the day, she thought at first she was observing a dust whirl far down the highway. Then it firmed into a car. As it came closer, she saw it was an older-model sedan with paint oxidized to an unappealing gray.

Just what she would expect from a hardworking gumshoe.

The car slowed and had almost reached her before she got a clear look at the man behind the wheel. Thin face, shiny pate and an expression of cruel satisfaction.

Hank.

She must be hallucinating. How could Hank have found her? If he'd managed to follow Alice and Mary Anne, he would have arrived hours ago.

There was only one plausible explanation. Hank Torrance was James Dunaway. He'd known she would be waiting here, alone and helpless.

Twisting the ignition key, Samantha shot her car into Reverse toward town. Hank sped past and skidded across the highway, blocking both lanes. He jumped out, gun in hand.

Samantha shifted into Drive and stepped on the gas, hearing her tires squeal in protest. As she surged forward, two shots rang out. The vehicle plunged ahead, rocked, then tilted dangerously to the right.

The tire rims scraped the pavement and for a stomach-wrenching moment Samantha thought the car would flip. She fought to bring it under control.

Finally it groaned to a halt. Stunned by her near disaster, she gasped for breath.

Hank had caught up with the car. "Get out," he snarled.

He was standing at the wrong angle for her to whack him with the door. Reluctantly, Samantha slid out. The car listed sharply, the two right tires blown completely flat.

"Over there." The gun waved her to the side of the road as Hank leaned into her car. He fiddled with a switch and the driver's seat slid backward.

Samantha glanced toward the cabin. If she ran inside, she might have time to bar the door. There was no phone, but surely someone had heard the shots. . . .

"Don't even think about it." Hank leveled the gun at her. "Stay where you are and I might let you live."

"How did you manage it?" she asked as he pulled at something under the seat. "How did you trick the secretary? You couldn't have known I was going to ask for a recommendation."

"Shut up." Hank pried at the springs, cursing as he scraped his hand. Then, with a whoop, he jerked out something small and metallic.

When he held it up, Samantha saw that it was a key, the heavy kind that would fit a safe-deposit box.

Sweat broke out on her forehead, and it wasn't from the heat. All this time, she'd been driving around with the key to Hank's safe-deposit box under her seat. He must have put it there the night before the wedding.

So that's where he'd stashed the jewels. Now there was only one thing standing between him and a future of wealth and freedom—Samantha Avery, the only witness.

Hank took aim as he stepped forward. "We could have had a lot of fun together," he said. "Too bad you got so snoopy."

A blur moving toward them from town caught Samantha's eye. A truck. Kieran's truck.

Hank swung around as the pickup screeched to a halt. Kieran's startled gaze met hers through the windshield, and he jumped out.

Samantha's heart sank when she saw his empty hands. "Go back!" she shouted. "He's got a gun!"

Kieran leapt to take refuge behind Hank's car. A shot zinged through the air.

"That's a warning!" Hank yelled. "Get over here or I'm plugging your wife."

"Don't listen to him!" Samantha called. "He'll kill us both."

Kieran leaned out and lobbed a rock at Hank, narrowly missing. "Samantha, run!" A gunshot zinged against the hood as Kieran took cover again.

She fled toward the cabin, expecting to feel the sharp sting of a bullet at any moment. At least she could draw Hank's fire and give Kieran a chance to attack him.

She knew that Kieran would never flee. No matter how great the danger, he wouldn't leave her.

"Get back here! You're coming with me!" Hank's wiry body shoved her against the side of the cabin. "You're worth more to me as a hostage than a corpse, now that that jerk has seen me. Get in the car!" He held his gun to her head and called to Kieran, "Stay back or I'll blow her away, man."

"Just leave. You've got what you came for," Samantha began, when a low growl caught her attention.

She and Hank turned at the same time. Around the corner of the cabin padded the lion cub, its mouth curling into a snarl.

She felt the gun barrel waver against her temple, but apparently Hank didn't dare release her even for a moment. Instead, he pivoted and kicked the little cat in the chest. A shrill scream broke the air and the cub scurried away.

Kieran walked around Hank's car, into full view. "If you want a hostage, take me," he said. "Not Samantha."

"Yeah, right." The gun shifted until it targeted Kieran. "I'm not taking you anywhere."

"You're not taking anybody anywhere!" Samantha grabbed his wrist. Kieran lunged, but before he could reach them, Hank had torn his arm from her grasp.

"You're too much trouble," he said to Samantha. "You and your backwoods chum are getting on my nerves. Goodbye, jerks."

Hank was staring right at them, finger on the trigger, when his expression shifted from gloating to disbelief... to panic.

The gun twitched, and Hank took a shaky step backward. Samantha was about to risk a peek over her shoulder when a roar thundered through her, as deep and primitive and violent as an earthquake.

Kieran pushed her sideways and they both fell against the cabin as the mountain lion uncoiled past them, her sinewy body bristling with all the fury of outraged motherhood.

With an unearthly shriek, Hank fled. Kieran caught Samantha in his arms and pulled her into the cabin.

The shivers started at her knees and went up to her teeth. If not for Kieran's strong grip, she would have fallen.

"Thank God I followed you," he said. "I just couldn't leave you alone."

From outside came a series of shots, and then she heard voices. Lots of voices. The townspeople must have come to investigate. She hoped no one was hurt.

"Can you walk?" Kieran asked. "I'd like to see what's going on."

Samantha nodded. Despite her trembling, curiosity propelled her into the sunshine.

Pete and Mack were holding Hank while Alice inspected some claw marks across his shoulder. "He'll live, but he needs to get this wound cleaned," she said.

Hank's gun lay on the ground and there was no sign of the mountain lion. Samantha looked behind her and realized Beatrice was standing there.

"He had a hell of a nerve, trying to shoot an animal on *my* property," the thin woman said, stuffing a tiny gun into her purse. "I guess I scared the both of them pretty good."

"Where's the key?" Samantha forced between chattering teeth. "He has a key."

"Search him," Kieran ordered.

Hank tried to resist as Pete reached into his shirt pocket, then winced as he jostled his own shoulder.

Pete held up the safe-deposit key. "What's this?"

"A half-million dollars in jewels and a ticket to the state penitentiary," said Samantha.

"I don't get it." Kieran sounded confused. "How did he find you? And wasn't he supposed to be locked up?"

Suddenly the puzzle fell together, every last piece. Mrs. Gray had lied about Hank's being in jail. Mrs. Gray had recommended James Dunaway. Mrs. Gray had access to Samantha's address when she lived in Del Mar, and Mrs. Gray could have tracked Samantha that day in San Diego through Joel Phillips's phone number. "I think I know who—"

"You people have no right to hold me," Hank interrupted. "I'll sue."

"Maybe I should just shoot him," Beatrice offered. "One clear shot. Isn't that what they call frontier justice?"

"It's also what they call murder," said Kieran.

"Looks like our problems are solved." Lew, who had been keeping the onlookers from trampling the crime scene, nodded toward the open highway.

A sheriff's patrol car was rolling toward them. "Amazing," Kieran said. "Their substation is half an hour away."

The car halted and two deputies got out. "What seems to be the trouble?" The older one squinted at them, his skin creased from long exposure to the sun.

Kieran summed up the situation, then added, "How did you guys get here so fast?"

"Fast?" said the younger deputy, who had brown hair and a clipped mustache. "We got the call about gunshots a couple of hours ago. It didn't sound urgent, probably some hunters, so we took our time getting here."

Mack solved the mystery. "I'm the one who called them," he said. "When Beatrice shot at the mountain lion. I forgot to call back and cancel."

"Good thing," Kieran said.

As the deputies handcuffed Hank and took statements from witnesses, Samantha said, "You'd better not let him make any phone calls until you round up his accomplice. Her name is Mrs. Gray and she works at the district attorney's office."

Hank blanched. "Leave her out of this."

"Who is she?" Samantha asked.

"My sister," he said. "She was just helping."

"She nearly helped the two of us into an early grave," snapped Kieran.

"Not to mention that she held up jewelry stores with him," Samantha added.

"We'll take care of it," the older deputy assured them, stuffing Hank into the back of the patrol car.

As they drove off, Samantha felt a wave of relief that lasted until she saw Beatrice dusting off her hands.

"Guess we took care of that scum, all right," said the thin woman. "I'll let you people stay for the fireworks but I want this place cleared out by tomorrow."

"You have no right," Kieran said. "The injunction only stops work."

"And with no one working, no one has any business being here." His cousin smirked.

A muscle tightened in Kieran's jaw. Samantha wondered if he were going to toss his cousin bodily off the property.

The lengthy silence was interrupted by a squeal from Mary Anne around the side of the cabin. "Oh, look! Here's that cute little cub!"

Her legs feeling steadier with the immediate danger past, Samantha hurried to her friend. "Be careful. The mother's close by."

Then she caught her breath. The cub was working its way up from beneath the cabin through a screen of bushes. "So that's where it's been hiding."

A strong hand gripped Samantha's shoulder. "Are you two crazy? Move away."

"Look over there!" Pete pointed toward the open brush.

Fifty feet from them, the mother lion stood stock-still, her tan body camouflaged against the dry landscape. Then those powerful jaws parted and she uttered a throaty call that sent spikes of fear up Samantha's back.

The cub, unfazed by the nearness of humans, bounded toward its mother. The big cat covered half-a-dozen feet in one leap as she met her offspring.

The mother licked her baby, and then the two of them loped away, the little cat frolicking beside the big one. They disappeared into a grove of trees.

Beatrice broke the mood by sneering, "Don't you just love happy endings?"

Thanks to the cub, this ending might be happier than Beatrice anticipated, Samantha thought as she pushed back the screen of bushes behind the cabin. "Kieran, look at this."

He peered past her. "Anybody got a flashlight?"

Lew produced a penlight. Kieran kicked away a mound of moldering leaves, uncovering a short flight of stone steps and a hidden door.

"Looks like we've found Uncle Albert's hiding place," he said.

Beatrice pushed toward them. "This is my property. I forbid you to enter."

Kieran turned to Lew. "You read the injunction. Did it bar me from the property?"

"Absolutely not," said the architect.

"Did it give my cousin the right to take possession of Hidden Hot Springs?"

"Negative, again."

"Then I believe the only person trespassing around here is you," Kieran told Beatrice, and strode down the steps with Samantha right behind him. The door, which tilted crookedly on its hinges, swung open at a touch.

They found themselves in a room not much larger than a closet. A musky smell arose from a flattened drift of old leaves that must have served as the cat's bed. Illuminated by a single overhead bulb, shelves along one side held an array of canned foods, cleaning supplies and hand tools.

"None of the other cabins has a basement like this," Kieran said. "It never occurred to me to look for one."

In one corner sat a metal safe. Its door creaked open when he pulled on it.

Samantha heard his swift intake of breath. "It's here," he said. "The diary. And some papers."

They crouched together, Kieran flipping through the journal and Samantha examining the sheets of paper. She leafed through, disappointed to find only copies of supply orders, receipts and other routine documents.

"This might be useful." Kieran's finger traced a line of spidery writing in the diary. "'It is with profound sorrow that I have come to realize I cannot trust or respect my daughter. She has no more love for me than a baby rattlesnake for its father.'"

"It does testify to his state of mind," Samantha said. "And his intentions."

Kieran nodded. "But it's dated three years before his death. The will naming me as heir was written only a few months before."

Samantha plunged into the remaining papers with renewed determination. But as they went one by one into the discard pile and the minutes ticked by, her hopes began to sag.

Kieran made another discovery in the journal, dated eight months before Albert's death.

"Apparently Beatrice came by and they quarreled," he summarized. "But he doesn't give any details. He sounds so disgusted, he doesn't even want to describe it in his own diary."

"That's something, isn't it?"

Kieran lowered the book. "It might help our case. I don't know if it's enough."

Daylight flared as Lew peered in. "We're going back to the picnic grounds. I'm afraid a lot of the guys are planning to pack."

Kieran described the journal entry. "At least it proves he was of sound mind and unhappy with Beatrice." He stood up and dusted the back of his pants. "Samantha, you've been through a lot today. Why don't you knock off?"

She didn't answer. From the bottom of the stack she'd pulled a crumpled sheet that looked as if it had been wadded and then smoothed out again. As if, she thought, Albert had almost thrown it away.

"Samantha?" Kieran prompted her again.

She couldn't tear her eyes from the page. It was too much to hope for; she wondered if she could be hallucinating.

Handing the sheet to Kieran for confirmation, she told Lew, "Beatrice renounces all claim to her father's property in exchange for his forgiving a ten-thousand-dollar debt."

Kieran glanced up from the paper. "She signed it. So did he. And listen to this: 'I further agree that if I breach the terms of this agreement and challenge my father's will, my debt becomes immediately due and payable.'"

"Good Lord," Lew said. "Beatrice owes us ten-thousand dollars. Of course, she probably doesn't have it, but it's a nice club to hold over her head."

He let out a whoop. Kieran joined in, and then Samantha.

"I think," Kieran said, "that it's time we got back to the party."

HE FOUND HIS COUSIN ordering the dining hall staff to put the evening's steaks back in the freezer. "They're too expensive for this lot," she commanded in a voice that must have carried over half the property. "Haven't you got some hamburgers?"

Kieran walked toward her, keenly aware of Samantha at his heels. There were so many things he wanted to say to her, but pent-up anger and a yearning for justice drove him forward. He had to deal with Beatrice, first.

"You owe me ten-thousand dollars," he told his cousin.

She waved a hand dismissively. "We've already dealt with that. It's nothing but slander."

He waved the sheet of paper. "I believe this is your signature. I'm prepared to have an expert verify it."

"Give it here!" Beatrice's angular hand slashed toward the page, but he pulled it away.

Kieran felt no glee, just a surge of relief as if he'd emerged from a long, dark tunnel. Around him, people were clustering close, eyeing the letter and whispering.

"I'm sorry," he said. "I really am, Beatrice. I'm sorry you broke your father's heart. I'm sorry you threw away the land that should have been yours. I'm sorry you've become so greedy you tried to rob these people of years of hard work. But I'm not sorry to tell you that according to this paper, not only do you have no claim to Hidden Hot Springs, but you owe me ten-thousand dollars."

"I don't have ten-thousand dollars," she snapped.

"You're paying a lawyer with something," he said pointedly.

"He's working on contingency." She squared her shoulders, her sharp face even paler than usual. "I'm not giving up, Kieran. That document is forged."

"You've forgotten one thing." Samantha moved forward, her small shape braced defiantly in front of the taller woman. "You've been lying all along, and now we can prove it. When you went to court to get that injunction, you committed perjury. That's a felony, Beatrice. This isn't just a civil matter anymore. You could go to prison."

The thin lips pressed together so hard they turned white. Then, so fast Kieran almost missed it, the bony hand lashed out toward Samantha's cheek.

He caught his cousin's wrist in a tight grip before she made contact. "We can add assault to that charge," he said. "If I were you, Beatrice, I'd drop that suit and get as far away from here as possible."

It occurred to him for one gut-twisting moment that his cousin still had a gun in her purse. He didn't doubt that, if there hadn't been a whole townful of witnesses, she might have used it.

Instead, she glared at him for one last vicious moment. In those eyes he saw not only hatred but desperation. Then she turned and stalked down the hill and out of his life.

A cheer went up, a spontaneous cry of joy that started in the midst of the crowd and rose into a chorus of hoots and hollers.

Kieran slipped his arm around Samantha's waist. "You're quite a woman," he said.

She rested her head on his chest. "I guess this is the best Independence Day I've ever spent. Or ever will."

Before Kieran could answer, people clustered around them, thumping his back and shaking her hand. He had something important to say, but it would have to wait.

THEY WERE SITTING on a blanket watching fireworks burst into the sky. It wasn't a huge display, and had been angled so the sparks fell on a patch of the highway rimmed with water buckets, but Kieran could swear he'd never seen colors so vivid.

He gazed down at Samantha, who was nestling against him with her face uptilted to watch the fireworks.

He could no longer hide from himself how much he loved this woman. He loved the light in her eyes, the vivacity in her face, her wild and unpredictable spirit.

When he'd seen her drive away that afternoon, he'd tried to tell himself that he had no right to interfere in whatever she chose to do. But it hadn't taken more than a few restless minutes before he realized that he had to make sure she was safe. Wherever she went, in his heart he would always be watching over her.

Of course, it would be easier to watch over her here than if she were in the Caribbean.

Above them, a great green glob popped upward through the darkness and burst into a shower of stars. That was when Kieran got the idea. Kind of farfetched, he supposed, but it was the best he could do under the circumstances.

"I'll be back," he murmured, and slipped away from Samantha.

"Hey!" she said, but he was already loping across the hill.

Samantha couldn't believe Kieran had left her just when the fireworks were reaching their crescendo.

As columns of white and blue ripped upward into the darkness, the cold emptiness where he had been sitting took on a shape and substance of its own. The vivid colors only intensified Samantha's sense of loneliness.

Around her in the semidarkness, she was aware of little huddles of people sitting close together. Some of the couples had just met; others were already making wedding plans. She imagined she could hear them whispering and chuckling, although in reality the noise from the fireworks blotted out everything else.

It was hard to believe the threat that had hung over their heads since she arrived had finally been dispelled. Samantha knew she ought to feel tremendously relieved. Instead, she felt dispirited.

Didn't Kieran want to enjoy the little time they had left together? Was he so excited about besting Beatrice that he couldn't sit still, even to share the fireworks with her?

As if for emphasis, a final triumphant shower of light boomed into the sky. Red-and-green, blue-and-white flowers dominated the darkness in a seemingly endless series of explosions.

Gasps went up from the onlookers, followed by applause. A silvery cloud hung motionless for a moment after the fireworks ended, and then dispersed.

That was when Samantha noticed something bright and sparkling moving toward them across the hill.

"What's that?" Someone pointed it out.

"It's the ghost of Pegleg Smith!" shouted Mack, and everyone laughed.

"Looks like sparklers," came Ernie's voice. "A whole bunch of them."

There'd been plenty left from earlier, but Samantha couldn't imagine who would be playing with them now.

Oddly, she realized, the sparklers were held in close formation, as if they spelled out a word. "What's it say?" she asked Pete and Mary Anne, who were sitting nearby.

"Kinda hard to make out," Pete admitted.

The twinkling array approached closer. It was heading directly toward Samantha, and now she could tell that the sparklers had been stuck into some kind of rectangular board.

The letters said: KLUVSS.

"What?" she muttered.

The sparklers stopped a few feet away. She could make out Kieran's face behind the board as he lifted it higher, and now Samantha realized what it said.

"K LUVS S." She started to laugh and then discovered that tears were running down her cheeks. "Oh, Kieran."

"It's the best I could do," he said. "I tried to spell out 'Marry Me' but it wouldn't fit."

"You mean this is a proposal?" she managed to ask.

"Technically, no," he said. "We're already married. But I'm asking you to stay."

She couldn't get any words through the emotions clogging her throat. After a moment, Pete called, "Say yes, for heaven's sake!"

Mack added, "Put the guy out of his misery!"

Samantha managed to force out a single, unsatisfactory "Okay."

People cheered.

"But only on one condition," added Kieran.

His friends hissed.

"I want another wedding," he said. "I want to put a real ring on your finger and know it's going to stay there."

"Yes." Samantha's voice rang out louder than she'd expected over the cheers of their friends. She waited until Kieran put out the sparklers and sat beside her before she added, "But only for one reason."

"What's that?"

"I want to get my money's worth out of that dress."

At the startled look on his face, she began to laugh, and was still laughing when he kissed her.

Chapter Eighteen

With three brides, Samantha thought, it's a good thing they built the ballroom big.

There were four sections of seating and three aisles, but only one minister, who had come from Mary Anne's church in San Diego.

As she paced toward Kieran, Samantha peeked at Beth to her left and then Mary Anne to her right. The only one missing was Alice, who stood among the attendants, but her turn would come soon.

Masses of flowers arranged over trellises transformed the giant room into a bower. A wall of windows on the interior side revealed splashing fountains amid a pool surrounded by greenery.

Samantha could hardly believe how quickly work had progressed. The hotel was scheduled to open in another two weeks.

The trial had taken place in late August. Mrs. Gray—whose real name was Margaret Torrance—had plea-bargained in exchange for testifying against her brother. By the time he got out of the lockup, he'd be looking for a retirement home.

So much for sisterly devotion.

As for the lion and her cub, they'd been relocated to a remote mountain area. The rangers had said it was for the cub's own protection, since it had lost its fear of humans.

Samantha hoped the cats were happy. Without them, Hank would have shot her, and Beatrice would have destroyed Hidden Hot Springs.

Now here Samantha was, draped in white, hat perched atop her head, making her third trip down the aisle.

She forgot everything when she saw the glow in Kieran's eyes. Shaggy hair tamed for the occasion, broad shoulders molding the tuxedo, he looked every inch the man of her dreams.

Samantha reached him, peripherally aware that Lew had met Beth and Mary Anne had taken Pete's arm at the same time. To her, though, nothing mattered except the love shining on Kieran's face.

As she listened to the ceremony, as she repeated her vows knowing this time it was forever, Samantha marveled that so far she hadn't felt trapped or restless at the prospect of being stuck in one place for always.

The ceremony ended and the minister introduced the three newlywed pairs to their guests. Samantha exchanged broad smiles with Beth and Mary Anne. Along with Alice, they had become the sisters she'd never had.

"Make sure you throw me the bouquet," muttered Alice from nearby.

"You'll probably catch all three," Samantha replied.

"That's fitting. It'll be my third time around," said her friend.

"Me, too," said Samantha. "In a manner of speaking."

In a haze of happiness, she marched up the aisle with Kieran. When they reached the lobby, friends closed around them, showering them with good wishes and hugs.

A band began playing in the second ballroom, where the newly hired hotel staff had set up lunch tables and a dance floor. Kieran led Samantha to the head table.

She wished her brain weren't swimming with excitement. She wanted to capture every moment, like an image in an album, to cherish for the rest of her life.

Even the photographers snapping pictures of the wedding parties would never be able to match the kaleidoscope of impressions streaming across Samantha's senses: the tickle of champagne against her palate, the aroma of lunch being prepared, the sparkles in the eyes of so many friends.

Other couples were planning to be wed here during the next two weeks. Besides being romantic, it was a perfect way to test the hotel staff before paying customers arrived.

Samantha wished she could freeze this moment, when Hidden Hot Springs still belonged exclusively to the people who had created it. But of course she wouldn't, even if she could.

The fall season was booked solid. Hank's capture and the recovery of the jewels had made headlines all over Southern California, creating a blaze of publicity that no advertising budget could have rivaled.

"Lost in a daze?" Kieran teased as waiters served their salad. "Where are you?"

"On cloud nine," she answered.

After lunch came dancing. The three bridal couples took the first turn, a waltz, and then the floor filled with celebrants gyrating to a rock beat.

They proceeded through a polka and a cha-cha. The fifth dance proved to be a tango.

"This is where we came in," Kieran murmured in Samantha's ear.

With a rush of emotion, she remembered that first night and the dance that had stirred her. She was afraid if she tried it again, she might cry; but weren't brides expected to cry?

"I'm game if you are," she said.

Kieran caught her against him, one arm claiming her waist, the other cradling her hand.

No matter how well she knew his body, Samantha felt the same heart-thumping response that had aroused her the first night. She could trace the hardness of his chest and the taut muscles of his thighs with her own softness.

As he'd done before, Kieran spun her around, but this time she was ready for him. And when she struck a pose draped over his arm, he held rock-steady.

Bodies tight together, the two of them dominated the dance floor. They extended their long steps dramatically, then tapped sharply during the short ones.

As before, Samantha knew instinctively what Kieran's next move would be as soon as she felt the slightest shift in his balance. But this time, as never before, he transported her into a private world that only the two of them could enter.

As they twirled and stamped, the room faded around Samantha. They were flying through the streets of New Orleans at Mardi Gras, buoyed by music so vibrant it renewed the soul. They strolled and posed, transported to Spain, to Africa, to a Pacific island whose name no foreigner could pronounce.

Only in the grasp of a man so strong could a dancer enjoy true freedom. When Kieran spun Samantha around, there was no fear, no possibility of falling. When she pulled away from him, clapping her hands and clicking the floor flamenco-style, she knew he would wait until the exact right moment, then claim her again.

How could all the realms of the world coexist on one small dance floor? How could the highways and flight paths of Samantha's universe merge into the endless path of the tango?

Finally, she understood why she would never feel restless again. Staying with Kieran didn't tie her down, it set her free.

She ended the dance breathlessly, in his arms. She wanted to tell him what she'd discovered, but Lew and Pete were pulling him away for a series of toasts.

THEY WATCHED THE SUNSET from the glider on Kieran's porch. It was the first time the two of them had been alone since early morning.

Samantha had put on a yellow sundress. Kieran thought she looked softer, as if the wedding had changed her.

The gold ring on her finger was much too simple for his taste. He wished he could have afforded a huge diamond, instead of three small ones, but Samantha hadn't seemed to mind. In fact, she'd said, it would be easier to bake cheesecake without worrying about getting goop caught in her stone.

He wanted to give her so many things—an elegant house, beautiful clothes, whatever she wanted. And someday, he would.

Looking beside him, he realized that Samantha hadn't merely been acting polite about the ring. She really didn't care about jewels or money or a fancy house. She was gazing into the sunset as if she'd found heaven on earth.

She would have stayed even if Beatrice had won, Kieran thought in amazement. He hadn't realized it mattered, until now, but it did. The only thing that could have drawn her away was her own restlessness.

They were rocking back and forth, a slight movement like sleepy breathing. "Happy?" he asked.

"I figured it out." Samantha's cheeks turned pink in the rosy light.

"Figured what out?"

"Why I don't miss traveling," she said. "Why I'll never want to leave."

Kieran slid his arm around her. Her bare back felt smooth and warm. "Why is that?"

"Because the funny thing about total freedom is that it limits you." Samantha tilted her face toward his. "If you aren't free to stay, then you aren't really free."

"I never thought about it that way." He pretended to heave a sigh. "Well, I guess I'll just have to send the tickets back, then."

"Tickets?" She asked suspiciously.

"We're going to have a slightly delayed honeymoon," he informed her. "I have to stick around for the opening, but following that, I've arranged for a week on a private island in Fiji. And then a week in Australia. The cook's recommended some places we could visit off the beaten track. But of course, if you'd rather not . . ."

She wrapped her arms around him. "Just try to send them back, Kieran. I dare you."

"I'd rather make love to you."

"Do we have to wait until we get to Fiji?" she teased.

Instead of answering, he scooped her up and carried her over the threshold. It was, Kieran decided as they headed for the bedroom, the very best way to enter a house.

Once in a while, there's a story so special, a story so unusual,
that your pulse races, your blood rushes. We call this

THE COWBOY & THE BELLY DANCER is one such book.

When rancher Parker Dunlap acquired guardianship of his niece and nephew, he got
a beautiful woman in the bargain! Trouble was, she said her name was Nesrin and
claimed she'd appeared out of a brass lamp! She was a genius with kids and a great
kisser—but was she a marriage-minded genie?

THE COWBOY & THE BELLY DANCER
by
Charlotte Maclay

Available in June wherever Harlequin books are sold. Watch for more Heartbeat
stories, coming your way soon!

HARLEQUIN®

AMERICAN ◆ ROMANCE®

In Name Only

With the advent of spring, American Romance
is pleased to be presenting exciting couples, each
with their own unique reasons for needing a new
beginning...for needing to enter into a marriage
of convenience.

In April we brought you #580 MARRIAGE
INCORPORATED by Debbi Rawlins, and in
May we offered #583 THE RUNAWAY BRIDE
by Jacqueline Diamond. Next, meet the reluctant
newlyweds in:

#587 A SHOTGUN WEDDING
Cathy Gillen Thacker
June 1995

Find out why some couples marry first...and learn to
love later. Watch for the upcoming "In Name Only"
promotion.

INO-3

Relive the romance... This June, Harlequin and
Silhouette are proud to bring you

by Request®

THERE'S SOMETHING
ABOUT A
Cowboy

Hard livin', hard lovin', hard to resist...

Three complete novels by your favorite authors—
in one special collection!

WILDCAT by Candace Schuler
THE BLACK SHEEP by Susan Fox
DIAMOND VALLEY by Margaret Way

Long on pride, short on patience, these sexy cowboys
will ride right into your dreams!

Available wherever
Harlequin and Silhouette books are sold.

HARLEQUIN®   Silhouette®

HREQ695

ANNOUNCING THE

FLYAWAY VACATION SWEEPSTAKES!

This month's destination:

Beautiful SAN FRANCISCO!

This month, as a special surprise, we're offering an exciting FREE VACATION!

Think how much fun it would be to visit San Francisco "on us"! You could ride cable cars, visit Chinatown, see the Golden Gate Bridge and dine in some of the finest restaurants in America!

The facing page contains two Entry Coupons (as does every book you received this shipment). Complete and return *all* the entry coupons; **the more times you enter, the better your chances of winning!**

Then keep your fingers crossed, because you'll find out by June 15, 1995 if you're the winner! If you are, here's what you'll get:

- Round-trip airfare for two to beautiful San Francisco!
- 4 days/3 nights at a first-class hotel!
- $500.00 pocket money for meals and sightseeing!

Remember: The more times you enter, the better your chances of winning!*

*NO PURCHASE OR OBLIGATION TO CONTINUE BEING A SUBSCRIBER NECESSARY TO ENTER. SEE REVERSE SIDE OR ANY ENTRY COUPON FOR ALTERNATIVE MEANS OF ENTRY.

VSF KAL

OFFICIAL RULES

FLYAWAY VACATION SWEEPSTAKES 3449
NO PURCHASE OR OBLIGATION NECESSARY

Three Harlequin Reader Service 1995 shipments will contain respectively, coupons for entry into three different prize drawings, one for a trip for two to San Francisco, another for a trip for two to Las Vegas and the third for a trip for two to Orlando, Florida. To enter any drawing using an Entry Coupon, simply complete and mail according to directions.

There is no obligation to continue using the Reader Service to enter and be eligible for any prize drawing. You may also enter any drawing by hand printing the words "Flyaway Vacation," your name and address on a 3"x5" card and the destination of the prize you wish that entry to be considered for (i.e., San Francisco trip, Las Vegas trip or Orlando trip). Send your 3"x5" entries via first-class mail (limit: one entry per envelope) to: Flyaway Vacation Sweepstakes 3449, c/o Prize Destination you wish that entry to be considered for, P.O. Box 1315, Buffalo, NY 14269-1315, USA or P.O. Box 610, Fort Erie, Ontario L2A 5X3, Canada.

To be eligible for the San Francisco trip, entries must be received by 5/30/95; for the Las Vegas trip, 7/30/95; and for the Orlando trip, 9/30/95.

Winners will be determined in random drawings conducted under the supervision of D.L. Blair, Inc., an independent judging organization whose decisions are final, from among all eligible entries received for that drawing. San Francisco trip prize includes round-trip airfare for two, 4-day/3-night weekend accommodations at a first-class hotel, and $500 in cash (trip must be taken between 7/30/95—7/30/96, approximate prize value—$3,500); Las Vegas trip includes round-trip airfare for two, 4-day/3-night weekend accommodations at a first-class hotel, and $500 in cash (trip must be taken between 9/30/95—9/30/96, approximate prize value—$3,500); Orlando trip includes round-trip airfare for two, 4-day/3-night weekend accommodations at a first-class hotel, and $500 in cash (trip must be taken between 11/30/95—11/30/96, approximate prize value—$3,500). All travelers must sign and return a Release of Liability prior to travel. Hotel accommodations and flights are subject to accommodation and schedule availability. Sweepstakes open to residents of the U.S. (except Puerto Rico) and Canada, 18 years of age or older. Employees and immediate family members of Harlequin Enterprises, Ltd., D.L. Blair, Inc., their affiliates, subsidiaries and all other agencies, entities and persons connected with the use, marketing or conduct of this sweepstakes are not eligible. Odds of winning a prize are dependent upon the number of eligible entries received for that drawing. Prize drawing and winner notification for each drawing will occur no later than 15 days after deadline for entry eligibility for that drawing. Limit: one prize to an individual, family or organization. All applicable laws and regulations apply. Sweepstakes offer void wherever prohibited by law. Any litigation within the province of Quebec respecting the conduct and awarding of the prizes in this sweepstakes must be submitted to the Regies des loteries et Courses du Quebec. In order to win a prize, residents of Canada will be required to correctly answer a time-limited arithmetical skill-testing question. Value of prizes are in U.S. currency.

Winners will be obligated to sign and return an Affidavit of Eligibility within 30 days of notification. In the event of noncompliance within this time period, prize may not be awarded. If any prize or prize notification is returned as undeliverable, that prize will not be awarded. By acceptance of a prize, winner consents to use of his/her name, photograph or other likeness for purposes of advertising, trade and promotion on behalf of Harlequin Enterprises, Ltd., without further compensation, unless prohibited by law.

For the names of prizewinners (available after 12/31/95), send a self-addressed, stamped envelope to: Flyaway Vacation Sweepstakes 3449 Winners, P.O. Box 4200, Blair, NE 68009.

RVC KAL